MW00914805

Hunter

Alice Honeyands

ISBN: 9798360653639

I choose you,

and I'll choose you,

over and over,

and over.

Without pause,

without doubt,

in a heartbeat.

I'll keep choosing you.

CONTENTS

Acknowledgements

About the Author

Chapter 1

Another night in paradise, Hunter thought sarcastically to himself as he strolled down the line of people waiting to get into the only rock and metal club in town, the Cellar.

He was in a shitty mood, and what was making it worse was that he was late for his weekly meeting with his brothers that they had been having since, well, as long as he could remember.

They were going to be pissed at him, not because he was late but because he hadn't checked in to tell them that he was going to be, which in their line of work could mean he was laying half dead in a ditch somewhere.

His saving grace was that technically, it was his night off from his job as an Enforcer. Not that the title made him any safer out there, but having the night off meant that hopefully his brothers would give him a little slack for not texting in.

The town of Foston Hall, where the club was, had a good reputation in itself, with the good neighbourhoods outweighing the bad, creating a place that people generally felt safe in. Unbeknownst to them, he and his brothers were partly to thank for that.

As he walked down the waiting line, all heads turned in his direction as he put on his usual mask of indifference, trying to cover the low mood he was in. The sound of giggling came from a group of girls up ahead as they stood huddled together as he walked towards them. Mists of warm air puffed in front of their faces as they rubbed at their arms in an attempt to keep warm in the crisp autumn air. Straightening up, they stared after him for a little longer than was polite as he passed them by, but it didn't bother him, he was used to the attention.

He stood out. At a towering 6'6, his genetic makeup had him attracting women like bees to honey, so the stares were just business as usual for him.

The methodical thump from the base inside the club carried outside to the waiting line, promising the people standing out in the cold a good atmosphere when they finally made it inside. Set on four floors, the club was the best thing going for the town and the best thing going in his shitty life. It was strange how a place so loud and busy gave him the only peace he'd ever had. He had a feeling his recent mood was due to him being bone tired of the same thing day in, day out. Get up, go to work, eat, go to work, eat, sleep, and repeat. It was getting real old, real quick.

He felt lost, like he was just stumbling along, existing rather than actually living. The feeling had

10

been a constant shadow lurking over him for months now, and he was starting to panic at the possibility that this was going to be his new reality. The club and his brothers gave him purpose and stopped him from going insane at least, but he despised the constant need for female attention. Still, it was no revelation that this was the hand that he had been dealt in life, and the show must go on.

Tonight was no different to any other night, he thought as he tried to suppress the miserable mood he was in by spinning around and calling back to the group, "Evening ladies," forcing himself to smile at them. They were obviously part of a small hen party, and his nature couldn't help itself as he checked them all out in their short skirts and tutus.

At the 'hi's' that followed, he carried on down the line, the fake smile dropping as soon as he reached the front doors.

Looking back over his shoulder, he was glad to see more humans than demons tonight, hopefully that meant there wouldn't be any trouble and he could enjoy a few beers with his friends for once in an attempt to brighten the current funk he was in.

He strode into the foyer, nodding to the two workers who were on the front desk as he passed. They always had a demon up front of the club, keeping an eye on who was coming in and out.

Tonight it was a fury demon- Nesh, a big blonde, angry son of a bitch who was acting as security guard.

"Any trouble?" Hunter asked him.

"All smooth sailing, boss." Nesh said, stepping aside to let him pass by.

Hunter clapped him on the back before taking the stairs up two at a time. Jogging up, he bypassed the main part of the club, where music pumped around him and through the glass doors, strobe lights shining to the beat. He went up to the floor above, which was slightly quieter- more tables, less dance floor.

Heading over to the VIP section, he saw that the guys were already there at their regular table.

"What the fuck time do you call this?" Viden asked as Hunter pulled off his coat and sat down, "Why are you so late?" He demanded as he stared into eyes the same grey as his own, a common similarity in incubus demons, with a humourless look on his face.

"You're late. It's your round," Theo said.

"It's never anyone's round when we own the alcohol jackass," Hunter replied, rolling his eyes.

12

He leaned forward, resting his arms on his knees, looking up at them through the table of empty beer bottles and glasses.

"I ran into some work that's why I'm late."

"Work? As in Enforcer work?" Theo asked, "But you're off rotation tonight." He said at Hunter's nod.

"I couldn't help it. I came across four furies brawling in the street right in front of me."

That got them all sitting up.

"Shit, why didn't you call us in?" Adriel said.

Hunter smirked at him, "Because I wanted to keep all the fun for myself."

It was a stupid thing to do, Hunter knew that- go off radar and take on not one, but four furies who were known for their lack of morals and hatred for Enforcers, but tonight Hunter hadn't been in self preservation mode. He had wanted something- anything that would make his heart beat and his adrenaline spike. There was nothing like taking on four of the bastards alone, with the possible threat of death to do that.

He'd enjoyed himself, and that was worrying. Viden was the one known for his suicidal tendencies in the job, not him. His smirk faded as he looked at his friends; his brothers, as he suddenly realised what he had risked.

Shit, what was he doing?

They were all bound by the same contract to Hell as Enforcers- to keep the peace between demons on the streets, and the knowledge that they existed secret from humans- but they worked as a team, and he had been wrong not to call them in, he knew that.

"So what happened?" Theo asked.

"Same old fury business," he mumbled.

When he didn't elaborate, they all looked at him and frowned. Hunter usually liked to dish out all the details on his heroic, albeit stupid behaviours, so he needed to keep face and deflect off his current mood before they realised something was up with him.

"One of them had only just received clearance out of Hell," he forced a smirk, reaching for a bottle of beer from the table. "I gave them some valuable life advice, and when that didn't work, I used my fists and then sent them on their way with a warning."

He caught Viden watching him. The smirk hadn't reached Hunter's eyes, and he'd spotted it.

14

Nothing like a dead soul spotting another dead soul.

"Did you log it with the Guild?" Adriel asked.

"I *am* not technically working tonight...and I couldn't be bothered with all the paperwork. I told them that I would though, that will get them shitting themselves for a while."

As Adriel turned to Theo and started asking him about their last job and whether he'd logged it, Viden turned to Hunter. "I'm not buying it, this little everything is alright act that you've got going on here," he whispered, leaning in close. "What really went on tonight? Did you go out looking for trouble?"

"And why would I do that? We're not all like you, V. Get off my case."

Viden's lip curled, "You're more like me than you think."

"Anything happening here?" Hunter asked the others loudly, ignoring any further accusations from him.

"We need to hire some more bar girls, mainly for weekends, but a few extra in the week would help too," Theo said.

The four of them had owned the club for years now, and they were natural owners. Their staff loved them, and patrons travelled from miles around to get there ever since they turned it from a quiet humans-only club into a landmark for all species.

They were well known by all demons for their brutality on law breakers topside, which helped in the smooth running of their club with so many species under the same roof on any one night. It helped that as Enforcers, they had the capability to strip a demon's clearance to be topside, which tended to make even the baddest of bad behave themselves in their presence. They weren't the only demon club in town, but they were the best. Hunter was proud of their achievements there. He just had to remind himself that he was one of the reasons for the clubs popularity too.

"Have we got any possibilities?"

"I ran an add on the website. We've got three interviews tomorrow night and another two the night after."

"I'll be there for them," Hunter said before his brain could stop him.

Theo's eyebrows raised, he usually dealt with recruitments on his own. Being the oldest of the four, he was the most business-minded of them all.

"Unless you don't want me to?"

"Uh no, it will be good to get a second pair of eyes on them…it's just…"

"I know, I know off limits. Don't worry, I can keep it professional."

They worked by a strict rule: no sleeping or relations with the staff. Hunter didn't need reminding of it. Viden, on the other hand…

"One of them is an ex of yours."

Hunter nearly spat out the beer he was drinking. Not likely, he thought. He never dated. Regular demon hookups sure, but never anything serious.

"Who?"

"Ashley."

Oh, he bet she'd applied for the job the second it got posted. She was a regular at the club and had become a casual hookup for him, but she'd got way too clingy, telling a few people that they were an item when they most certainly were not. It had made him pull the plug on their rendezvous, but she wasn't great at dealing with rejection.

"Ugh," he groaned.

"She knows the setup, Hunter, and she knows everyone here. I think we should give her a position on the bar."

He'd already had her in a few positions on the bar, he thought, but he didn't voice that little fact, "She's going to be a pain in my arse."

"Then you can prove just how professional you can be." Theo smirked.

He was a sex demon and a club owner, which certainly had its perks. The constant stream of willing females at his beck and call, ready to feed his Demon's need for sexual contact, was the main one, and his physique did all the work for him. Tall and strong, along with his black hair and grey eyes, Hunter was most women's wet dream. His genetic makeup ensuring that his needs could be met easily.

He couldn't blame Ashley for her inability to take no for an answer. The ladies didn't just have the time of their lives with him sexually. As his Demon fed off their energy, they also got a free high, which kept them coming back for more.

Ashley had obviously become a little hooked on this without him noticing, which was just another reason to keep her at arm's length now.

He was a total pro at keeping his Demon in check on the recharge. Unlike Viden, Hunter could only use humans, so it was important to keep him under control and not take too much from them, a kiss here and there usually kept him ticking over nicely.

"I'll make a point of it that work place relationships are strictly forbidden and see if she still wants the job," Theo laughed.

"You're just jealous. You wish you could get that kind of attention."

"Oh yeah, everyone wants a hot stalker in their life, throwing themselves at you every opportunity they get. No thanks, I'm quite happy with my level of normal."

Theo *was* normal for a demon. He took his job as an Enforcer seriously, making it his life ambition to keep everyone he possibly could safe from harm whenever he had the chance. The others had labelled him as a jobsworth from early on, but he hadn't taken offence to it- quite the opposite. As an abraxas demon, he was all about the rules, so it came naturally to him.

More Enforcer work= less female attention.

All the more for Hunter.

He wasn't going to have an issue with finding a girl tonight, he thought as he spotted the hen group he'd seen outside eying him up from over by the bar.

"I can't tell if you're being sarcastic or not."

Theo rolled his eyes, putting down his empty glass.

Hunter stretched in his seat, unfurling his massive frame. "Guess you want me to get the drinks in then."

"Well, you were late. You're three rounds down." Adriel said, shaking his empty bottle at him.

Just before he got up to go to the bar, a girl appeared from the the staff area, obviously just starting her shift. Wearing her wavy, long brown hair loose, Kali was shorter than the other girls working, but super hot as she hustled behind the bar to help with the backlog of people waiting to be served.

Hunter turned in his seat as Viden growled from where he sat, looking over at her.

Wearing tight-fitting black jeans, she had on a little top that showed off all her assets, not that Hunter would ever show her any interest. Her and Viden's love story was the type you read about- in horror stories.

Seeming to feel Viden's gaze on her, her brown eyes swung around to his. Instantly looking guilty, she reached for a work top that was under the bar and pulled it on over her head, even though she was already easily wearing more than any of the other girls working there. Viden seemed satisfied, nodding to her as she carried on her work. Some of the other bar girls looked at her, rolling their eyes as they carried on serving the increasing number of waiting customers, not about to get involved but clearly not impressed either.

Another reason not to have work-place relations.

"You need to cut her some slack V."

Wow, ok, so Adriel was going to go there tonight. Good, he needed a bit of entertainment. Drinks forgotten, he sat back in his chair, crossing his legs, and waited for the showdown to commence.

"You need to mind your own goddamn business."

"If you want her working here, then it is my business. We've told you a thousand times- cut her loose already. Stop tormenting the poor girl."

Viden's Demon bristled, his eyes momentarily turning black.

The three of them knew he'd bonded with her. Hell, V knew it, he just tried and failed to hide it, not that he'd ever tell her or complete the bonding link.

"You need to back the fuck off. There's nothing going on. I'm not breaking any of your rules."

"Your rules too, V. This club is yours too remember."

"Then leave her out of our conversations."

"When you stop being a dick to her, I'll leave it out."

As Viden moved to get up, Hunter got ready to pull Ade out of his reach, but the saving grace came in the form of Tess, one of the club's regular succubus, coming over to their table.

She was one of Viden's casual hookups, and it didn't go unnoticed by Kali, as she stole glances in his direction, her face falling.

Ah, Viden and Kali, how they lived to torment each other.

Viden waved Tess away with his hand, a scowl on his face as usual as he glared at Adriel, before standing up and storming off towards the toilets.

"Man, he needs to sort his shit out sooner rather than later for Kali's sake," Adriel said, looking after him.

"Give him a bit of slack. He is trying at least," Theo said.

"Trying to what exactly though?"

"Trying to stay away from her. We need to keep him focused on work for now until he works out what he wants," Theo said.

"I'm pretty sure she should get a say in that too. He may act like he owns her, but he doesn't. We all know that a bonded male without completing the link is a dangerous thing, and he's just getting worse. If he doesn't get it together soon and just admit to himself that his Demon has chosen her, then it's going to end in a world of hurt for everyone."

"And what happens then if they do become fully bonded? Do we sack her? She's been here from the start and she's one of our best employees," Hunter said.

"We bring her in as management. She can share V's cut of the club if it comes to it." Theo shrugged.

That was part of, but not all, of Viden's hesitation to complete the link with Kali, Hunter was sure of it.

Fully bonding as a demon was a life sentence. No going back, no changing your mind after. You were in it for life together. He could see why he didn't want to. That kind of commitment was too much to even comprehend.

The thought of spending your life with just one female, especially as an incubus, he could laugh at it.

The others didn't understand the same way that he did- they weren't the same species as them, but Hunter got it. They were programmed as drifters to work through females like they would eat meals. Unlike Theo, who lived in harmony with his demon side, and Adriel, who hadn't even discovered his yet, Hunter and Viden were in a forever battle of dominance with theirs. Keeping a neutral mood and them well sated was the only way to keep their demons under control.

"He needs to get focused on Enforcer work again," Hunter spoke in his defence, knowing that it helped him with his control.

"We all need to start concentrating on our Enforcer work. There is a weird vibe out there. I don't know about you guys, but I've got this feeling that something monumental is coming. It's weird out on the streets, quieter. I don't trust it," Adriel said.

Adriel may be having a quieter time of late, but Hunter wasn't. His patch on the right side of town the past few nights had been a total shitshow, and he was beat.

Tonight was his only night off work for a week, and he planned on getting wasted and then getting a recharge.

"Well, while you decide on what it is that's coming, I'll go and get us those drinks."

Chapter 2

"Hey Kali, you got another couple of bottles of Jack for us?" Hunter asked, leaning on the bar top.

She gave him a smile before reaching behind her to the stacked bottles and passing him two. Her attention suddenly swung around to Viden as he re-emerged from the bathroom, chugging on a bottle from god knows where that was already half empty.

"You know Viden is a complex creature. He doesn't mean to act like an ogre, he just can't help himself." He rubbed the back of his neck, looking over to the brute that was the closest thing he had to family. The four of them had all been fucked up in some way or another and it was only by sheer luck that they had all stumbled upon each other when they did, the chance meetings causing them all to turn their lives around for the better.

"He cares about you more than he lets on." He should so shut his mouth right about now. Viden would string him up for talking to Kali about him like this. Hunter looked down as Viden walked past narrowing his eyes at them both before returning to their table. He knew that Hunter would never try anything with her- their trust ran deep. It didn't stop Viden's Demon's possessiveness, though. All the regulars knew that she was a total no-go, but every now and again, a new guy would show up in town with a death wish.

"It's not enough, though, is it. I'm not enough for him."

When she had showed up a few years back looking for a bar job, Viden had tried to hide it, but he'd been so into her, and it had been obvious that she was more than just a bit of skirt to him. It had become apparent to his brothers that his Demon had chosen her as his mate when his behaviour had turned catatonic whenever she was near. Possessive, protective, and an obsession bordering on crazy were the obvious indicators that he was bonded and that he was screwed.

When he seemed to realise what was happening, he cut all communication with her, and he had kept her at arm's length ever since. She didn't realise the extent of his connection to her. If she did, Hunter wondered if she would act any differently around him.

Hunter had tried to bring it up with him once before and learnt that some things were best left unsaid.

"Don't give up on him," He said quietly, reaching over to squeeze her hand before taking the bottles back over to their table.

"What was that about?" Viden asked as Hunter sat down, poring himself a large glass of amber liquid.

"Just getting refills, V, chill." Hunter took a deep drink and sat back, determined to relax even just a little. "So what's the plan tonight?"

"Me and Theo are taking Western Avenue up," Adriel said.

"Viden?"

"I'm on Trade," Viden replied, reaching for the new bottle.

Theo grabbed it before he got a hold, earning him a growl. "You'll thank me tomorrow when you wake up alive." Theo stated, "You sure you don't want us to come and back you? You shouldn't be working Trade alone," he said, pouring himself a refill.

Trade street was known for being where the underbelly of the demon population did their dealings, and was notoriously the hotspot for bad shit going down.

The look Viden gave him was the clear no he didn't need spoken.

Hunter scratched at the stubble under his chin "You want me with you? We can go and sort out some other, personal business after." He would forgo his night off tonight if it meant having Viden's back.

They always worked in pairs, and he and Viden were always together unless someone was off rotation. Finding a girl and getting his recharge could wait until later, and Viden could act as his wing man.

"I don't need a god damn babysitter. Look, I only come in here because of the free drink. If you lot are going to start pansy-arsing me constantly, I'm just not going to show for these fun little catch ups."

Ok, maybe no wingman tonight. Hunter raised his hands in surrender. "We hear you. Just be safe is all."

Viden rolled his eyes and snatched the bottle from Theo's hand. "Whatever. I'm out of here."

The crowd parted as he left, a ripple of unease following him through the club before he disappeared out of the door.

"Don't worry, I'll go and find him later." Hunter said, watching him leave.

"Well, until then, you entertain yourself, Hunt. We've got places to be..." Adriel and Theo got up and clapped him on the back as they left him alone with his thoughts.

Within seconds he was back to his shitty mood and still in major need of a recharge. He'd put it off for as long as he could, like usual. Sexual activity for him was as important as breathing to keep his energy up and his Demon calm. He fronted to the others that he loved the need to screw random females, but the truth was, it ate him up inside to use them. He loathed it, and it was just another thing to stoke his bad mood at the moment.

Another idea for how he could blow off steam crossed his mind. The others would be super pissed at him for it, but before his sensible brain could kick in and stop him, he pulled out his phone and shot off the text. He felt instant regret but also a weird sense of relief at hopefully something exciting to do.

Placing his mobile phone on the table he sat back, scanning the club. All the usual types were milling around.

God, he needed more alcohol for this shit tonight.

He leaned forward to grab his drink off the table when his phone pinged. Staring at the thing like it had done him some wrong, he reached over and picked it up.

Well, he did ask for it, he thought as he cast a look over the message before putting it back down again.

After a few minutes, his dark brows dropped low as he finished his drink, instantly pouring another and downing that too. It seemed like he was going to end up on Trade Street after all tonight, doing some under hand dealings himself.

His other night time activities would just have to wait.

Chapter 3

Hunter left the club undetected, going around the back of the building to find the love of his life and the one thing that guaranteed to lighten his mood—his motorbike.

The sleek custom built black panther Harley was, other than the club, the one thing in his life that he'd done right. He'd owned her for a decade now, and she was as reliable as they came. Every added extra he could get when he'd had her built, he'd had done, and she had never let him down.

Running his hand over the smooth metal, he felt bad for having left her unattended in a generic parking space when he'd parked up the night before, but he'd had little choice due to the ugly yellow skip that was taking up residence in front of the underground parking lot beneath the club. He'd called the company straight away to move it, but apparently skip firms didn't operate over the weekend. He made a mental note to call them first thing tomorrow morning to get them to move it before he had to leave her out in the open again.

Hopping on board, he turned the key, and as she roared to life, he gave himself a few seconds just to feel the power beneath him. His eyes closed on their own accord as he breathed in the smell of diesel and her engine fumes before kicking up the stand and heading off down town to his other job- as a demon assassin. Unlike being an Enforcer, this was a title he wasn't proud of. He didn't do it for or need the money that was associated with the high- payout assassin work, unlike a lot of the others that worked for Bacchus, the demon warlord of the area, which, more times than not, caused bad blood between them and the other assassins. They all had it in their heads from the beginning that Hunter and his brothers thought that they were better than them due to their Enforcer titles and their higher financial status, but being ashamed of a role and thinking you're above others that do the same job, were two very different things.

The reality was, they were all in the same shitty situation, just for many different reasons. It didn't make him any better or worse than them.

It was a shit situation gone bad for him and his brothers; how they'd found themselves owing a debt to an assassin demon warlord, but with only five years left of service, after the century they had already endured, it was nothing.

They all counted down the hours until they were free, and hopefully Hunter's job tonight would knock a little more time off for them.

Baccus's assassin den was hidden about five miles away from the Cellar, on Trade Street, and about the same distance from Hunter's apartment. If you didn't know where it was, you'd never find it. On a strict need-to-know basis, the entrance was hidden by a spell that only demons with Bacchus' brand could see. Hunter and his brothers had had his mark branded on their wrists the day they were initiated into the den, essentially linking them to him until their debt was paid. Usually a message or call would come through with a job, stating the information on the hit along with the amount of time it would take off their remaining debt, but if you texted in and requested a job like he had earlier, you'd get a better payout, but with it came a shittier, more dangerous job.

Viden had had his ability to text in for jobs revoked after he'd taken it upon himself to try and clear their debt single-handedly. He'd made the mistake that got them into the assassin situation, but it wasn't his job to fix it. They were all in agreement over that. Roles reversed Hunter would have done exactly the same thing.

This was the first time that Hunter himself had ever texted in for a job, but he didn't regret it. He was sure that the feeling would change later in face of what job he was assigned, and if not that, then the grief he was going to get from the others when they found out about it.

These days, there were more and more hit for hire type jobs coming through, so he hoped that he'd just be given one of those, get it done, and meet up with Viden before the night wore on. He guessed the den needed the high payouts that came from the outside jobs. It wasn't his place to ask questions, but as an Enforcer, it was his job to wonder where the jobs were coming in from.

Hunter hated it, but his hands were tied. He'd never risk his brothers over refusing a job. They could do what they wanted to him, but Bacchus knew that his brothers were his weakness, and he wasn't above threatening them, but refusing jobs meant more time added, and nothing was worth that.

He pulled up on his bike and left her in his usual parking spot, away from the entrance to the den, and walked the rest of the way. Slipping unnoticed down the alleyway between two office-looking buildings, with his black leather jacket pulled tight along with his black jeans and dark hair, he quickly disappeared into the shadows.

His boots ate up the ground as he strode quickly towards the shitty-looking emergency escape door nestled deep in the shadows. Crouching down, he pretended to tie his laces while checking for any followers or nosey homeless people out and about.

Seeing no one, he straightened up slowly and pushed through the metal door.

Inside, he was greeted by an empty room, save for Lana the lash demon, who always worked the front desk. Her eyes lit up when she saw him.

Quickly getting up, she smoothed down her super short red dress and came around the front of the desk. She tottered over to him on stilettos and got way up in his personal space, rubbing her hands over his pecs.

"Hunter, you haven't been here in so long. I thought you'd forgotten about me."

Batting her heavily mascaraed eyes at him, he took hold of her hands and moved them away from his chest. She made his skin crawl, but he may need her later on, depending on what this 'job' was. Although for him, demons didn't give him the recharge of energy he needed, they did serve the purpose of keeping his Demon sated, which was just as important. No energy and a rage-filled demon would be bad news.

He'd been there, done that, and he didn't want a retake.

"I'd never forget you, baby girl, but I've got business to deal with first," he said as he moved past her and punched his way through the double doors behind the desk before she could reply.

As soon as he was through the doors, a wall of heat hit him square in the face, causing him to miss a breath.

Going down the concrete stairs, he didn't rush. Taking his phone out, he thought about texting Viden but decided against it. Pocketing the thing again, he walked down the next three flights of stairs to the bottom level, going through another set of heavy doors.

The heat and humidity down here reminded him of Hell, not that he'd been there for years now. The corridors were narrow, with noises sounding from all directions, above and below him, it was hard to decipher whether they were noises of pain or pleasure, knowing the den it was probably a mixture of both. The walls seemed to writhe on their own- ooze and blood- and god knows what came out of them.

Hunter always hated coming here. He'd hoped that by texting in, they would just send him the job through, but he should have known better.

The corridor opened up to the large area where subjects were brought in to be punished and where arranged fights took place. He looked up at the metal walkway that ran around the floor above that acted as a viewing platform, so demons could watch the fights below and cheer on the ones they had put bets on. Last time Hunter had been here, a couple of demons who'd wronged each other were duelling to the death right where he was standing now. He hadn't waited around to see who had won the fight, but if the bloodstains surrounding him were any indication, it hadn't been a quick win for whoever was the victor.

Many demons were milling around upstairs on the platform. The sight of him sending a ripple of whispered words and growls in his direction, but he couldn't care less. He played by the rules, and he could take care of himself.

"Well, if it isn't our very own law-abiding citizen," a voice boomed from the top level.

Hunter raised his eyes to see Kane, a valker demon, leaning over the balcony, his arms propped up on the railings. He was pretty tall but wasn't packing the sort of muscle that Hunter was, and with a head of crazy red hair, he was handsome in his own way and pretty much a permanent fixture of the den, being Bacchus's brains of the operation. One look from him had the other demons scurrying away.

Lucky for him, he liked the guy.

"It's been a while, Kane. So...what's the job you've brought me in for?"

Kane smirked before volting over the ledge and landing right in front of him. "Oh, we've got you a hit alright."

"Well, yeah, I guessed as much. Why couldn't you text it through like usual?"

A loud groan echoed down through the halls, which had Hunter's Demon stirring. He needed to take care of him soon before he started getting pissy.

"This one is a bit...different. We're talking top-end, high payout."

"Keep the money you know I'm not interested in it. Give me the information so I can get out of here." He was getting angsty being this close to so much pleasure and pain.

Kane narrowed his eyes at Hunter and lowered his voice. "Heads up. This is just a suggestion, but you might want to let your Demon out for this one."

Hunter looked him in the eye.

Kane knew the shitshow that letting his Demon loose again would create, so this job must be bad. His Demon had ruled the show a few years ago, back before he was an assassin or an Enforcer- ever since Hunter's whole family were butchered in front of him. The sane, humanised part of him had regressed back, letting his Demon have 100% control. The trauma of losing his only relatives had left his mind weak, and it was the easiest and most cowardly way out of dealing with the heartache that he had refused to face.

His Demon purred at the memory of the control. Wandering alone, he'd been a regular in the darkest of demon pits. He had been ruthless and brutal, and no rules could keep him in check. The den had become his regular hangout; it was where the darker types all hung out. Down here, as long as it didn't involve humans, pretty much anything went, and his Demon had thrived in the environment.

He was one mistake away from being thrown back down to Hell for good when he'd picked a fight with the wrong incubus demon- Viden. They had beat each other shitless, but they had recognised something within each other before it had become fatal.

Afterwards, they had stuck together, neither having met another incubus before other than their fathers. They acted as a buffer to each others most heinous traits and worked together to suppress their Demons so they could get back to a level of normal and live in a more civilised way.

It was hard- one of the hardest things Hunter had ever had to do- to rebuild his life after the mess his Demon left.

Not long after, they found Theo and then Adriel, and he'd learnt to love them all. Love- a feeling that he thought himself incapable of since the loss of his family. He'd be damned if he lost control again.

It had been Viden that had saved him. Shit, what was he doing here? Out of them all, it would be Viden that suffered the most by his actions of messaging in for a job. He had to get in and out and hope that his brother didn't hear of what he'd done.

"Not a chance, Kane. Now give me the intel."

Kane thrust a bit of parchment into his hands.

S.T.K

A.Logan

Frequent at Sin the downtown strip club

72 hours until completion

$1 million

He read it twice, then three times.

One million dollars? Who the hell was worth that kind of price tag? Hunter thought.

"What the fuck is this? Nothing else? How am I meant to find someone if I don't even know what their full name is? What they look like? Age or anything? The chances of me offing the wrong person is way up there," he said, thrusting the parchment back at him. "Where's the normal ID?" At Kane's nonchalant shrug he carried on. "Eye colour? Hair colour? The dude's favourite takeout? Anything? Help me out here, Kane"

"You have 72 hours," was all he replied.

Quick hits weren't exactly unheard of, but usually at least a few other assassins were in on it, or all of them for a bit of sport.

Hunter itched at his jaw, where stubble had grown in. "Why's this one different? Other than no info, why the high price tag?"

A few other demons started to enter the arena then, followed by some creatures Hunter had no clue of their origins.

Kane motioned for him to follow him over to a sheltered corner away from them. "I told Bacchus that you wouldn't give a shit about the money, so this one is worth two years."

Hunter's head whipped up to him. He didn't even dare breathe.

Walking back up the stairs in a daze, he still couldn't quite believe that one hit could be worth two years less to him. It had never happened before. A normal hit was usually only worth a few hours, maybe a day if Bacchus had a personal interest in them.

As he walked into the foyer, he was glad to see that Lana was preoccupied with a group of young furies by her desk. Keeping his head down, he quickly ducked out of the door and out into the night. For the first time all night, and in he didn't know how long, he felt like he had a challenge and something good he could do that would actually make a difference, not just to him but to the guys too.

Heaven help this Logan guy. He wouldn't know what hit him.

Striding back down the street to his bike, he threw his leg over and hit the gas, heading downtown.

Chapter 4

Evie was late for work, like usual. She frantically ran through her small apartment, looking for her car keys. She always put them in the same place when she came home- always by the door- but they weren't there. She'd come in late from her shift the night before and was so tired that she couldn't even remember how she got into bed, let alone where she'd put her damned keys.

On her third pass around, feeling deflated, she sat with a huff on the arm of her sofa, putting her head in her hands.

Argh!! Life wasn't meant to be this hard, she thought. It wasn't the missing keys, but everything else. She wasn't quite sure what she'd done to deserve the shit hand that she had been dealt in life, but at 24, she had already had to deal with far more than any normal person should ever have too.

Her whole adult life she had spent looking over her shoulder for her abusive foster father, who had vowed to her that there was no place on Earth that she could hide where he wouldn't find her.

She'd left home at 19 and had moved from place to place ever since then, never settling for more than a few months before moving on again. He had been catatonic when she had left him the first time, and the promise of a monthly pay check for having her there. He'd found her easily the first two times that she had run. The memory of the beatings he'd given her still raw in her memory, but she had been sloppy at hiding where she had gone back then. She had learned from her mistakes, and this time was different. She had changed everything, going totally off-grid, walking, and hitching to a remote location before working and borrowing her way to where she was now.

It wasn't all just in her head that he was still chasing her. He'd always been just one step behind her, tracking her from place to place. She had to keep an eye on his movements as well as figure out where she was going to move next. Getting to where she was now had been hard, but so worth it.

She'd been living in Foston Hall for nearly a year, but it was getting to the point where she'd have to move on again soon. Just the thought had her fighting back tears. She liked it here and didn't want to have to leave again.

She was momentarily distracted from her pity party by a ping coming from her phone. Grabbing it, she saw it was a message from Jax, the hunky security guard from the club where she worked.

Are you coming in?

She quickly fired back a reply

I'm running late and can't find my keys. Be there asap.

Leaning back, she moved her sofa cushion, and finally, the sound of jangling keys had her looking up to the ceiling and thanking god.

Need me to come and get you?

Ah, Jax, he was so perfect. She'd known him for the year that she had been in the town, meeting him shortly after getting the job at the club. There had been an interest in each other from both parties when they'd first met, which resulted in a couple of awkward dates, but they got along so well that it was more like a brother-sister bond rather than a romantic one. Definitely on her side, at least. She wasn't 100% sure he was on the same wave length as she was, though.

It's ok I've found them. I'm on my way!

Grabbing her bag and red coat, she locked the door behind her as she left and jogged over to her faded white Dodge pickup, jumping inside. Turning the key, she had to give it a couple of tries before the old girl fired up. She cranked up the heat and checked for puffy eyes in the mirror, putting on a generous amount of concealer and mascara to hide the fact that she'd been a hot mess for most of the day before she drove out of the car park and took the 10-minute drive downtown to the strip club where she worked, Sin.

Evie dashed though the back door of the club, where she prayed that she still had a job. She checked the time on her phone: 11:17p.m. She was so screwed. Her shift was meant to start at 11, and even though she had floored her old truck to get there on time, there was just no way she would have made it. She could try and give the excuse that her watch had stopped working or her alarm hadn't gone off, or she could just hope that no one had noticed, but Jax's text had shown that at least one person had noted her absence.

Dropping her bag on the dressing room shelf, she looked out to the bar area and realised that no amount of excuses were going to work this time as Scarlet stood drumming her fake red nails on the bar top where Evie always worked, and there was no sign of Lizzy, the other girl that usually worked the bar with her.

Evie looked at Scarlet who hadn't noticed her yet. She was wearing her usual get-up of a tarty red dress that set off her flame-red hair- Scarlet by name and all that. As she wiped down the bar, she looked more than pissed off at having to cover Evie's slack.

"I'm so sorry!" Evie called out, hurrying through the doorway, pulling her long, ash blonde hair out of her messy bun and running her fingers through it to get the knots out.

"How about you stop saying you're sorry constantly and just get here on time from now on. How about that? We're all sick of covering your arse and losing out on money because we are stuck behind your bar rather than earning proper money out on the floor." Scarlet looked her up and down, taking in her thrown on fitted grey t-shirt and black jeans that had holes in them. Thank god for the current fashion to hide her wealth, or lack of it. "If you weren't so fridged, you could be doing the same, and then you wouldn't have to be working every hour of the day and night rushing between jobs."

Evie just caught the sodden bar towel before it hit her in the face, but it didn't stop the excess liquid that splattered her in its projection.

She watched as Scarlet strutted away, stopping by the first table she reached and dropping down onto one of her regular's laps. As she stroked her fingers through his hair, she reached behind his back and flipped Evie the bird.

Leaning her back against the wall, Evie looked up at the mirror-covered ceiling. Maybe it was a good thing that it was time to leave this place, she thought, leaning her head back on the wall and closing her eyes.

"She's a bitch." A deep, rumbling voice came from the edge of the bar, pulling her head around to the sound of it.

On the furthest stool from the stage, propping up her bar, was a huge man that she hadn't spotted when she'd first arrived. Hidden in the most heavily shadowed corner, he blended in well with the wall; wearing all black he was nothing at all like the club's usual clientele. Even with his head bowed nursing a beer, she could tell that he was quite possibly the best-looking man she had ever seen. With black, messy hair and a Hollywood handsomeness she wasn't used to entertaining, she was suddenly at a loss for words.

He didn't look up from his drink as he picked at the label with hands bigger than she'd ever seen and arms as thick as her thighs, his muscles straining the tight t-shirt he was wearing.

"Ain't that the truth," she breathed.

At her words, he looked up at her.

As their eyes locked, Evie felt as if she was being stripped naked, right down to her soul.

It wasn't that he was looking at her all seedy like the other guys in the club did, it was just his eyes and the grey intensity of them at which he was taking her in.

She'd never been looked at like that before.

"You've obviously never been in here before," she said, breaking eye contact before it got overly awkward. Gathering all the empty beer bottles from the side of the bar that Scarlet had neglected to tidy away, just to give her hands something to do, she threw them down the chute a little more forceful than necessary and winced at the sound of breaking glass that reverberated up from the metal container.

Shit, she needed a break in life. A hot guy giving her the eye was not her biggest problem here.

She looked up at him to see his eyebrows raised and his beer bottle paused at his lips.

"You having a tough day?" He asked, lowering it without taking a drink.

"Yeah, something like that," she mumbled, leaning back against the doorframe she had just entered through again. How was she going to get enough money behind her to skip town again? She was only just scraping by as it were. Another red letter this morning was going to force her hand. Maybe Scarlet was right, and she needed to do more at the club. It wouldn't be for long, just until she had enough money to leave.

"What makes you think that I haven't been in here before?" The man's deep voice brought her back into the present and away from her inner turmoil.

"Well, I just thought..." She looked around desperately, trying to think of something, rather than admitting that she would have definitely remembered him if she'd seen him in here before, and the other girls would most definitely have mentioned him.

He smirked at her. "Relax, you're right, I haven't been in here before."

Oh yeh, she doubted he'd ever needed to pay for a female's attention. The guy just oozed confidence and fuck-me vibes. "Are you here for a security job or something?"

"No." He watched her while drinking from his beer bottle, his eyes narrowing suspiciously.

Evie didn't trust him. Had her father caught up with her, and this guy was here to drag her back to him? "So what brings you in here then?"

What a dumb question. What else brings a guy to a strip club? She rolled her eyes at her own stupidity. She needed to rein in her paranoia, or at least be less obvious about it.

"I fancied a change of scenery is all." He drank from his bottle again and gave her a look that made her feel as if he wanted to eat her for dinner. "Turns out the scenery is quite nice."

She snorted at the cheesy remark. Shaking her head, she went to the other end of the bar to the waiting patrons. If he wasn't here because of Drew, then the guy was looking in the wrong place for an easy ride. She was pretty good with showing that she was not on the menu at the strip club, but maybe he wasn't very observant of her clothing attire compared to the other girls and the fact that she was stationed behind a bar and not on the main floor. It could be that he truly had never been to a strip club before, and she was the most un-intimidating girl in the place which was attracting him to her.

She would just keep to the other end of the bar when she could, and if he carried on, then she'd tell him black and white that she wasn't available.

However nice he was to look at.

~~~~~~~

Hunter's eyebrows shot up at this woman's ability to shun his incubus vibes.

It was the first time that he could ever remember his Demon stir by just looking at a female, but he'd stirred alright, taking notice of this girl and pushing him to get her attention again for a little more air time.

When he'd first arrived at the club, he'd asked the first few workers he'd come across if an A Logan was working there or if they were a regular, but no one knew anyone of the name.

He was frustrated at himself for getting into this situation, knowing that if he was going to forgo his night off work for more work, then he should be with Viden right now, not hanging out in a strip club on his own. Ever since then, he'd been sat at that bar, listening to the redhead moan about the missing bar girl. Little did he know that she would become his new focus at the club.

She'd not even spoken more than a few words to him, and his Demon had woken right up. Something was up with that.

Recharge target for the night identified, he did love a challenge, and by the way that she was now trying to avoid him at the other end of the bar, she would definitely be that.

He remained where he was but started to pay more attention to her without being too obvious about it. Her hair was long and had that mused just woken up look that Hunter wasn't used to seeing- he was more of a wham bam, thank you, mam, kind of a guy. He didn't think he'd ever actually woken up with a girl in a bed before.

His Demon was all into the idea of getting this girl into a bed and keeping her there until he'd had his fill.

Hunter shook his head to try and get a grip on him and went back to looking at the girl again, trying to work out what had gotten him so hot and bothered.

Her features were perfect. Eyes a little big for her face, but she looked to be trying to blend in, rather than the other girls he was used to seeing who all tried their hardest to look a quarter of her natural beauty.

Her big, ice-blue eyes seemed to look right at his Demon when their eyes had met, but it had been when he'd first heard her voice that Hunter had truly taken notice. It had been as if she had been speaking directly to his Demon, bypassing the more humanised part of him and going directly to his beast.

He was used to being around women- hello, sex demon- but they were usually throwing themselves at him, not trying to avoid him like she was now.

She was something entirely different.

Hunter didn't trust it.

He looked out to the floor of people and to the obvious working girls, in their revealing outfits or no outfits at all. He couldn't say that he'd been in many strip clubs in his life, but he'd seen them on TV and this one didn't seem like a typical one. It was clean and all the girls looked healthy, and other than the bar girl, they all looked reasonably happy too.

The red neon lights that shone from the walls and reflected off the mirrored ceiling illuminated the two stages where the girls were dancing and a handful of men sat watching them. He tried to let the atmosphere of the place keep his attention, but his Demon was demanding that he go back to the bar girl again, and before he knew what he was doing, his eyes whipped back to her.

He should be all over the half-naked women in the club for a quick bump and grind to charge up and get his Demon to chill the fuck out. He could even be doing that while he pumped them for any information on this Logan guy that was on the assassin hit. He told himself this, but he seemed to be rooted to the spot, and he couldn't pull his eyes away from her.

She had just finished serving a guy when she turned around and noticed him watching her. He tried to act non-fussed by spinning in his seat so that he was facing out at the dancing girls on stage again, but he felt her as she walked back over to him.

"Do you know who I am?" she asked, putting her hands on her hips. As he turned his head back to face her, she whispered, "If Drew has paid you to find me, I can pay you more to leave me alone, just give me a little time..." Her voice died in her throat as she saw the confused look that he was giving her. "You have no idea what I'm talking about, do you?" As he raised his eyebrow, she continued, "ok, if you could just forget that I'd said anything at all, that would be great."

"I have no idea who you are."

A few seconds passed before she shook her head and said, "Don't worry, I'm no one."

"Is this Drew guy trying to hurt you?" He frowned, leaning in closer to her.

She looked at him, searching for some link to this Drew prick, he guessed as he felt her fear- an old, deep fear that she thought she was hiding so well behind a wall, but he felt it like it was his own.

"It's nothing I can't handle. Honestly."

He didn't believe her, but that could wait. "Well, your not no one. What's your name?"

She looked him up and down, obviously still not trusting him, but replied, "It's Evie...I'm Evie, and yours?"

"Hunter"

Fuck, did he honestly just give her his real name. Usually if he was working a job he'd give an alias at least.

He was so in trouble here.

His Demon suddenly surged forwards and started fighting his way to take Hunter over and claim this girl, to protect her from this *Drew*. Squeezing his eyes shut quickly, he managed to hide his all-black demon eyes that came out whenever the guy was in control.

"Are you ok?" She asked, placing her cold hand on his forearm.

He fought his Demon back easily this time, as the guy was running on empty energy wise, and as soon as he knew his eyes were back to their normal grey, he opened them to find a concerned look on her face. He couldn't even blame his Demon this time, he couldn't help himself as he checked her out. Her blue eyes widened as he inched closer to her, as she searched his face and settled on his lips, just as he caught himself.

"Look, I know where we are, but I'm not available like that." She flushed. "I'm sorry if I gave you the wrong impression."

He looked momentarily confused before getting with the programme. "I didn't think you were a..." he rubbed his hand over the back of his neck.

"You do know where you are, though?" She raised an eyebrow, smiling. It quickly disappeared as she frowned. "Hang on, why didn't you think I was a stripper?"

Shit, was there any answer he could give her that wasn't an insult? The saving grace came in the form of a couple of guys stumbling into the bar, a few seats away from him.

His Demon growled at the intrusion, causing him to have to cough to hide the noise.

"Yo, sexy lady. Two lagers when you're ready."

She stayed standing with her hands on her hips, looking at Hunter.

"Hey, you deaf? Is that why you're behind the bar and wearing so much?" his friend sniggered.

Hunter looked at them sideways and said, "you want to keep all your teeth you'll speak to her with a little bit more respect."

"Being the boyfriend of a whore, hey Billy, isn't that your life ambition?" The drunk, slimy, 30-something-year old slapped his mate 'Billy' on the back, finding himself hilarious.

Hunter sighed loudly before standing to his full height. Even Evie took in a breath and stepped back from the bar at the sight of him. The two guys soon lost their smiles as they looked him up and down.

"We meant no disrespect, sorry, Miss," Billy stuttered, moving away from the bar and Hunter quickly.

He sat back down, picking up his drink again.

"Thanks, but there was really no need, it comes part and parcel with this job" Evie looked flushed, like she didn't quite know where to look. "Well, have a good night." She didn't look him in the eye as she turned around and disappeared out the back quickly.

What the actual fuck had just happened? He blinked. Had he just been handed his arse on a plate by a cute little blonde that right about now should be putty in his hands? And then possibly scared her off with his physique rather than draw her in? He couldn't remember the last time, ok, ever that his Demon's tricks hadn't got him what he wanted, and right now he really wanted some attention from that bar girl.

He got up from his stool and walked around the bar to look out of the door that she had disappeared into, but she was gone.

His Demon let out a growl that he couldn't cover this time, earning him a few unwanted glances in his direction. Feeling his eyes turn black again, he clung to his control over the beast.

Casting his eyes down, he prayed that they hadn't been noticed by anyone and that he didn't lose control over his Demon in this club.

Chapter 5

Evie tried to slow down her racing heart.

Wow, that guy.

Hunter.

In all of his size and muscle, it was as soon as their eyes had met that she had felt things. Sure, there was always some guy at the bar trying his luck with her, and she had her regulars who kept her company on her shifts- hell, she'd even been out on a date with one guy a couple of times that had come into Sin for his mates stag do once before. Yeh, he'd been nice, but this was totally different. One look from this Hunter guy, and she had wanted more. Even now, she was fighting the need to go back to him.

Crouching down, she put her back to the girls lockers and looked up to the ceiling. "Pull it together, Evie, you need this job," she mumbled to herself.

She needed more than this job. She had all of twenty dollars to get her through until her next pay check in two weeks, which was fine by her. She didn't need luxuries, but she did need to put more aside for her next town hop. She had been putting it off because she didn't want to leave this town, but she had to stick to her plan, and that was to disappear again, and the clock was ticking. Tomorrow she'd put on something different, she'd borrow something skimpy, and she'd try to get a different gig at Sin so she could leave this place behind. As for the man at her bar, yeah he was hot and obviously the protective type, but that didn't mean she was having a moment with him.

"Evie?" A male voice came through the door just as Jax appeared around the corner. Noticing her sitting against the lockers, he went into instant security guard mode as he rushed forward to kneel in front of her. "Shit, are you ok?"

"Just a guy getting me all hot and bothered," she fake-fanned her face.

"You mean it's not just me that gets your heart rate up?" He said, helping her to her feet, offering up one of his drop-dead grins. "So you found your keys then?"

She looked up at him, his brown hair falling over his onyx eyes, and wished again that she felt something romantic towards the only man to have ever cared about her- well, about all the girls in the club.

"Not always, and yes, they were on my sofa. Must have missed them when I looked the first ten times," she said, giving him a shy smile. Just before it could get weird between them, she asked. "Hey Jax, you're tight with the owner of Sin, right?"

"Sure, we know each other," he nodded.

"You think you could get me a meeting with them tomorrow night?" She looked up at him, from her 5'6 he towered over her, and he was packing the same kind of muscle that the guy at her bar had been.

"That depends. What are you thinking, Evie? If it's what I think it is, then no, not even no, but hell no," he held out his hands before she could protest. "You're too good for this place as it is. Let me help you out for a while to take some of the pressure off."

She shook her head. "I need to look after myself, J, and I couldn't bare owing you money too." ...and being stuck in this place longer trying to pay you back, she thought to herself. She smiled up at him. "That doesn't mean that I don't appreciate the offer, though." She took his offered arm so he could lead her back out towards the bar area.

Just before they got there, Jax stopped and turned to her again. "Listen, Evie, it's not a good idea you meeting with the owners of this place, especially to ask them if you can start stripping here," he shook his head to stop her come back. "Let me speak to them about getting you a raise for working the bar."

She thought about it, and even though she was late more times than early recently, she had been a good worker, and in truth, she really didn't want to be a stripper. No one had ever seen her naked body except herself, and she didn't want to start off with random strangers paying to see it. Not if she could avoid it, but unfortunately, she didn't have the luxury of time on her side to wait for a raise to come through. She needed extra cash, like yesterday. The reality of her situation hit her, but she couldn't tell Jax that, and she truly did appreciate him trying to help her out.

"Ok Jax...thanks. I don't know what we'd do without you." She said as she was already forming a plan in her head to try and fix a meeting with her bosses herself.

~~~~~~~

Hunter walked into the gent's toilets. He did a quick check around and was relieved to find himself alone. Flicking the lock on the main door, he leaned back against it, silently hitting his head against the frame. What was wrong with his damned Demon? Maybe she had put some kind of spell on him- a witch, maybe? Although she seemed far too innocent for that kind of business, maybe a witch had put a spell on her- that she attracted demons- unheard of and super unlikely, but a possibility.

He'd spent years in the human world and had always managed to keep his Demon under careful supervision. Now, because of this girl, he was at serious risk of losing control over him. If the bastard had decided that he wanted her fine, he'd happily screw her, but he was trying to take over Hunter to get to her, which was not fine.

He walked over to the mirrors, leaning in and taking a good look at his reflection, trying to find anything different about himself or see a glimpse of his other self as he brewed and paced just under the surface. He was relieved to see his eyes were their normal grey colour.

Frowning, he moved closer to the mirror. "Who are you, Evie? And what have you done to us?" He looked over to the door from which he'd come and without conscious thought, he was suddenly in front of it. His Demon made his hand reach for the door handle that would take him back to her.

"You need to back the fuck off," he said, turning back to the mirror.

"Let me have her." His voice came through deeper, warped, and...involuntary.

Fuck.

"You don't even know her. What you've had one sniff? Leave her alone."

No reply.

Walking over, he leaned closer to the mirror again as he waited for his eyes to turn black or for the Demon to speak again, but he remained silent. It was the first time he'd ever spoken when Hunter was in control, and he didn't know what it meant. He needed to speak to his brothers about it, but he couldn't let on that he was on an assassin job.

Leaning down to the sink, he ran the cold water and splashed some onto his face, trying to regain some kind of clarity. She was effecting him, and he was determined to find out why, even if he was on his own in this.
As he walked back out to the bar area, he saw that Evie had reappeared and was making drinks down at the other end of the bar again.

Shaking his head, he decided to stay at arm's length until he worked out what had his Demon all worked up and told his brain to get back in the game and work out how to find this A. Logan on the hit. He didn't have much time on this one, and even without the usual file on who he was taking out with a picture, he had still hoped that he would be done by now. He could have taken the time given and been meeting up with V already to celebrate.

He walked past the dancing girls on stage and found a quiet, dark corner away from the flashing lights and neon signs. He could disappear here for a little while and look for any demon activity. His eyes travelled to the bar girl, Evie, again. That, and he could keep an eye on her from here to try and work out what her deal was without raising any suspicions.

A couple of hours later, Hunter had learned nothing, but then his eyes had rarely left the bar girl. She only drank lime and soda when a drink was bought for her, and she was highly professional at telling guys that she wasn't on the menu. The other patrons didn't seem particularly drawn to her, as soon as they knew she wouldn't give them what they were looking for, they would move on to the dance floor. No demons anywhere, either, although she obviously had some inner demons of her own, it seemed.

He had noticed that whenever she laughed or sported a genuine smile, her face would fall as if she shouldn't be doing it. He would bet his left nut that it was the guy who was looking for her that had caused it.

When she did let herself smile, her whole face lit up and transformed, which, even low on energy, perked his Demon right up. He was a sap, but he needed something to pass the time, and she wasn't anything like the other girls that worked there. He literally couldn't take his eyes of her.

Did Drew pay you? He wondered who this Drew guy was that was out looking for her and why she was hiding from him?

Someone had paid him to find someone, he reminded himself of that and the fact that she wasn't who he was looking for. He told himself this as he went back to looking at her again.

All of a sudden, his view was blocked by a giant of a man- well, not to his 6'6 but to other human men. This guy was about 6'4 and built like Viden.

Strong and deadly.

The stranger crossed his arms over his massive chest, obviously trying to throw his testosterone at Hunter as a way of intimidating him.

Ha, yeh, nice try.

One thing was for sure- whoever he was, he was messing with the wrong guy.

"Can I help you? You're kind of ruining the view," Hunter said, looking him up and down before trying to look around the hulk of meat.

"You're looking at the wrong girl," he said, pointing in the direction of the girls dancing on the stage. "I'm Jax, the security guard here, and a few people have reported back that you're taking a lot of interest in Evie," he said, narrowing his eyes.

"What of it?" Hunter didn't let on that he gave no shits about the fact that he'd been caught ogling her.

"She would have told you that she wasn't for sale, and I'm telling you again now. I can see you watching her from back here. I don't know who or what you are, but you need to back off."

And what do you know? This guy Jax's eye's flashed all black, the demon equivalent of fuck off.

Hunter scowled.

He wasn't getting any demon vibes off the guy other than his size and build, which was weird seeing as how they could instinctively tell each other's species apart and especially tell demons from humans. For all intents and purposes, this Jax seemed human, which was very, very interesting.

Hunter gave him a cold grin and responded by flashing the all-blacks right back at him along with his Enforcer badge.

Mr. security guard wasn't as quick to hide his oh shit.

Chapter 6

Hunter used some guy's inability to keep his hands to himself from one of the dancing girls on stage as his chance to slip away from Jax, the security guy, before any questions such as what the fuck are you came about.

Jax had simply poked his finger into Hunter's chest and told him not to move until he got back. Yeh, that would be a solid no, he thought as he left the club through the front door. It was late, and he hadn't managed to find this Logan guy or anything about him at all, which didn't bode well for his time frame.

It was a wasted night, but not totally, as he thought of Evie.

He should have used one of the girls there to chill his Demon out, but just the thought of using anyone other than her made him bristle.

This wasn't good, and he wasn't stupid. As much as he didn't want to admit it, his Demon was showing all the first signs of bonding to this girl, which he really, really didn't need right now.

Writing off the night for the den's hit, he decided to scratch his Demon's itch and try and find out more about her.

He milled around outside Sin like a total creeper until the club began to wind down and eventually shut for the night.

Moving into the shadows opposite the staff exit, he waited for Evie to emerge. Every time the door opened, he held his breath, but Evie remained elusive. He hoped that she hadn't left through some other door. The thought vanished as, linked arm in arm with that security bastard, she walked out wearing a red coat with her bag in her hand.

Were they together? Was that why he'd been so protective of her? The thought gave him a sliver of hope that it wasn't his Demon bonding and some other reason he was so attached to her already. If another demon was being drawn to her, then maybe something else was at play here.

Hunter watched as Jax walked her right up to her car door and opened it for her, leaning in on the window frame after she'd hopped inside. He could tell the guy was trying in all his gentleman chivalry to impress her, he could also tell that she just wasn't interested in him like that, and that's what saved the arsehole.

They spoke for a few minutes more, until the security guy straightened and waved her off as she pulled out of the parking lot. The guy swung around from where he stood, his eyes immediately looking to where Hunter was standing.

He was certain he wasn't visible from the parking lot, but still he held his breath. He wasn't scared of being caught, he just couldn't deal with the effort of getting rid of the guy again. It wasn't why he was here.

After a few seconds more staring, Jax looked away and walked over to the motorcycle that was parked next to his. A dark blue bonneville that had caught his attention when he'd parked up earlier.

Guy was still a dick.

He hopped on it, kicking it to life, and disappeared off into the night.

Hunter jogged over and jumped on his own bike. Doing the same thing, he peeled out of the parking lot and followed the direction that Evie's car had gone.

Luckily, she didn't live far from Sin, and he kept up with her easily, making sure to keep enough distance so that she didn't notice him, although if she had, she'd probably just think it was the security guard keeping an eye on her.

Her apartment was in one of the rougher parts of town, but it wasn't known for its demon activity, which was a bonus in his eyes.

She pulled her car around the back of the complex as he spun his bike around and ditched it in a dark alley leading to another street next to where she was parking. He tried to hide his bike as best he could. He just had to hope that she was still there when he got back.

He raced around just in time to see her walking up to the condo steps, rummaging in her bag for her keys. Quickly flattening his back against the wall, he willed his racing heart to slow down.

Feeling like a total peeping Tom, he watched as the ground-floor apartment's living room light came on as he crept towards the window. The curtains were so thin that he could see her shape moving around inside. Through the gap in them, he could see the small apartment, bed, kitchenette, and sofa all in one room, and a small TV off to the left. She disappeared into what he guessed was the bathroom and appeared a few minutes later, wearing the cutest mint green tank top and shorts nightie combo.

He should leave. He totally shouldn't be watching her like this.

She grabbed the blanket off the back of the sofa and a book that was resting on the top and settled down on the cushions.

He took one last lingering look at her and willed himself away, much to his Demon's disappointment.

As he walked back to his bike, he shot Viden a text message to see where he was.

He'd at least do one thing right tonight.

It was later that night that Hunter truly realised what shit he was in, as the further he moved away from Evie and her apartment, the more frantic he began to feel at wanting to get back to her.

Viden hadn't answered his messages or calls, but that wasn't anything new for him, especially when he knew Hunter wasn't on rotation.

Out of options, he decided that Viden would call him back later, and so he headed back downtown to his place to try and get some sleep. He was back on Enforcer rotation tomorrow, and he was still running low on energy for his Demon. He didn't want to make a mistake on a job because he was tired too.

As he walked in through the front foyer, he felt a strange feeling of detachment as he entered the apartment he'd owned for 3 years now. It was usually his happy place. Only he and his brothers ever came here.

Tonight, it felt cold.

Lonely.

He had to speak to Viden about his situation with Kali as soon as possible to see if this was what he suspected. That was going to be a conversation he would very much rather not have.

Exhausted but determined to get to the bottom of this new link he felt towards Evie and to find this A Logan quickly, he went to bed. Tomorrow would be another day, and one he hoped would be full of answers.

The thought kept him awake long into the morning.

His plans for the next day never materialised. He couldn't think straight, he couldn't eat properly, and when he finally fell asleep, he hadn't slept well.

His energy level had dropped significantly, and his Demon prowled just under the surface. Ready and waiting. He wouldn't be shy about getting what he needed from Evie.

His next two days passed in the same way.

Viden had called numerous times, but he hadn't answered. He was too busy in his own head to have his friend's input added right now, and it was most definitely a conversation they needed to have face-to-face.

He needed to get back to the mission of finding and eliminating Logan, but he just couldn't keep away from her. He shared his time between visiting Sin, lurking outside Evie's apartment, and following her around in the daytime. She worked long hours at Sin and worked in a book store during the day, but she still somehow found the time to go the gym most days for hours on end too.

Following her was the only way to keep his Demon off his back and satisfied.

He'd also found out that she had a fake ID, probably to do with that dude Drew who was after her, but he couldn't find anything about him or where she was from.

Every lead he got led him to a dead end.

He wasn't in a good place mentally, but tonight he'd reach out for help.

Hunter went to find the one person who might understand what he was going through.

He went to the Cellar.

He walked down the line of waiting people outside. It was busy as usual, even at this late time of night, and like usual, more than one girl tried to get his attention as he passed by, but his mind was fixed purely on another girl. Still, he was running on dry. He'd need to force himself to take care of business sooner rather than later.

His Demon growled at the nearest girl, causing her to back away from him before she made contact with his arm as he walked past her.

He strode through the dark club quickly, nodding to the various people and demons that worked there along the way. Heading straight for their VIP table, he found Viden already there with two drinks in front of him.

He was dressed in his black Enforcer fighting clothes, and his gaze was fixated on Kali, who was working her usual bar across from their section.

As soon as he noticed Hunter approaching, his eyes narrowed. "Where the hell have you been, Hunter? You've not been to the club in days, and I've been patrolling on my own. Your Enforcer jobs are stacking up. I can't keep covering for you." As he sat down across from him, Viden seemed to notice just how bad he looked. "What's going on, and don't bullshit me."

"I'm in trouble, V"

"What kind of trouble, and why am I only just hearing about it?"

"It's sensitive, especially for you."

"Spill"

"I think I've bonded to a human."

His eyes narrowed. "And why is that sensitive for me?" After a few seconds, his gaze followed Hunter's to Kali, and he huffed.

"You're the only one that can help me work out if that's what's happening to me."

"Demons don't bond with humans."

"Maybe I'm different. You know that demon hookups don't work for me the same as they do for you."

He shrugged. "Maybe. I don't know how you expect me to help you, though. I haven't bonded to anyone."

Hunter just stared at him.

"I haven't. You're better off asking the Guild about it."

He had thought about asking the Enforcer Guild about bondings, but he didn't want to give any of them reasons to put him under surveillance, or Evie. They knew he had to use human females for strength, but as a rule, demons had to leave them well alone.

"You know I can't."

Viden seemed to be contemplating what to say next. His gaze slid over to Kali again, where she stood, pouring drinks for a group of girls.

"It feels like your soul belongs somewhere else when you're not around her," he said quietly.

Hunter didn't dare breathe in case he stopped talking.

"The minute you wake up to the minute you try to sleep, your thoughts are solely on what she's doing, where she is, who she's with, if she's ok, or if she needs you. Using other girls makes you feel sick, but there is a way around it. I suggest you do just that and move on with your life."

Viden had never spoken like that with him or anyone else that he knew of. His heart hurt for what he'd been living through all of this time without them knowing.

"How? How do you block something like this out?"

"Alcohol, and a lot of it. Vodka is the only thing that works for me. Two bottles, and I can convince my Demon that anyone I want is her."

His sadness deepend.

"You need to do it, Hunt. You look like shit, and it will only get worse."

Hunter leaned his arms forward on his knees. He knew he was right, and he was running out of time for the Den job.

He had to go back to Sin.

Nodding solemnly at him, he agreed, "She isn't working tonight. I'll go for a last check-in to see if she's ok, and then meet you at that strip joint, Sin."

He didn't like the thought of using a girl from where Evie worked, but it was better than meeting back at the Cellar. Now Hunter knew what Viden went through on a daily basis, he'd try and make his life easier anyway he could. Sin was definitely the better option. Hunter would stay away from the workers, they all knew his face by now, and none approached him for work anymore. A few had tried to talk to him when he first started going in to watch Evie, but he had stayed in the shadows, trying to act inconspicuous, and they soon left him alone. She was as much of a mystery to him now as she had been the first time he'd seen her.

He thought about the security guard, Jax the demon, who he couldn't get a read on, and wondered if she was the same as him. Had she somehow suppressed her demon side the same way he had? If so, then perhaps he wouldn't be able to keep them from the knowledge of the Enforcer's Guild after all, but she never went to any demon parts of town and wasn't part of any other worldly groups. Other than Jax, the security guard-no demons. She had a few friends, but none seemed close to her, like she kept them at arm's length.

Again, he thought to the guy she mentioned, Drew.

The mystery of her made her even more attractive to Hunter's Demon and his need to know and protect her.

"Message me when you're heading over there, and I'll follow." Viden said, bringing Hunter's attention back to the table.

He appreciated the fact that he hadn't call him out on them meeting at a strip club, and clapped V on the back as he stood up. "I appreciate this more than you'll ever know, brother."

"This conversation never happened. Don't forget what I said about the alcohol."

Hunter nodded, leaving him.

Striding across to the main bar, he grabbed two bottles of vodka as he went.

Just before he left the main room, his inner club owner and Enforcer role made him turn to a darkened corner of the dance floor, where a low-life bael demon was getting a bit hands-on with an obviously very drunk human woman. She seemed to be trying to get away from him without attracting too much attention.

Scrubbing a hand down his face, Hunter willed the thought of Evie and him and Viden's conversation away as he strolled over to them, leaning on the wall beside the pair.

"Miss, are you alright?"

The bael looked at Hunter with pure disgust in his eyes.

"Don't get involved with stuff that doesn't involve you, incubus," he sneered the last word.

Yeh, it was no revelation that incubus demons were seen as the lower society in the demon hierarchy, but that didn't bother Hunter one bit, especially when it came to his club's patrons.

"That's Mr.Incubus to you, and you're in *my* club, so you need to watch your tongue if you want to be welcome here again."

The woman looked to him with glassy eyes. Her dress had been pushed up her legs, and one of her shoulder straps hung off her arm.

"I want to go home," she slurred.

"Then home you shall go," he said, placing his arm under hers and steering her away from the fuming bael.

Pissing off other demons was one of Hunter's favourite hobbies, it's why he'd become an Enforcer in the first place. That, paired with rescuing a damsel in distress, meant that his night had just gotten a little bit better.

He cast a look over his shoulder as he steered the woman towards the stairs that led out to the front of the club and waiting taxis. The bael had gone and disappeared into another part of the club.

As Hunter helped the woman into a taxi, he pulled his phone out and texted one of his security guards, telling him to keep an eye out for the douchebag and to add him to the blacklist based on cctv images.

"Hey, thank you," the woman said, placing her hand on his forearm, before he shut the car door and watched the taxi's tail lights disappear around the corner.

It was the first time in a while that he felt inside the good deed that he had done.

When this Logan guy was dealt with, he was going to immerse himself in Enforcer work to keep his mind off of Evie.

With a slight spring in his step, he started down the street in the direction of Sin.

Evie would be finishing work at the bookstore soon, and he wanted to make sure she got home safely too.

He strode down the street to his bike, happy that he'd managed to piss off at least one demon tonight.

That was until he realised he'd be pissing another one of very shortly.

His own.

Chapter 7

When he arrived at Evie's place, he pulled his bike off the road and headed for his usual spot to hide it.

His mind was still going over what Viden had said to him as he pulled the makeshift cover he'd stashed away over his bike, so he wasn't paying attention as he turned around and walked straight into a super pissed-off Evie.

"Fancy seeing you here," she said, putting her hands on her hips.

Busted.

His Demon almost sighed in relief at the nearness of her after being parted for so long.

"Er, have we met? You look familiar, but..." He asked, rubbing the back of his neck.

"I know you've been following me, I just want to know why."

Well, shit how to answer that one?

"You either lied to me the first time we met about working for Drew or you're a stalker? I don't know what's worse. You might be all muscly and hot, but I'm not available, and I'm like a wild animal when cornered or if I'm feeling threatened." She narrowed her eyes at him.

He couldn't help the grin that came. She was just too cute, and she thought he was hot. He had to respect her for waiting for him and then calling him out. Even if it was the middle of the night.

"You think I'm hot?"

She just stared at him.

"Look, I don't know any Drew's, and I'm not stalking you. I just find you...interesting."

"That sounds like a very stalkerish thing to say. Well, news flash, mister, I've been keeping an eye on you too." His grin suddenly vanished, "I know your name, the fact that you're somehow involved with the Cellar club in town, you live at..."

Just before she could rattle off god knows who's address, he checked no one was around to have heard her and steered her arm towards her apartment. "You mind if we carry on this conversation inside?" He asked while walking.

She pulled out of his hold, stopping dead. "You want to come into my house after I tell you I know you're following me? Are you crazy?"

"I won't hurt you, Evie. At any second you feel uncomfortable with me being there, I'll be gone. You have my word," he said, reaching into his jacket pocket and taking out his Enforcer badge, showing it to her.

To humans, it looked like a regular police badge with an odd emblem behind it. Demons knew that it meant he was a demon Enforcer, and not a cop.

She looked at it and breathed out a breath, obviously thinking that he was a policeman, but still, she narrowed her eyes at him. "You mind if I tell Jax? You know the big security guard from Sin?"

Hunter couldn't stop his Demon's growl, "Who is he to you?" He caught himself but couldn't help the question that came next, "Are you two together?"

Evie looked up at him as if weighing up her options before blowing out another breath. "We're not together. He's just a friend, but my brain is telling me that I should let someone know that you're coming into my apartment with me, badge or no badge."

"Text him, but like I say, I'm not going to hurt you."

She seemed to realise that he wasn't a threat to her, and the knowledge of that had his Demon rejoicing. The overbearing feeling of exhaustion and being antsy and not in control of himself had gone the moment she had appeared before him.

As she walked with him to her apartment, she took out her phone and sent Jax a message.

With that Hunter guy at mine I am ok. I will call in half hour.

She showed it to him as they walked. "If he doesn't hear from me, he'll be around here quicker than you can blink, all guns blazing."

A few seconds later, her phone started ringing. She answered it, and he heard Jax's voice through the handset saying "Put him on."

Hunter looked down at her as she tapped him on the shoulder and passed him the phone. "He wants to talk to you."

He nodded for her to keep walking ahead as he put the phone to his ear.

"If you try any of your incubus shit with her, I'll rip you a new one. I'm not fucking about. I know about you, that club you own, and the other 'business' you deal in. I'm telling you now that Evie isn't part of our world. I'm taking it that, for whatever reason you might think that she is, but you need to leave her alone. The only reason I'm not there right now is that you're an Enforcer, but I will report you if you continue to harass her after this."

"Bye then," Hunter replied, hanging up and jogging to catch up with Evie.

"That guys a touch possessive, isn't he?" He said handing back her phone.

"He's been there for me for a long time now." He followed her up the steps to her front door. "Jax is like a brother to me."

Ah brother. Hunter had never liked that word so much.

As she unlocked the door, he reached over her head to hold it open for her.

"A stalker and a gentleman. Who'd have thought"

"Don't go around telling everyone I'm a gentleman now. I have my stalker reputation to keep up." He grinned down at her.

She rolled her eyes, but he caught her smile as she turned and walked through the door, as he followed her into her small flat.

His Demon purred at being in her living space. Maybe this wasn't such a good idea, he thought, but he needed answers, so he started taking note of things about the space that he couldn't or hadn't seen before.

It was cold inside. Looking around, he noticed the piles of blankets laying around. He wondered if she liked the cold or if it was a choice out of her hands. Cold-blooded demon breeds ran through his head, but he just couldn't picture her as one.

He already knew the layout inside- two sofas on the left, facing each other, with a small table in the middle and a tiny kitchen straight ahead. Bed on the right, bathroom opposite the bed. Hell, he'd watched her enough through her window.

Even so, he still saw things he'd never noticed before- she had a small aquarium on a table in the corner that wasn't quite visible from the window. The little chubby goldfish swam around, gulping at the surface water as it spotted her, as she walked over, sprinkling some flake food in for it, causing little smacking noises to come from the water as it hoovered it up.

Underneath the tank littering the floor were stacks and stacks of books. A few were cook books, but most were novels.

"So you like reading, huh?" He asked the question to deflect the fact that he already knew she worked in a book shop.

"I do," she replied, walking over to the kitchen. "Would you like a coffee? Or water? I don't have much else I can offer you, I'm afraid."

"A coffee would be great, thanks," Hunter said, sitting down on one of the sofas.

His Demon was humming with energy, and he willed himself to calm the fuck down.

This wasn't planned, but the lucky break was all about getting information, nothing else.

Flicking the kettle on, Evie took off her coat and hung it on the back of the front door.

Taking two cups out of the cupboard, she placed them on the side. "Do you take sugar?"

"No, just milk please, or blacks fine, whatever works."

A few seconds later, a cup of milky coffee sat in front of him. Whether it was her way of saying that she wasn't poor, he couldn't tell. It was obvious that she wasn't well off like he was, but she wasn't living like a slob either, which he totally respected her for. Everything matched in some way.

His Demon got even more with the programme when he looked over at her bed. It was a decent-sized double. Two duvets and a blanket sat neatly on the top.

"If you think that we are going to be having sex, then you have another thing coming. You're taking a little too long checking out my bed there, buddy."

She sat down on the sofa opposite him, warming both her hands on her coffee cup as she sipped the contents.

"The sofa works just fine too," he smiled, reaching for his coffee. "I really think we should get to know each other a little first, though. You could class this as our first date, and I'm not that kind of man."

He was. He so was.

He didn't miss her grin before she could hide it by taking a sip from her cup.

"So, how long have you lived here?" He asked.

"We're really doing this, are we?"

He leaned forward, resting his elbows on his knees. "Yep. I want to know everything."

She looked at him suspiciously. "I don't usually share things about myself. First, tell me why you want to know and why you're following me around. Have I been reported for something?"

"No, no, nothing like that. I find you interesting, that's all, but the cop in me knows that you're hiding something."

Close enough. Not technically a lie.

She stood up and walked back over to the kitchen, leaning on the worktop.

He couldn't help himself but get up and follow, stopping in front of her. "Evie, who is this Drew guy?"

She smiled at him and released a breath, her face relaxing a little. "I don't need a protector or the law- I mean, I really appreciate that you feel like you need to look out for me after what I said the other night, but I have things under control," she said, placing her hand on the forearm he'd crossed, and as her hand connected with his flesh, it was the first time in ever that he felt proper desire, an all-consuming need for this other being. She'd touched him in the club, but this time it was stronger- so strong that his Demon pushed forward to gain access and act for him.

He spun around, needing to get away from her, far away, and never look back like Viden had told him to.

His Demon growled at the thought, but instead of acting on it, he did the opposite, and before he knew what he was doing, he shook off his Demon's hold and turned towards her, opening his eyes as he reached for her.

She let out a little squeal of surprise as his large hand curled around her upper arm.

A vibration ran through him at the contact, and his heartbeat picked up speed as he started to feel his control slip away. His Demon was demanding that he fully bond with her right here, right now.

The vibration pulsed just under his skin. Every pulse trying to push Hunter further down so his Demon could step into his shoes and take her.

One kiss, no more.

He bargained with the beast internally.

Mine

The voice came from his lips but didn't sound like him.

Evie's eyes narrowed at the word.

The Demon managed to gain enough control at that second that he leaned Hunter forward, pressing her back up against the counter. He managed to close his eyes just before she got a look at his black peepers as he leaned in and kissed her.

As their lips met, Hunter was right there with his Demon and her. It was like nothing he'd ever experienced before. He hated hooking up with random females so much that he'd worked out a way to let his Demon out just enough that he could regress back and fuzz out the details each time. Not very sex demon like, but he'd had his fill and then some of endless hookups.

He was never going to get his fill of this- of her, he thought.

She gasped in surprise as his hands came up to cup her face, but then an amazing thing happened, and she started to kiss him back.

Emboldened, he deepened the kiss, sweeping his tongue into her mouth.

His Demon started to tremble, but luckily Hunter managed to hold in the movement, so she didn't think he was having some type of seizure, thank god.

He and his Demon were being supercharged. Buzzing with energy, he felt as though he'd just had sex with ten women, all at the same time. His bone tiredness vanishing in an instant.

Breaking apart, they both breathed heavily. Oh, she was so not just a human to get that kind of response from him, and he very much doubted it was a bonding thing.

Just as he was about to do something really stupid, like kiss her again, his phone started to ring.

She reached up and put her hand on his chest, as he stared at her for a second more before reaching into his back pocket and answering it.

"Your deadline is in 19 hours. You know how Bacchus doesn't like to be kept waiting." He pushed back from the counter and moved away from her as Kane's voice came over the line.

Shit, he'd been so sucked in by Evie and this whole bonding thing that he put his job, his important job, on the back burner.

"It'll be done," he said, hung up, and grabbed his coat. Before he could change his mind, he said, "Sorry. I've got to go."

He thought for a second that whatever she was, that Jax guy was right. He was a demon assassin for Christ's sake, he shouldn't drag her into his fucked-up world.

"My curiosity has been fulfilled. See you around." He strode past her to the door.

"That's it? What the actual fuck! You can't come into someone's apartment, kiss them, and then leave with no explanation."

"Sorry babe, it's been fun." He opened the door and walked out, hearing it slam shut behind him.

Well, that was at least one thing he'd done right tonight.

At his Demon's roar, he pushed his presence back down. Now he was running on full energy, he wouldn't be as much of a problem for a while.

Getting out his phone, he sent Viden a message.

Chapter 8

"You're playing with fire, Hunter. If your Demon has chosen her as a mate, then you need to keep her at arm's length. You keep giving him little tasters of what he could have, and it's not going to end well for any of you. If you need to be near her, tell me, and I'll come with you to keep a check that he doesn't get too excited."

They were quiet for a few seconds as they watched the girls at Sin dance around their poles.

"Is it the same for you? When you kiss her?"

Viden looked over at him. "The same as what?"

He blew out a breath, "like getting plugged into the mains. We just kissed, and it was like she super charged me, like I'd banged a whole netball team all at once."

Viden smirked before he could help himself. "It's more intense than just getting with a stranger, but it has the same level of energy transfer for me. They seem to be immune to incubus tendencies, and they don't get the same high as your normal Jane off the street would, which is a relief."

Hunter scratched at the back of his neck. That explained why she'd not jumped on him the first time they'd met when he'd thrown his incubus pheromones at her.

"It wasn't like that, though, V. She did something to me. My first thought was that she is some type of unknown demon?" He phrased it as a question, as the likelihood of there being an unknown species out there was pretty much nil.

"Maybe she's some type of hybrid, and that's why you can use her?"

"If she were a hybrid, I'd get some hint at what her demon half was, surely." They could sense Adriel's shifter side even though he didn't have the ability to shift, it lay dormant just under the surface, but they could still sense it.

"Maybe she's managed to hide her demon side somehow?"

His thoughts went immediately to Jax and the fact that he couldn't tell what he was.

"Maybe, but that doesn't answer what type of demon could give me a supercharge like she did, though."

"Did you find out anything else about her other than what type of toothpaste she uses?"

"Funny, but no nothing. The only demon she knows is that security guard who works here." He nodded over to where Jax was standing, glaring at them both. "He says that Evie is human and that she doesn't know anything about him in that sense, or about demons plural."

"Then I think you should leave her well alone."

"Already done brother," Hunter said, knocking back his drink. "I kissed her, then ran. She isn't going to want me anywhere near her again." He rubbed the back of his neck as he nursed his beer.

"Good. Try and keep it that way. It's hard at first but it gets easier with time. Now, whats the business you have here? Other than my needs, of course, seeing as you've already been taken care of, apparently." Viden signalled for one of the working girls to bring over another couple of drinks for them.

After she left, Hunter leant back in his seat and said, "Its den business."

Viden stiffened. He hated that it was his fault that they were all stuck owing the den a debt."They called in a job? What is it?"

Hunter didn't want to lie to the guy, but he also couldn't be bothered with the lecture that would come with telling him the truth, so he dodged it.

"Just normal den stuff."

"What can I do to help?" He asked, knowing full well that helping out with an assassin hit was strictly forbidden.

"Take care of yourself, V. It's all good."

Viden went from being quite chipper- well, for Viden- to his normal pissed-off, brooding self. Hunter didn't judge him though, Viden carried a big weight on his shoulder, all he could do was try and help him to carry it.

His mind wandered to the girls who worked with Evie.

"That girl over there," Hunter said, pointing to Scarlet, who was leaning up against one of the pool tables at the back of the room. "She'll be able to sort you out tonight."

Viden grumbled in his seat but got up, looking at Hunter for a long while.

Hunter was a bastard for putting him through the fresh inner turmoil that the den business brought him, but he didn't regret it. He did it to feel something, and yeah, it wasn't exactly what he had expected to happen, but it had brought him to Evie, which had definitely made him feel something.

"Catch you later." Viden broke the silence, grabbing his arm in a hand shake before making his way over to Scarlet.

Hunter felt better knowing that the working girl was made of tough stuff and wouldn't take any of Viden's shit in the mood he was in.

Walking in the opposite direction, Hunter went over to Evie's usual bar. He always sat in the same seat, the one he had occupied when he'd first come into Sin, but only when she wasn't working.

Buying himself a double-straight vodka, he started getting down to business by chatting up one of the girls behind the bar. She was tall and skinny, with long, straight brown hair. Sure, she was attractive, in a fake kind of way, but that wasn't important right now.

He found out her name was Janey and that she was quite new to the job, never having worked this side of the club before was good news for him, as she hadn't seen him lurking about before.

Half an hour later, she was putty in his hands. Leaning across the bar, her small hand rested on his forearm as she told him all about her life, as if he was going to become some part of it or something.

Why couldn't Evie have been this open with him?

And why was he thinking about her again?

This bonding thing was going to get real old, real quick.

As if his thoughts had somehow summoned her, she was suddenly there, walking out of the back room.

Instantly, his Demon was present and content at the sight of her being so close.

She stopped dead as she noticed him, her eyes narrowing as she looked down at where Janey's hand was resting on his arm.

His Demon went to pull away from her, but Hunter remembered Viden's words. That, and the reason why he was actually there, so he reached across the bar, tucking Janey whoever's hair behind her ear and whispering that she was beautiful to her.

Evie seemed to take stock of herself as Janey smiled up at him.

His Demon growled at him inwardly.

He should have left, or at least gone to a different bar to try and get some information on this Logan guy, but he didn't. His Demon wanted to be close to her, and he was a selfish bastard and would get it anyway he could.

She solved the problem for him, though, by walking to the other end of the bar and turning her back on him.

Hunter's eyes were glued to her as she moved.

Janey noticed his interest shift towards Evie and quickly jogged around the bar to him. Plopping herself onto his lap, she wrapped her arms around his neck, pulling his attention back to her.

"So what do you say we go make use of one of the private rooms here? No charge," She purred into his ear.

His Demon would usually wake up at this point and demand some action, but he didn't even stir at the attention. Well, other than to throw out some repulsion Hunter's way.

He looked over to the other end of the bar at Evie, she was smiling and laughing at a guy who'd come in a little while ago with a group of his friends.

This was the perfect way to push her away for good, he thought.

Looking back at Janey, he sighed, picking her up off his lap and placing her down.

He held out his hand for her to lead the way.

~~~~~~~~

Evie watched Hunter and Janey leave, her smile instantly vanishing as they walked away in the direction of the private rooms. She'd been called into work at the last minute, but on the plus side, she had managed to haggle a meeting with the manager of Sin for covering the shift on short notice. It wasn't with the owners, but the manager was just as able to promote her to a stripper.

Oh god, even the thought of it brought out her nerves. Did she even have the ability to seduce a man for money? They would be paying for a service, and she was pretty sure they would be expecting a level of experience and professionalism that she simply didn't have. Her mind drifted to earlier in the night. She hoped that Hunter hadn't picked up on her inexperience when they'd kissed and that hadn't been the reason he'd turned tail and run out on her. That guy was just another reason that it was time she sucked it up and started making more money at Sin so she could leave the town for good.

Excusing herself from the best man of the bachelor party, she went in search of Scarlet. Hopefully she had received her message in time and had brought in some clothes for Evie to borrow for her meeting.

She found her a little while later in a dark corner of the club. At first, she thought she'd stumbled upon Hunter in the shadows, but the guy with Scarlet had the wrong hair colour, for starts. Man, he was big, though. He was all over Scarlet, and she seemed to be having the time of her life.

Trying to back track quickly, she walked backwards, and right into a table, knocking over the couple of glasses that were on top. None broke, but the noise was enough to bring the big guy and Scarlet's heads around.

It was so dark where they were at the back of the room, away from the stages and bars, but Evie could see that Scarlet was flushed and looked a little unsteady on her feet, as if she'd had a few drinks, which wasn't like Scarlet when she was working.

"Sorry!...are you alright, Scarlet?" Evie asked her.

"Never better. Oh yeah, clothes are in the back on my hook. Use them for as long as you want." Scarlet slurred slightly, waving her away impatiently.

The big man looked at her, like he really looked at her then, and narrowed his eyes, which were the same colour as Hunter's and she wondered if they were related somehow.

"You're Evie" His deep voice asked as if he already knew.

Scarlet looked pissed that one, they had been interrupted, and two, at his sudden interest in Evie. She tugged at his arm, trying to regain his attention, but he held her at arm's length.

"Who are you?" Evie asked him suspiciously.

A couple of awkward seconds ticked by as the man looked at her as if trying to find something in her appearance, "I'm Viden. Hunter is my brother."

Well, that answered the relation question, but now, as she looked at him, she wouldn't have pegged them as related. Other than their size, eye colour, and the fact they were both packing some serious muscle, they didn't look alike. Sure, they were both off the Richter scale hot, but hang on, if this Viden knew her name, then Hunter must have spoken about her to him. It was probably just to laugh at her expense, but the look Viden was giving her was making her think, possibly not.

"Well, you can tell Hunter that he's an arsehole." She looked at Scarlet and said, "thanks for the clothes. I'll get them back to you as soon as I can." She didn't wait for a reply, as she turned and walked away, praying that she didn't bump into Hunter and Janey.

~~~~~~~

Hunter pulled Janey to a stop before they reached the corridor where the private rooms came off.

"Do you know anyone with the surname Logan who comes in here?"

She opened her mouth as if to talk, then thought better of it and shut it again. "After," she said, tugging at his arm.

"Not tonight, baby," he said, pulling her to a stop again.

"I don't even know why you're all into Evie anyway. I heard she's frigid. Never even had a boyfriend, apparently. There must be something wrong with her looking the way she does." Janey said, crossing her arms over her quite obviously fake chest.

Hunter's Demon surged to the surface, pushing her up against the wall. He leaned in close, growling, just as his 'frigid' Evie walked around the corner. He blinked his black eyes away, hoping that Janey hadn't noticed them.

As he turned back towards Evie, he did a double take at what she was wearing or wasn't wearing as it were. She had on a skimpy black bustier, dark leather short shorts, and heavens above, short lace-up black boots with red heels.

Holy shit, what the fuck was she doing?

Instantly aroused, he pushed away from Janey and stalked towards her, grabbing her arm. She squealed in surprise as he steered her into one of the private rooms, flicking the engaged sign before shutting the door.

"Explain." He looked her up and down before beginning to pace the small space "If this is to get back at me, then you need to cut it out."

Other than a long bench in the corner, a sink, and a mirror on the wall to project the mirrored ceiling, the room was empty of objects.

"Funnily enough, Hunter, not everything is about you."

She was furious, but so was he, as his body moved before his brain could keep up, kissing her with everything he had.

After a beat of hesitation, she was right there with him, kissing him back. Emboldened by her enthusiasm towards him, his hands slid down her waist, pushing her back with his body until she was pressed up against the wall behind her.

Reaching up, she wrapped her arms around his neck as his hands came around to grip her backside. Hunter and his Demon moaned, even fully charged, they still wanted more of her.

His Demon pushed him to complete the bond. The primaeval need to bury his teeth into her neck as he buried himself into her was almost too much to bare.

Chapter 9

The sound of his moan and his obvious need for her had Evie panting harder. She'd never been kissed like this before. She felt like she was drowning, but she needed more- every part of her throbbing.

She grabbed his jacket and pulled it from his shoulders, dropping it on the floor, before pulling at the bottom of his black t-shirt and tugging it up. As she let out a grunt of frustration, he got with the programme and broke away from the kiss, tugging his shirt up and over his head before bunching it in hands. He tossed it onto the floor as Evie stared at his bare chest, transfixed. He looked like some kind of Greek god standing before her. No way was she this lucky.

"Evie," He whispered.

"Hunter," she whispered back. "Wait," she said, putting her hand out on his chest, pushing him back slightly. "You said you weren't interested before. This isn't...I'm not..."

She didn't know why, but she needed to know what exactly had changed his mind, and him thinking that she was now a working girl was bad news.

"I lied to you before, my curiosity most definitely hasn't been filled. I can't keep away from you," he admitted, taking her hand away from his chest. "And you totally like me," he grinned, closing the distance between their mouths and kissing her again.

She couldn't help herself, and she couldn't deny the insane pull she had towards him. He was trouble, that was for sure, but she literally couldn't say no to him.

He picked her up, and her legs automatically wrapped around his waist as he walked, carrying her, before he sat on the edge of the bench, settling her onto his lap so she was straddling him. Her hands travelled from his shoulders down to his chest, and then further down his sculpted body. As he tilted his hips forwards, she couldn't help but rub up against him, the friction on his dark jeans doing nothing but heightening the ache growing between her legs.

As his kisses travelled down her neck, his hand moved from the top of her thigh inwards, his thumb resting on the part of her that ached the most, rubbing firmly over her underwear. She let out a moan, which brought his face up to hers.

Noticing the unsure look on her face, he stopped immediately, seeming to read the look on her face easily.

"Don't stop," she pleaded with him.

He looked at her uncertainly. "You *have* done this before right?" he asked, narrowing his eyes.

"I told you I don't work as a..."

"I know you're not a stripper or a prostitute, Evie, but you have done this before?" He gestured between the two of them.

How could she be that transparent? Not for the first time, she cursed her stupid, on-the-run life.

She took a deep breath before blowing it out.

"Not exactly," she said, closing her eyes.

He stared at her, obviously having some kind of moral dilemma with himself.

"We shouldn't be doing this." He shook his head as if trying to clear it.

Evie looked back at him, trying to gauge whether or not she could get him back to the place where they had just been.

After a moment, she sighed, "You're probably right."

Setting her feet down on the floor, she pushed away from him and took her last opportunity to look at his amazing body- his wide, muscled shoulders, thick tattooed arms, and washboard abs. He had a lot of scars, but that just seemed to add to the appeal.

She reached down and picked up his shirt, tossing it over to him as he stood up slowly. Indecision warred on his face before he pulled the shirt back over his head.

Looking up at her, they locked eyes and she gasped, stepping back. Her face instantly changing to shock as her hand reached up to his face. "Your eyes..."

He slammed them shut, turning away from her quickly. "Uh, yeah, I think I've got something in them," he said, reaching up and rubbing them.

She reached for his shoulder and said, "I can take a look."

He turned back towards her, blinking as he opened them, his grey stare intense. "It's ok, I think I got it."

She looked at him sceptically, narrowing her eyes, and was just going to question him further when the noise of someone's fist banging on the door had them both jumping apart.

~~~~~~~~

Seconds after the banging, a furious-looking Jax punched his way into the room. "I told you to leave her the fuck alone!"

Hunter stepped in front of Evie, pushing her behind him. "This is none of your business."

The two stepped forward towards each other, growling, causing Evie to spring out from behind Hunter and put herself in between them, placing her hands on each of their chests.

"Ok, you both need to chill out...Jax, it's alright."

"The fuck it's alright. Janey said that he grabbed you and pulled you in here."

"Of course she did," she said, shaking her head and putting her hands on her hips.

Viden, of course, chose that moment to walk past the open door. Looking in, he did a double take at the group and stopped dead. "Is this a private party, or can anyone join?"

Jax growled again.

"Hunter, can I talk to you outside for a second?" Viden looked between them all before moving aside to give him space to pass.

Hunter sighed, knowing Viden was going to chew him out for this, but knowing it was also an inevitable conversation, he leant down and grabbed his jacket, pulling it on before walking out past them.

Viden followed him out into the main club area, pulling him over to where he'd been with Scarlet moments before. "You're doing a really good job at leaving her alone," he said, glaring at him.

"I don't know what to tell you, V."

"Well, you're obviously not listening to anything I'm saying."

"I'm sorry. Look, I'm trying, really I am, but the pull towards her is just too much."

"And there's me thinking you were the strong one capable of anything." His face gave away the fact that he was being sarcastic.

"We can't all be as strong and uncaring as you..." As soon as the words were out of his mouth, he regretted them. "V..."

"Yeh, ok, I don't care. Fuck you, Hunter, work it out on your own." He stormed away, going straight for the exit.

Hunter stared after him, scrubbing a hand down his face. He had to pull it together. What the fuck had happened to his life, where he was pissing off his best friend over a girl?

As his hands dropped from his face, he looked up to see Jax standing straight in front of him.

They stared at each other, the tension building, before finally Jax spoke. "I told Evie I wouldn't get involved, so this is me getting involved. You're quite obviously not playing by any rules here, so what do you want with her? Is it just an incubus thing?" Hunter opened his mouth to answer, but Jax spoke first. "I'll help you find out about her *if* you protect her as an Enforcer. You think that she's something other than human, right? That's why you're sniffing around her. Well, if that is the case, then she will need protection, and who better than an Enforcer bound by Enforcer laws?"

He smiled. Jax thought he knew something about Enforcer laws, obviously. He was probably thinking of the law that protects those that don't know about demons from their knowledge, meaning that this thing between Hunter and Evie would only be a fleeting thing. What Jax didn't know was that a bonding link superseded all Enforcer laws.

He tried to hide his smirk as he stuck out his hand. "Deal," he said as they shook.

Hunter leaned back against the wall, crossing his arms. "First, though, what type of demon are you? You're off the radar, and I want to know why."

"That's none of your concern, and if you want my help then you will stay out of my business."

Hunter narrowed his eyes at him suspiciously. "I will find out."

"I'm not what's important at the moment. You want to know what I know about Evie, right? Evie Morgan- she goes by that at the moment, but I'm pretty sure she's had a few surnames. Randall, Evans, Jones, Logan..."

Taking a minute for his brain to catch up with what Jax had just said, he cursed, "Wait a minute, her surname has been Logan? Evie Logan?"

It had to be a coincidence. Surely it couldn't be the same person as his hit. A.Logan was on the parchment, not E.Logan. He still panicked, and a weird, ominous feeling started running through his veins.

"She's been through some shit so she had to change her name a few times, but Logan is her adoptive name. Not many people know it, but I found it out when I did a background check for her job here."

His heart was beating out of his chest. "Has she ever changed her first name?"

Jax looked at him and said, "You swear you don't know her past or anyone from it?"

"I swear it to you, on my Enforcer title."

Jax blew out a breath. "Her name when she was adopted was Aimee"

Fuck!

Hunter quickly shoved Jax aside, running to the room they had just been in, but she wasn't anywhere to be seen.

He scanned the club, but he couldn't see her.

"Woah, demon, what's going on? What do you actually want with her?" Jax ran up behind him, pulling Hunter around "She's good people, not like us. I'm sure she's a human."

Hunter tore free of his grip and beat feet back over to her bar.

She wasn't there.

He hopped across the bar, closely followed by the security guard. Running through the staff door, he came to a long corridor with a dressing room and lockers off to the side, but it was empty.

He still had 12 hours left for the hit to work all of this out.

Suddenly, he was slammed back into the lockers. Jax leaning into him with an explain-now face.

"If she is a human, which I highly doubt, then why is there an assassin demon hit out on her?"

"A hit as in marked for death? " Jax asked, grabbing the front of Hunter's t-shirt, "Is this part of an Enforcer job?"

"The opposite...I'm the demon that's been given the hit." He pushed the guy off him just as his phone pinged.

"Wait, what? You're meant to protect! How have you been given orders to do that? All this interest in her just so you can kill her? That doesn't make any sense."

Hunter's phone pinged in his pocket again. Pulling it out, he looked at it and cursed. There were no 12 hours left, it seemed.

"We don't have time for this...I didn't know that she was the one on the hit until just now. Look, I don't want to hurt her, but we have find her and quickly. The hit has just been put out to all the other assassins, and this time with an ID to follow." He flipped his phone around to Jax, showing him the picture of Evie he'd just been sent.

Turns out the security guard was a good guy to have on hand.

"Hey Cherry, did you see where Evie went?" He asked the first working girl they came across.

"I think she went out round the back. She must be on a break. Anything I can help with?" She called after them.

"It's all good, but if you see her before we do, tell her to come find me asap."

"Sure thing," she smiled.

Jax led him out through the side emergency exit door and into a dark alley way lit only by the sign above the door, which buzzed EXIT.

The cool, fresh air slammed into him. His breath fogging as he looked left and right. There was nothing. Know one.

"Which way? Actually, you go left, I'll go right," Jax said from in front of him.

"I appreciate the help, but I've got this. It's assassin business, and I'll get in shit if you're involved. I need to get it cleared up, and it's obviously some mistake if what you say about her is true."

"If it involves Evie, then it involves me."

Hunter looked him up and down, taking him in. "What is she to you?" Why he was asking, he didn't know, and why he was anxious about the answer he didn't want to admit.

Jax shut his mouth. That was obviously a question he didn't want to answer, which had Hunter's Demon bristling with anger. Evie had said that she thought of him as a brother, but he was obviously into her.

118

Hunter was just turning to tell him to go back inside when a gunshot rang out.

He didn't even hesitate. He ran full speed in the direction of the sound, praying he wasn't too late.

Chapter 10

Turning the corner of the club, his heart dropped at the sight of a body slumped on the alleyway floor while two skinny guys stood over the shape, high-fiving each other and sniggering.

"Personal best that, Neuro!" Neuro was a demon name that he'd heard of at the den.

"Well, let's bag her and get out of here already. Be time to get a few beers in after we collect the payout," the guy, Neuro, replied as he wiped clean his gun before holstering it. They seemed to be completely oblivious to Hunter's presence. Good assassins they were not.

Hunter didn't hesitate as he reached into his inside jacket pocket, unholstered his gun, and took aim, shooting the guy Neuro in the thigh as he was throwing a blanket over the body. The scream of pain was instant as he dropped to the ground, where he stood.

The guy still standing looked down momentarily confused before grappling inside his black puffa jacket for his weapon as his friend lay gripping his injured leg under him. Fumbling, he took out a handheld of some type and started swinging it all around, shooting bullets everywhere.

The den really was scraping the barrel these days, Hunter thought.

He and Jax ducked down either side of the alley. Jax stopping behind a car, and Hunter behind a dumpster.

Hunter pulled out his other gun, checking the barrel, before he slid it across the alley into Jax's waiting hand. The assassin noticed the gun exchange and went full on cowboys and Indians, shooting off round after round in their direction. His friend seemed to be pulled out of his pain haze at the noise and joined in with the party from where he lay, shooting off rounds too.

Hunter sighed before taking a deep breath. Looking over the lip of the bin, he squeezed off one round, right into the other guy's shoulder, before dropping back down again for cover. There was a curse of pain as he ran clutching his arm to his side with his gun hand, taking cover behind a car, leaving his friend still writhing on the floor unguarded.

Surprise, surprise, they ran out of ammo a few seconds later.

Jax and Hunter looked at each other and both nodded. Standing up simultaneously, they both shot the guy on the floor. One bullet went into his head, the other into his eye.

He slumped forward, unmoving.

The remaining assassin started backing away quickly, looking from his dead friend to behind him for an escape route before he took off at a sprint down the alleyway.

"Get after him. Make sure he doesn't survive. I'll find Evie."

They shared a knowing look as their eyes swung over to the body lying on the road. Jax looked like he wanted to argue but instead took off after the man. Hunter didn't hesitate as he ran past the dead guy on the floor and crouched down in front of the covered body, which was lying facedown.

"Don't be dead," he whispered as he gently turned her over.

It was Evie.

Cursing at the sight of her blood on the asphalt and soaking through her bustier, he reached to her neck, feeling for a pulse, and could have cried when he felt it beat under his finger tips. He ripped the bustier open from the bottom, popping the buttons from it and throwing it away from her as he pushed her thin top up that was underneath. There was no missing the bloody hole that was now in her side.

Moving her forward, he breathed a sigh of relief at the small exit wound on her back.

No vitals hit, and no bullet inside.

She let out a soft groan as he quickly dropped the fabric back down and checked the bump on her forehead.

Glancing back to the dead assassin on the floor, he placed Evie down carefully before he got up and walked over to him. Reaching inside his pockets, he hit jackpot at the car keys he found there. Clicking the unlock button, lights flashed from behind him where a shit brown ford was parked. He jogged over to it and opened the back door before going back to Evie and gathering her up into his arms.

He placed her as carefully as he could onto the back seat of the car before getting into the front and driving in the opposite direction of where Jax had gone.

He drove the 10 minutes it took to get to his apartment, constantly checking for anyone tailing them. When he was confident that no one was, he pulled the car into a dark alley, a block away from his place.

Evie was still unconscious as he lifted her out of the car, pressing his back against the alleyway wall, he listened, but there were no sounds of pursuit. Holding her close, he stuck to the shadows as he moved swiftly down the streets to his building. Turning the corner into another alleyway, he gently sat her down against the building before reaching up to pull down the emergency exit steps. With a clank, they hit the bottom rung.

Hunter crouched down in the alley in front of her, pushing the hair back from her face. "I'm going to have to manhandle you a little for this bit. I'm sorry it's going to hurt, but there's nothing I can do about it." He hoped to hell that she was still out of it while he moved her.

Pulling her into his arms, she shocked the shit out of him by hooking her arms around his neck, freeing him up so he could climb better, and five seconds later, he was shutting the window behind them that he'd just climbed through.

"Fuck! Answer the goddamn phone, Theo," Hunter cursed, pacing his living room with his phone to his ear.

He'd propped Evie up against the wall while he tried to work out what to do. Her blonde hair had fallen over her eyes, and he had to stop his Demon from reaching out to touch her to make sure that she was still ok.

A voice suddenly came from over the phone. "Hello?"

"About time! I have a situation," he said.

"Sorry, man, it's loud at the club. Hang on a sec." The sound of music and movement was closely followed by a door clicking shut and Theo's voice coming back through the line, "What's up?"

"Did you get the hit tonight? Actually, you know what it doesn't matter. She's here. Bacchus put a hit out on a girl, and now she's in my apartment." He scrubbed a hand down his face. "Theo, there's more to this...I need to talk to you and Ade, but I'm pretty sure she's a human."

"Wait...what? Slow down a bit. The den put out a hit on a human girl? It must be a mistake. They don't put out hits on humans ever, but more importantly why the fuck is she in your apartment?"

"I know, I know," he said, not sure if he wanted Theo and Adriel to know about his Demon bonding with her yet. He trusted them with his life, but knowing what Viden went through with Kali with them all watching was not how he wanted things to go down with her. "I was chatting to her in a club."

"In the cellar?"

"No, the one in town, Sin."

The line was quiet for a minute before Theo's voice sounded, "Bit of a coincidence, Hunt."

"Look, I'll explain more later, but some other assassins shot her. I'm going to patch her up here, but we need to get to the bottom of this sooner rather than later for her sake. If she is human, then we need to protect her as Enforcers."

"Ok...I'll head down to the den and see what's going on. Keep your head down. I won't let on where you are, but it won't be long before someone comes looking. Turn this phone off and keep your burner on."

He hit the end button and turned the phone over, taking the battery and SIM out.

Looking over at the unconscious girl on his floor, he went over to her and crouched down. His pulse was thumping, but as he got closer to her, even in the situation they were in, he felt the most at peace he'd ever felt having her there in his home with him. Still, he couldn't help but wonder what her deal was. What if this Drew guy was the one that was after her, and he was a demon? It was the most likely answer here and would prove his theory that she, in fact, wasn't human. It would also explain his Demon bonding to her.

Right now, it didn't matter what she was, he needed to fix her.

Reaching for the hem of her top, he pulled it up exposing the bullet wound that was oozing blood all over his floor. Cursing, he stalked to the bathroom, where he kept his medical supplies, and grabbed an armful of saline packs, gauze, needles, thread, tape, and bandages. Making his way back over to her, he picked her up and carried her over to his couch, laying her down before pulling out her phone from her shorts and taking the SIM card out. He then set to work stitching her up.

About half an hour and half a bottle of vodka (for the wound and his nerves) later, he looked down at the neat row of stitches and bandaged her up.

Smirking at his good work, he dumped the bloody rags in the trash along with her bloody shirt and replaced it with one of his own t-shirts. At least she'd had a bra on underneath. He guessed he should have left her modesty intact, but it wasn't like he looked much. He could blame his Demon, but it hadn't been his eyes that had travelled down her smooth, lightly tanned skin on their own accord.

Hearing his burner phone going off in his bedside draw, he went over and pulled it out. Answering the unknown number, he didn't say a thing.

"Hunt, it's me, Theo."

"What have you got?"

"The hit wasn't a mistake. Don't ask me why it's there, they wouldn't tell me, but it's legit. She can't be human. Word is out that you disappeared with her, and if you don't take her out, then the hit will get transferred to you. Hunter, do you know the payout on her? It's a million dollars! The whole place is buzzing. Listen, Kane told me that Bacchus has offered you two years for her. I wouldn't say this on a normal hit, but...it's two years, Hunter, think about this. There is never no reason for a hit to be put out on someone."

Fucking Jax, he was meant to kill that other assassin.

His eyes closed as the reality of the situation and what Theo had just said hit him.

"I've heard you," He rumbled.

Shit, shit double-fucking shit.

He ended the call.

Well, she was obviously a demon of some kind for the hit to be legal. The question was whether he would find out which type before she died.

Could a bonded male even kill his intended mate? He reasoned with his Demon about it, but he wouldn't listen to him.

Maybe if he let him out just enough so that his consciousness was between them both? Could he actually kill her? He'd done worse in his life.

He called on his Demon just enough, eyes turning black- he was the infamous stone cold killer after all, and if Hunter remained in control of who he was, then he may just act on instinct, but as he stalked into the living room, the determination he'd felt, and his Demon just bled right out of him at the sight of her curled on her side on his sofa in his shirt. He blinked, trying to retain some of that stone cold killer in him, but his Demon had abandoned him in this.

Coward.

"Fuck." He blinked again, leaning back against the wall. That last bit of killer bled straight out as his arse slid to the floor.

He sat there for god knows how long, his head hanging on his shoulders with his eyes closed, trying to figure out what the hell he should do, when he nearly jumped out of his skin as a small hand fell on his arm.

"Jesus! Give a guy a heart attack!"

"I'm sorry!" Evie's voice snapped him to attention. "Are you ok?"

She was crouching in front of him, holding her bandaged side, with her stupidly big blue eyes locked on his.

Oh yeah, he was fan-fucking tastic. He'd lost his job- probably both jobs, to be fair- and just signed both of their death certificates because he'd turned into a pussy, while she had just been shot and was now in some random apartment, and her first thing to ask was whether he was okay. He opened his mouth to question her, but he was stumped.

"Hunter? What's happening? Where am I?"

Ugh, that voice.

She reached out, placing her hand on his cheek. His Demon vibrated and came back full force. He had to fight him from demanding air time. Clenching and unclenching his fists, he squeezed his undoubtedly black eyes shut.

This was dangerous.

He surged up, walking past her to the other side of the living room, putting as much distance between them as he could as he fought for control. "What are you? because you sure as hell aren't a human, and whatever you're doing to me is pissing me off!"

Her eyes widened at his snarl. "What do you mean, what am I?" She sat down where he'd just been, obviously still in pain from the gunshot wound. A crease appeared between her eyebrows. She genuinely looked like she had no clue.

Hunter studied her closely. There was a chance, all be it a small one, that she was a demon and, in fact, had no clue what she was. Either that, or she was one hell of an actress.

He leaned back against the wall where he stood, scrubbing his hand down his face as he concentrated on his breathing, in and out, as he regained control.

"Did I get shot? I can remember two guys walking up to me outside Sin and a bang...and now..." she said, looking down at her bandaged side. "My side is killing me."

"Ok," he said, blowing out a breath. "We don't have a lot of time on our hands here, so cards on the table, don't freak out. I work as an assassin." Her eyebrows shot up. "And there is a hit out on you." He gauged her reaction, which was one of complete shock, before continuing. "At first, it was just me with the intel, but now everyone where I work has it. Two guys from the assassin den shot you outside the club, but I patched you up. You have a lot of guys out for you, and if I don't take you out, then it's my neck on the line. That's why you were shot, and that's why I'm fucked."

Evie looked down at her delicate hands and frowned. She didn't say a thing for a long while. Her thoughts going straight to that bastard Drew, no doubt. Hunter could tell because he'd jumped to the same conclusion.

"You were getting close to me so you could kill me? So why didn't you? It doesn't make any sense. We were alone enough for you to do it."

"I didn't know that it was you I was suppose to kill...until tonight."

"Oh," she said, looking down at her hands again. "So why am I still sitting here, and why did you bandage me up if you're suppose to kill me?"

When he didn't answer immediately, she looked up. He was standing right in front of her, staring straight into her eyes.

"Because I can't kill you," he said, closing his eyes. "Evie, I won't kill you, but we need to work this out quickly." Sitting down with his back against the wall next to her, he went for a different approach. "That Jax guy said that you were adopted? Your real name is Aimee Logan, right? This might be an odd question, but...do you know who your birth parents were?"

~~~~~~~

Ok, that wasn't what Evie had expected to come out of his mouth, but her mind had gone to a similar place. "You think this is down to Drew too?"

"Who is this Drew?"

She looked up to the ceiling, trying to compose herself before speaking. "He's my psycho foster

132

father, who has been looking for me for the past five years. I've moved from place to place since I was 19. He named me Aimee, and his surname is Logan, but I've changed my name more times than I can remember just so I could stay still for more than a few weeks. Sin is the longest job I've ever had, and I earn just enough for my appartment and my shit car, but I needed to earn more money, so that I can move on again."

He thought to when she'd come around the corner at Sin and looked down at her clothes, "You were going to work as a stripper?" There was no disgust in his voice, just the question.

She turned and looked him in the eye, wiping the tear away that was falling down her cheek. "If he's the one that's after me, it's not his usual style. He prefers me knowing he's close. He likes the chase."

Even if he wasn't the reason for all of this, Hunter looked like he had already decided that he was going to kill the guy.

"I don't know who my birth parents are. I was left outside an orphanage as a baby with no name, so it wouldn't be them. It's got to be Drew. I know we have only just met, but will you help me get away from him and out of this town? I just need a ride out of here. I can disappear off my own back."

"I wish it were that easy." He ran his hand over the back of his neck, making his bicep bulge. "This

Drew guy...did you ever notice anything off about him? Anything...demonic?"

"He was a demon alright, total male shovanist with a power complex."

"That wasn't quite what I meant. Look, don't freak out, ok?"

She looked at him questioningly as he took a deep breath and closed his eyes.

Chapter 11

When he was sure that he was in complete control, he opened them, flashing his black pupils and looking out of his eyes as his Demon did.

Her sharp intake of breath was predictable, but her hand reaching for his face was not. He watched her with trepidation as her fingers brushed the skin beside his eye, making his Demon purr- actually fucking purr- the bastard.

"Ok, so I guess that answers the what am I question." She raised her eyebrows, flipping the question back at him.

Well, here goes everything. It was totally against the rules to inform humans of demons existence, especially as an Enforcer, but having a demon hit out on you kind of took precedence on what she needed to know right now.

"I'm a demon and not the shovanistic, power complex type," he said.

He didn't dare look at her, but in the end, he couldn't not. Her expression didn't waver. Maybe she was in shock.

She just sat there, staring straight at him.

~~~~~~~

She should be scared- hell, self-preservation should have set in the moment she woke up in a random apartment with a gunshot wound, however nice the apartment was. And now she was in a room with a demon? Demons were a thing?

Weirdly, she wasn't surprised. Sure, she felt a little like she'd fallen down the rabbit hole, but stranger things had happened. She didn't know what exactly, but she was sure that they had.

She felt like she knew this man, and she still felt drawn to him rather than afraid, and even with his revelation, he'd done nothing but protect her so far.

~~~~~~~

Flipping his eyes back to their natural grey, he brought his hand up to cup her cheek and was emboldened when she didn't cringe away from him. "I won't hurt you, Evie, that's why you're still sitting here."

They just looked at each other for a long while then.

"I'm going to work this all out. I showed you my badge before, I'm kind of the demon equivalent of a cop, so you're safe with me. If you are in fact a human, then I can go to the Guild and get you protected."

Maybe Viden was right, and his Demon had bonded with her for some other reason, but he definitely had, and whatever the reason was, it had happened, and his Demon was back in full protection mode.

To his surprise, she leaned into his touch before she seemed to realise what he'd said and froze. "What do you mean *if* I am human?"

"Demon hits can't be put on humans." At her look of shock, he rubbed his thumb along her cheek. "We're going to work this out, don't worry."

After a few seconds, she stood up and started pacing in front of him, right where he'd done the same trying to get through to Theo on the phone.

She stopped and turned to look at him. "Ok, what have I got to lose?" She seemed to be saying to herself. "In the spirit of all cards on the table, Drew's a prick, but no way is he anything other than that. As for the other stuff, I've always felt kind of off, like I'm spinning on a different axis than everyone else. Your little revelation isn't that much of a shock to me, but I've never had any proof of anything...different." She eyed him warily to double-check that she hadn't insulted him. "I've stayed off the radar a lot and have never upset anyone enough to have them want to kill me."

"Any ex's that might hold a grudge?"

She blushed, looking down. "No chance of that."

"Why?"

"I've never been in a proper relationship before."

At that, he raised his eyebrows. No way had this girl never had a boyfriend. His mind travelled back to that room at Sin, and her nervous anticipation at his touch.

"My adoptive mum died when I was 9, and Drew was an abusive drunk. I first ran away at 16, but he found me, and I couldn't get away again until I was 19. Other than my late bill payments, I don't owe anyone anything, so I really don't know why I have people or...whatever after me."

Whatever he was about to say was cut off by the sound of his burner ringing again. He jumped up and grabbed it off the table where he'd left it.

"What the fuck is going on, Hunt? It's gone crazy down here. There is talk of you saving an assassin hit? Bacchus is gunning for you. He's going to put everyone he has out, including all of us. Don't pit us against the den, it won't end well for us." Adriel sounded more frantic than Hunter had ever heard him.

He looked to Evie before he got up and walked over to his kitchen, lowering his voice. "A.Logan-it's a girl, Ade. She doesn't know anything about demons."

There was a beat of silence.

"I got the ID Hunt. What's really going on here? Are you just thinking with your dick? We don't question the logistics of the jobs. Let her go and go pick up another plaything. I'm not taking you out, brother, but I'm not getting myself put on that list. You were meant to be rostered on to Enforcer business with me tonight, did you forget? That, and you totally forgot about the bar interviews the other night with Theo. Get your fucking priorities straight." The line went dead.

He scrubbed a hand down his face. He just needed to bide a little time so he could figure out what to do.

He found Viden's name on his cell and hit dial. He answered the call on the second ring. "What?"

"Viden, where are you?"

"What the hell is going on, Hunter? I've been trying to call you. I got the den's hit intel. It's Evie?"

Hunter blew out a breath. He was an arsehole, but at the moment he didn't care, Evie was in immediate danger here, not his brothers, and they could look after themselves. He knew that, out of all of them, Viden would never hurt her. He knew what she was to him, so no matter the price on her head, she would be safe with him.

"Look, I need you. Can I use your bolt hole to crash for a while? We need to disappear."

Chapter 12

They needed to hurry, Hunter thought as they walked down the corridor from his apartment. Who knew how many highly trained assassins were out there looking for them right this minute. His place was at the top end of the market, and he'd kept it under wraps as best he could, but you could never be too careful in his line of work.

A door opened from behind them, which had him reaching under his leather jacket to the gun he had holstered there as he turned his head towards the noise. Luckily it was just one of his high-flying neighbours. He had his phone pressed up to his ear and was barking orders into it as he fumbled to lock his door behind him.

Hunter put his free hand to Evie's back, hustling her along as he gripped the bag of essentials he had packed quickly, mostly guns, ammo, and a few clothes.

Viden had messaged him that he was waiting out the front and that the coast looked clear, but that didn't stop Hunter from taking his time to leave the building. He feigned hugging her close and kissing her hair, all the while looking and listening for anything that could be a threat. To her credit, she didn't push him away or act surprised at his overfondness. Again, she shocked him by reaching up and intertwining her fingers with his, holding his hand where it rested over her shoulders.

He pressed the exit button by the door, trying not to breathe in her scent too much and trying to retain as much of his senses as possible. Her touch, smell, and just her being so near had his brain short circuiting, and he seriously needed to keep his wits about him.

Seeing Viden's car idling on the curb was a sweet mercy.

He smiled at her to reassure her as he pushed open the foyer doors and stepped out into the cool night.

~~~~~~~

The car Hunter's brother had turned up in was huge- a hummer or something Hunter had told her, reassuring her it was bullet proof as he pulled the door open for her. Hunter's eyes travelled immediately to the brunette sitting in the passenger seat of the car, looking surprised that the woman was there.

"Hey Kali, fancy seeing you here," he said, giving his brother a quizzical look.

The girl, Kali, smiled at him, turning in her seat. "Getting into trouble again, Hunter? And dragging a poor girl into it? Shame on you."

Evie's side screamed in pain as she hoisted herself into the car, and her wince didn't go unnoticed.

"You ok?" Hunter asked, getting in beside her.

She gave a meek nod, her eyes travelling to the girl who had spun in her seat and was looking between them both. She was petite, with long brown, wavy hair and a friendly face.

"It was actually me that did the dragging," Evie said to her.

She smiled and said, "I'm Kali. Viden told me the situation. Don't worry, you can trust us." Her smile turned sympathetic before turning back in her seat and looking at Hunter's brother shyly.

Evie's eyes travelled to the man who sat in the driver seat too. She remembered him from Sin, but, well he was something else.

He didn't acknowledge her, his eyes never stopped searching the area. Hunter was big, but this guy was huge, and where the former gave her reassurance, the latter gave her chills- and not the good kind.

"Evie, you've met my best friend, my brother Viden. Kali is right, you can trust them. We're going to go to Viden's place. No one else knows about it. Except apparently, Kali" Hunter and Viden's eyes met briefly in the rear view mirror.

In the light of the car's interior door sensor, she could now see more of Viden than when she was at the dark club. His grey eyes were the same colour as Hunter's but colder, and his brown hair was cut shorter than Hunter's black hair was. He looked to be packing more muscles than a monster truck and was really good-looking, if you liked that fresh-out-of-jail look.

Wearing a black wife beater and black combats, if you'd said demon before she'd met Hunter, the guy in front of her would have fit her description perfectly, not the looks but the coldness radiating from him. But Hunter trusted him over all others, it would seem, and so she decided to take him at his word and hope that she wasn't being led to her grisly death.

As the car peeled away from the curb, she looked at the girl up front again and wondered how she had ended up in the car with them all. She was wearing shorts and a t-shirt that said 'Cellar' on it and wondered if she worked in the club just outside of town.

Hunter seemed to be able to tell where her thoughts had gone. "Kali works at our club. We'll be safe at the bolt hole until we can work all this out."

She thought to the girls t-shirt and Hunter's words, 'Our club'. It was common knowledge that the Cellar was owned by four super-hot brothers. Could Hunter be one of them? She'd been there once before on a rare night out with some of the girls from Sin, but she hadn't seen the infamous brothers anywhere.

Relaxing back into the seat more now that she knew they were heading out of town, she thought about how she was glad to be out of Hunter's apartment, nice as it was, but she wanted to go somewhere more secure, and having another girl there made her breathe a little easier.

Picking up speed, they headed for the road that would lead them out of Foston hall, and hopefully away from any imminent danger.

"How are you holding up?' Hunters deep voice had her turning to him.

She blew out a breath she didn't know she was holding. "It's a lot, you know." She looked at him-this huge, strong, other being who owed her nothing but was willing to risk himself to protect her. He was so handsome in that moment, with the car's interior light casting a soft glow on his face, that she had to look away. They were obviously being drawn to each other over more than just appearances though. There was an invisible pull she was feeling towards him that she couldn't deny. The thought had her wondering if it was just a demon thing.

"So are there different types of demons, or is it just that you are a demon?" She asked, looking out of the window.

Hunter stiffened next to her. "Uh, yeh, there are different types."

She looked back at him and said, "So what type are you? And if I'm one, what am I?"

Viden smirked at him in the rear-view mirror.

"I'll explain all about that stuff later. You'll be ok, we'll get to the safe house then work out what's going on. As for the demon stuff, you can just forget about it all and go back to the way you were if you like, or we will try to work that out too," he said, looking at her like he may be nervous of her response to that one.

Definitely not just a demon thing.

She reached over and took his big hand in hers. She was already getting major feels for this guy she'd only just met, and that wasn't like her at all. She always kept guys at arms length, but then it had never been a two-way street with her before. They were all into her, and she hadn't been in the slightest bit interested in them. But she was interested in Hunter.

"I want to know. It's time I found out who I am."
She looked up and noticed Viden watching them
silently in the rear-view mirror.

Hunter noticed his attention too. "Try and get
some sleep. I'll wake you up when we get there."
He said putting his arm around her, tucking her
into his side, like he wanted to keep her close and
be touching her. She felt safe in his arms, and that,
along with the movement of the car, had her
drifting off into an uneasy sleep.

Soon after, she was vaguely aware of the hushed
voices of Hunter and Viden, who were in a heated
discussion about something. She tried to drag
herself awake so she could concentrate on what
they were saying, but exhaustion consumed her as
her body took every minute it could to repair and
recover.

She had no idea how long she'd slept, but what felt
like hours later she was waking up. It was still dark
outside, the moon shining through the car window
as she sleepily rubbed at her eyes.

Inhaling an amazing scent- an amazingly masculine
scent, she realised she had fallen asleep cuddling
against Hunter's massive chest, but before she
could move away from him, his arm came up
around her shoulders unashamedly, keeping her
where she was.

~~~~~~~~

"Hey sleepyhead," His voice rumbled.

Hunter just couldn't help himself, she was just too damn sexy with that just-woken-up look. He wanted to keep her close just for a few seconds more, but then thought to when she had asked about different types of demon. Ugh, he was going to come off as a serial creeper if he told her he was a sex demon anytime soon. His Demon stirred, getting with the programme.

You do realise that you're lusting after a girl that you have no clue about. She might turn out to be some suppressed demon that eats incubus after mating with them.

He thought at his Demon, but the guy didn't respond.

They had been travelling for a couple of hours now, and he'd finally managed to reason with his beast over her. After feeling so out of control and being this close to her for this long in the quiet as she slept, he'd finally managed to get the bastard to behave himself. The idea that perhaps his Demon had decided that he wanted to keep her long-term as a mate because she was the other half of him and his equal crossed his mind more than once. He couldn't say that he didn't want that if it was the case. He didn't know enough about bonding links to know the reasons behind it, but she had already proved herself to be his equal by the way she was handling everything that was being thrown at her right now. He respected the shit out of her.

They pulled up to the warehouse-looking building that Viden owned not long after.

Hunter looked down at her. "I'm going to go and check things out. Wait here, I'll be back in a sec." He reached up before he could stop himself and tucked her hair behind her ear, but then he remembered that they weren't alone and that he had no real business touching her.

Glancing to Viden in the front mirror, he gave him a clipped nod and quickly jumped out of the car.

~~~~~~~~

Viden immediately turned in his seat to glare at her.

Kali looked at him, rolling her eyes. "Be nice," she whispered.

"I've never seen Hunter act like this before over anyone." He narrowed his eyes at her.

She didn't want to think why that statement made her so happy, but there was no denying that it did.

"So what's your deal? If you're playing him and you know what's going on here, there is going to be a world of hurt for you and anyone involved with you. I specialise in pain more than those guys at the assassin den do, so if you're using Hunter to get away from some shit demon business you've got yourself into, then you need to tell me and then leave right now. It would take a while, but he'd get over it."

What a weird statement to make, she thought, that it would take him a while to get over her when they had only just met.

Whether it was the shock of everything that had happened, stress, fear, or just bad judgement, Evie had no clue, but she looked him straight in the eye. "What's *your* deal? Viden, isn't it? I don't specialise in pain, as you claim you do, but I'm sure I could improvise. I'm not lying when I say that I don't have any clue as to what's going on here. I got into this car trusting Hunter's word on you, why can't you do the same?"

Viden grunted, looking pissed.

"I'm done with being threatened tonight." She looked out of the window to see where Hunter had gone, but she couldn't see him. Maybe Viden would just kill her and be done with it, but instead of more threats, he barked out a laugh.

She couldn't help the smile that came at the sound. She doubted he found very much funny. Kali was looking at him as if he'd grown two heads.

"Well, you're certainly something."

"Are there many demons that are known for their humour and quick wit?"

"Answer me this. How are you acting so ok with all of this? Finding out demons exist, being shot, assassins...the list goes on."

"How else is there to act when you have an unknown number of people out trying to kill you for no reason? Does it really matter what they are? I got to know Hunter enough before all of this happened to realise that he isn't a bad guy. The fact he's not human makes me realise all the more that humans are the biggest villains that I know. Wait, you guys are demons too, right?"

"I'm the same as Hunter, an incubus demon. Kali is a half breed, half human, and half fury." Kali smiled at him, but he looked away.

"An incubus..." she knew enough about so-called fictional beings to know that that was a sex demon. "Wait, is that why I feel like I do about him?"

"How *do* you feel about him?" Viden asked, narrowing his eyes at her again.

She sat quietly, thinking of a way to describe what she felt for her stalker and protector in this scary new world. "I feel drawn to him, like he's a missing part of a puzzle."

He studied her closely for a while and then leaned back in his seat, facing out the window.

They were quiet for a while.

"We have certain tricks to get what we need from women," she swallowed. "Our incubus sides need sexual contact to keep strong, so anything from a kiss to sex works. If we don't get it, then we get weaker, and eventually we would die, but that would take a long time."

Evie glances at Kali, who'd frozen where she sat, looking wholly uncomfortable.

"What tricks?" Evie asked.

"Don't worry, he's already told me that his incubus charms don't work on you." He looked in the mirror again, wincing. He realised he'd probably said too much.

Saying that they didn't work meant that he had tried.

"He will stand by you no matter what. If a demon can't protect what is his, then what can he do?"

"His?" Evie questioned.

"You are obviously not something to just satisfy his Demon's hunger. You've awoken something within him. You've given me hope, and you've given my brother a reason to fight, for that, I am thankful, even if we do all die as a result."

His words ran through her head as they all sat in silence until Hunter returned, pulling the car door open.

"Ok, it's all clear. Lets go as quickly as we can. V, can you grab my bag?" He ushered her out of the car with his guns drawn.

Running through the door to the warehouse with Hunter and Viden with their weapons drawn, things began to feel a whole lot more real again.

It was dark inside, but there were candles lit all around the room, helping her to get her bearings better. As they walked into a big open-plan area on the ground floor, she looked over to the kitchen that was at the back, all shiny granite and sleek edges, and then over to a spiral staircase on the right of the living area, which led onto a balcony loft that had doors coming off of it- bedrooms, she guessed.

It was nice, really nice- nothing like she was used too. As she looked around the sleek living area, taking in a deep breath, she wasn't really taking anything in anymore. She needed a timeout. She just couldn't process anymore and keep functioning in this quite obviously crazy situation they were all in. Her mind was spinning, her side hurt like hell, and she was about ready to fall down where she stood when Hunter turned to her and seemed to notice.

"You want a shower while I get a room set up for you? I don't know about you, but I could do with a recharge."

Evie's mind went immediately to what Viden had said about what an incubus needed in order to stay strong. When he'd kissed her before, was it just a means to an end?

"Are you still with me?" He asked, ducking down so he was eye level with her, searching her face.

Pulling herself together, she smiled. "A shower sounds great, thanks," Alone, she thought to herself.

Following him over to the stairs, she looked over her shoulder to see Viden flop down onto the sofa in the main room, getting his phone out. For all his hard exterior, she felt like there was a lot going on in that closed book.

Kali walked into the kitchen. "I'll make us all something to eat- anything you don't like, Evie?"

"I'm good with everything, except mushrooms. Wait, you don't eat babies or anything weird, do you?" She stopped on the stairs, leaning over the side.

"Har har," She said.

The corner of Viden's mouth lifted. "Only at Christmas," he smirked.

Evie's smile vanished before Kali threw a spatula at him.

"I was thinking pizza or pasta?"

Hunter was looking over the banister at them as if Viden had grown two heads, before he carried on walking, scratching the back of his neck with a frown on his face.

"Either is good with me," She said, jogging up the last few steps and following Hunter into one of the rooms.

It was a large bedroom painted in greys and beiges with a giant-sized bed in the centre. Other than uplights either side of it, the room was otherwise empty.

Evie looked to the bed. God, she hoped he hadn't brought all of his conquests here. She watched as he walked over to the door at the back of the room and opened it, turning on the light inside. She followed him over, looking inside to find a big bathroom. It was probably the nicest bathroom she'd ever seen, with black marble everywhere. The shower was something out of a luxury magazine, with shower heads all along the open space. The place where she lived now was pretty decent, but that hadn't always been the case. She doubted that if she experienced this shower, she would ever want to get out of it.

She walked past Hunter into the room, looking around. He watched her as she took everything in. Stopping in front of the mirror, she lent on the sink and looked at herself, like she really looked at her reflection.

Poking at the side of her eye, "You think mine turn black too?"

Hunter walked up behind her, their eyes meeting in the mirror. "It's ok to tell me that you're not okay, you know." His hands came up to rest on her shoulders.

"I'm scared. I have no clue what's going on, where I am, or what to do next. I've dragged you all into this somehow, and I have no idea why you're helping me." She turned around to face him. "Why *are* you helping me, Hunter? For whatever reason I get that you don't want to hurt me and that you're a demon cop or whatever, but you could just let me go, this would all just be a bad memory for you. I'm not ungrateful, really, I'm not, but I wouldn't hold it against you if you asked me to leave here. I've disappeared on my own before more times than I can count, so I'd be ok, and you've done more than enough by getting me out of town already." He looked like he was having some inner war with himself. "Look, I'll have a quick shower, then I'll grab my stuff and head ou..."

His mouth was suddenly on hers, taking her completely off guard. He kissed her softly before stopping abruptly and pulling back to look down at her. Breathing hard, he searched her eyes, needing to know whether she was with him on this.

She looked up at him and couldn't help the question that came out, "Are you doing this because you need to, or because you want to?"

He frowned and stepped back. "What?" He looked more than confused, but he soon caught up. "Viden told you?" He said, leaning his big frame back against the wall.

"Yeh, Viden told me."

He heaved out a sigh.

"I don't know what to tell you, Evie" her heart dropped. "Other than, that's not what this is about. I was..I was trying to show you why I'm helping you. I probably wasn't doing it the right way or anything, but I'm no good with stuff like this. It's totally foreign to me. This isn't a demon thing," he paused, and she had a feeling he was leaving something out. "It isn't an Enforcer thing or anything other than me liking you. I like you, Evie, more than I should." He looked up at her nervously to where she was standing by the sink. "Have a shower, take as long as you want, and then come downstairs for something to eat. I'll wait down there for you." He pushed away from the wall and walked out of the bathroom door.

She let a couple of seconds pass before she
followed him. "I like you too, Hunter," she said,
gripping the door frame.

They both smiled at each other before she reached
over and shut the door between them.

Chapter 13

Hunter walked down the stairs with a silly grin on his face. His heart felt alive. For the first time- in he didn't know how long he felt he had a real purpose in his life. He could still feel her lips on his as he replayed her words, 'I like you too'. He'd find a way to make this work, he had to, consequences be damned. It was the first time that his Demon had ever been as close to happiness as he thought a demon could get.

Kali was in the kitchen chopping food up while listening to Linkin park, one step closer. Looking over, he saw Viden sitting on the arm of the sofa, watching her, before his gaze swung around to him.

Avoiding his eyes, Hunter quickly walked in the opposite direction.

"Hold up there, lover boy."

He stopped and turned towards Viden

"What are we doing here? I'm all for breaking the rules, Hunt, but what the fuck are you doing? We should be at the den trying to clean all this up, or at the very least we should be with Theo and Ade. You said before that your Demon was trying to take over around her. Is that still the case?"

He scrubbed his hand through his hair. "It's ok, I'm in control of him...Viden she's all alone, she doesn't have anyone. The guys will be fine, they have been through worse."

"Well, I'm glad you think that because when Theo and Adriel wind up dead, it can make you feel all warm and fuzzy inside knowing we were out here sitting on our arses hiding while looking after her when they needed us."

"What do you suggest I do? Leave her here? Or ask her to go? I'm telling you now, V, where she goes, I go. It's the den that's got the hit out on her. They won't hurt Theo and Ade over this."

"I'm not so sure. We need to decide on what we are going to do here."

"Agreed."

"You've got your Demon under control because you've promised him he can bond with her, right?" Viden asked with no emotion in his voice.

"I haven't promised him anything. I'm in control because she's near, and I'm keeping her safe. What about you, Viden? Why the hell is Kali here? She didn't seem to struggle finding where things were in the kitchen either, almost like she's been here before," he said, raising an eyebrow and folding his arms.

"If shit is going down because of you," Viden poked him in the chest, "then I'm keeping her close. It's none of your damn business if she's been here before."

He looked down at Viden's finger, still poking him.

"Dinners ready," Kali called out.

He pushed his hand away from him and walked over to the bottom of the stairs.

"Hunter, I found some clothes for her, could you give them to her for me? No doubt she wants to get changed after the night she's had," Kali pointed to a small pile of clothes she'd left on the kitchen side.

"Thanks Kali. I'll go up and get her. Start without us." He replied, wondering just how involved Kali was in Viden's life. It was obviously more than he and the others realised, or she wouldn't be here now giving him clothes that she quite clearly kept there.

He looked over to Viden again before he walked up the stairs, feeling beat. They were all conversations that could be had later and in private.

"Evie?" He called softly as he knocked on the bedroom door. When there was no answer, he opened up the door and stopped dead, just as Evie appeared from the bathroom wearing only a towel, her long blonde hair hanging wet around her shoulders.

He reached up and rubbed the back of his neck. "Uh, sorry. Foods ready. Kali gave me these to give you," he said, placing the pile of clothes on the bed.

"I'm not all that hungry now. You think she would mind if I just grabbed something later?"

"Not at all. I was thinking the same thing. I'll just shout down and let them know."

"Thank her for the clothes for me."

He nodded as he ducked out of the room.

A second later, he was walking back through the door, catching her inspecting her side.

"I think I need a new dressing. I got this one wet."

He looked at her, his pupils dilating, and cleared his throat. "I can help you with that."

Stepping into the room he closed the door behind him.

~~~~~~~

"I'll just go and change," she said, taking the bundle of clothes from the bed into the bathroom with her. He'd got her so hot and bothered from that

162

kiss, and earlier on at Sin in that room, that the cold shower she'd had had done nothing to diminish the fire running through her veins. Wearing just a towel in front of him was just too much of a temptation. She at least needed some clothing between them, but as she looked through the options Kali had given her, she either had to put on jeans and a t-shirt to sleep in or the thin camisole that was obviously intended for her to wear to bed alone.

She came back out a moment later, still wearing the towel. Walking over to the big bed, she sat down on the edge of it, her hands trembling as she reached up to the corner of the towel, releasing it. She was wearing the thin camisole top and boxer-cut underwear underneath. As the towel fell onto the bed around where she sat, Hunter's eyes roamed over her hungrily.

"Do you have another dressing?" He asked in a gruff voice, and she replied by holding one up from where she'd found it in the bathroom cupboard.

She lay back on the bed on her side and started picking at the corner of the wet dressing. Hunter walked over to her and pushed her hand away, taking the corner and carefully peeling it from her skin. She sucked in a breath as the cool air hit the wound.

As he inspected it carefully, he gave it a little prod with his finger. "It's not looking too bad. Does it hurt?"

"No, it's ok."

"You're pretty badass, you know. Not many people get shot and then walk around like nothing happened."

"Getting shot is a first for me, but what can I say? I roll with the punches."

Chuckling, he walked into the bathroom, rummaging through the draws until he found a few sterile wipes.

"How come you have so much medical stuff anyway?" She called after him as he walked back to her, ripping open the packet with his teeth, as she remembered the stash he had at his apartment too.

"We get a lot of injuries in our line of work. The others always come off worse though," he grinned at her before looking serious. "Right, lie back. This is probably going to sting a little."

She did as she was told and bit her lip, wincing as Hunter dabbed at the wound with the alcohol wipe, cleaning away the dried blood from her skin. Placing a dry cloth to it, he then replaced the dressing with a new one.

"All done," he said, looking satisfied as he put his hands on his hips.

"Not bad," she said as she looked down, feeling a surge of courage at his closeness to her. It was probably the traumas of the last 24 hours that had her suddenly throw her inhibitions out of the window. As his arms dropped, she reached up and grabbed his t-shirt at the neck, dragging him back down to her. He just managed to stop his fall before he landed straight on top of her.

Pushing her inexperience down, she decided that confidence would be the best course of action here, and so she pushed him onto his back, straddling his waist as his hands came up to grab her barely covered arse.

"These shorts are criminal," he groaned, dropping his head back onto the pillow.

He was criminal.

She smiled as she ground her hips on his. He grabbed hold of them, stopping the motion. "You're going to have to stop doing that." Of course, that just made her do it more.

Cursing, he pushed her shoulders back, switching their places and pressing her down into the mattress. She felt his need for her. She wanted this. She'd waited too damn long, and now she had some death threat hanging over her head that was making her think fuck it to all logical thoughts.

She wanted it, and she wanted it with Hunter now.

He blew out a long breath, looking down at her. His eyes were black, his Demon growling as he smirked.

Evie's eyes flew wide.

Cursing, he blinked rapidly, his eyes turning back to their normal grey. "Maybe we should press pause on this and try and get some sleep instead?"

She nodded solemnly against him as he reached behind himself, dragging his t-shirt up and over his head as he settled in behind her, tucking her into his chest.

Laying on the bed together, his arms wrapped around her, a few minutes passed before she asked quietly, "Can I ask you about your incubus side?"

~~~~~~~

He instantly tensed. "What do you want to know?"

"I'm not sure. What does it feel like to be a demon? Is it like sharing yourself with someone?"

"It's not really something I've ever thought about before. The demon side of me was born when I was born, so he's always been present. I guess it would feel a little lonely if I were on my own in here."

"So you were born? How old are you exactly?"

"I'm old, Evie. Demons can't die of natural causes, we have to be killed."

"How old is old?"

"I can't really remember now...I think 135, but I could be a little out on that."

She was quiet for a moment then, and he worried that he'd just given her a huge ick by revealing his age.

"So if I am a demon, then I would also have another soul in here with me?"

"Oh, demons aren't souls- kind of the opposite, I guess. Your demon side is most likely suppressed or dormant. Only pure bred males will have them present always."

"Huh, ok, I guess that makes sense. So what happens when they take control?"

"When I get angry or...turned on, my control can slip, giving my Demon full access. I don't have the best past, and my Demon used to have full reign...I gave it to him when things got too tough for me. It's not something I'm proud of. We did a lot of bad things back then, but I got through it. I'm more in control now than I ever have been."

"Except when it comes to me?" She turned to face him, raising her eyebrows.

"You heard me talking to Viden about that, hey?" He reached up, rubbing the back of his neck. "When I'm around you, sometimes my control slips."

"You think your Demon wants to hurt me?"

He looked at her long and hard. He didn't want to lie to her, but he couldn't tell her that his Demon wanted to fully bond with her. It was a commitment stronger than marriage, and she would freak for sure if he explained it to her.

"I'm not sure. I won't risk finding out by letting him have full rein. Don't worry, I've got it under control." His voice rumbled at her back as she turned around again.

"Okay," she whispered. A few minutes more passed. "So...I guess being a sex demon means you've had a lot of sex?"

He was quiet again. "I don't want to lie to you." Luckily, he couldn't see the look of disappointment on her face. "My nature compels me to act so my Demon gets the energy he needs, and the energy he needs comes from sexual contact." He reached up and trailed a hand down her arm. "I hate it. Wow, I've never said that out loud before, but I hate it so damn much- using people, taking for my own gain...I can't stand it."

Evie reached back, placing her hand over his. "I'm not judging you, it's just I haven't had much experience in that department, and I wouldn't want to disappoint you," she whispered.

He reached across the bed and wrapped an arm around her waist, pulling her across the bed closer to him.

He took a deep breath and then let it out in a whoosh across the back of her hair. He leaned back and clicked the light off, plunging the room into darkness. "You could never disappoint me. Get some sleep, Evie."

Chapter 14

Evie lay with her back to him as his big body relaxed. There was no way was she going to be able to actually sleep when she could feel every inch of him against her. She had never been in a bed with a guy before, let alone one like Hunter.

She moved back slightly, not knowing how to initiate anything, but arched into him, hoping that he was still awake enough to feel it.

"Hunter," she whispered into the dark.

"Mmm?" His chest rumbled on her back.

"Nothing, don't worry."

He chuckled quietly, rubbing his nose into the crook of her neck as if she was the best thing he'd ever smelled. His hand, from where it rested on her hip, started to move then, travelling upwards under her cami top, his large palm splaying over her rib cage and higher until his thumb and forefinger brushed the bottom of her chest. Every movement was so hypersensitive in the darkness that she stopped breathing.

Shifting a little to give him better access, his hand travelled higher still until it was cupping her completely. He squeezed gently, his thumb brushing back and forth across the tip. Groaning against her, he kissed her neck, and she couldn't help the moan that escaped her too.

"Can I touch you? God I've wanted to touch you so much, ever since I first saw you walk behind that bar."

She replied by turning to face him and kissing him deeply. He was on board with that idea as he pushed her back into the pillow, rising up over her, not breaking the link between their mouths as his hand travelled back down between the two of them.

"Are you sure you want to do this? And now?" He paused. "It's just I'm not sure I'll be able to stop if we go much further."

"I want to Hunter, I'm sure." She said this as her hand travelled up his tattooed bicep.

When his hand moved against her again, she tensed up before she could stop it. He froze immediately. "When you said that you haven't had much experience before..."

Chewing on her bottom lip, she couldn't believe that she was being so transparent.

He blew out a deep breath, dropping his head down against her collarbone. "Evie, we shouldn't be doing this here and now with everything that's going on."

He kissed where his head rested before turning so he was lying down next to her again.

She looked over to him before turning to face him, the light from the window showing the dubious look on his face. "Hunter, I need this."

"Ok, ok, but you need to be sure." At her quick nod, he chuckled as her hand reached down, trying to undo his jeans. "Slow down. There's no rush. We need to take our time here."

"I don't want to take our time. I want you now," she said, linking her arms around his neck and bringing his mouth back to hers.

He tried to keep the kisses light, but that was like trying to stop a flood as she wound her tongue in his mouth, pushing at his jeans. He had to help her remove them without breaking contact.

A second later, she dragged her lips away from his, tugging her top off and over her head and pulling her shorts down.

Stopping, they lay there both naked, breathing hard.

He reached up and cupped her cheek. "Evie, are you one hundred percent certain about this? A lot has happened, and you're still processing it all. This won't make it go away. If anything, it's just going to add in another emotion you don't need right now."

"Stop talking, Hunter," she said, reaching down and gripping onto his obvious need for her.

Dropping his head, he groaned as his hand reached down, covering hers with his before moving it up and down, showing her what felt good to him. Letting go of her, he moved his hand across her stomach and hips, lower still, until he was rubbing her thigh. Moving his mouth down, he kissed her neck, her shoulder, and her chest until his mouth landed on her nipple, sucking and nibbling at the tip. She arched up into him as he moved onto the other, teasing, pinching, and rubbing as he went.

As he moved further down, she lost her grip on him. Not knowing what he had planned, she clenched her thighs together, but he was quick to push his hand between her knees. Leaning down, he planted a kiss on her inner thigh, making her quivered at his touch. Trailing his lips up, his tongue snaked out, licking her core, making her hips jerk up involuntarily.

At the sound of her moans, he was emboldened, repeating the movement before sucking and licking at her, driving her to some precipice that she didn't know existed. Sure, she'd felt pleasure before, but never anything like this. This was something else. Hunter was right, she'd never been more vulnerable than she was right now, but she was glad that it was him here with her.

As his fingers and thumb started moving against her and he continued to lick, she thought she would explode from the sensation. Pushing one digit in and then another, she almost did, but he moved his face back up level with hers. "Not yet," he panted, his eyes swirling silver. Her hand instantly went straight back down to where it was before rubbing him up and down again.

Pushing her hand away gently, he moved upward, settling between her legs. He looked her dead in the eyes. Feeling a push against her, she nodded slightly to him as he guided himself to her.

"I don't think it's going to fit," she breathed.

As he chuckled, whispering "try and relax," he started rocking back and forth, gently pushing in and pulling back, slowly inch by inch.

The pressure felt too much, feeling stretched she shifted her hips slightly, taking him in further.

He stopped and hissed, grimacing as if it was hurting him to hold back. "Slowly Evie"

She moved her hips just as he was rocking forward, and she winced as he thrust the rest of the way in.

They both froze as she panted through the pain. He didn't dare move in case he hurt her more.

Resting their foreheads together, they just breathed for a second. She could feel him throbbing deep inside her, and then something amazing happened, he started moving against her slowly, and the pain morphed into pleasure.

~~~~~~~

Hunter had never felt anything like it before, it was like they were meant for each other. Funny, he thought, as that was exactly what the bonding link between them was. Her every move had stars burst behind his eyelids as he fought for control over his Demon, that and that he didn't blow his load before Evie knew how good sex could be.

If kissing her was like being plugged into the mains, sex with her was like being attached to the national grid.

"Are you ok?" he asked.

"Just keep doing that," she moaned.

Masculine pride surged through him as he thrust into her, each time going that bit deeper.

She was the sexiest thing he had ever seen in his life. He had to rein in his need for her as his Demon urged him to bite her to complete the bonding link and claim her as his own, but Hunter would never do something like that without her knowledge and consent. He was already pushing the boundaries just by sleeping with her.

No, he kept his mouth firmly away from her exposed neck and concentrated on what he was doing and feeling instead, pushing the bonding link away much to his Demon's disapproval.

Every other sexual experience of his life has paled in comparison to this. He felt like a teenage boy all over again, having his first ever sexual experience.

Gripping under her knee, he lifted her leg slightly, and just like that, she was moaning his name, clutching onto his arse as he pushed in deep as they both tensed up.

He came right along with her.

Her leg fell down from where he had been holding it up, as he hugged her close to him. They lay together, body to body, both breathing heavily.

Who knew how long later he withdrew and tucked her into his side as if she were his most valued possession in the world.

~~~~~~~

"That was...."

"Something else," he finished for her.

"Is it always like that?"

"Not for me. It's never felt like that before," he said, kissing her forehead.

That statement had her soaring all over again as she snuggled down into his side. Maybe it was her tortured past that was making the threat she was facing fade away, but she had a feeling that it was the man next to her that was making her feel safe and secure as she drifted off to a peaceful sleep.

A bang on the door woke Evie up. She squinted at the sunlight that was shining through a gap in the curtains towards the door.

"Breakfast is ready." Viden's voice sounded from the other side.

She tried to get up, but a strong arm pulled her back down. Looking down at the thick arm resting on her stomach, her heart started beating double time.

She was in bed, with Hunter. She'd spent the night in his arms after they'd...shit, they'd had sex.

Goodbye virginity.

"Not, now V," Hunter's voice rumbled from the pillow next to her.

"You guys have to take care of your other bodily needs, you know" Viden replied before his heavy footsteps sounded retreating down the hall.

Hunter dragged her back into him, turning he breathed in her hair. She felt him pressing against her thigh, where he lay, and instant lust shot through her.

"How are you feeling?"

"I'm feeling good," she replied, rubbing herself back onto him.

He chuckled deeply. "You'll be sore. We shouldn't."

She grabbed his hand, pulling it up to her chest.

"You're a temptress I can't resist." He squeezed his hand before removing it. "I'm going to go and have a cold shower, and then we should go and eat breakfast." He pulled the covers off of them and looked down at her naked body.

"You are the most beautiful thing I have ever seen."

Giving her butt a playful slap, he got up and walked into the bathroom. Evie watched his naked form move away until it was out of view, and the sound of running water came on through the door.

She gave it two seconds before she was up and following him into the bathroom.

Turns out the second time was just as good, if not better, than the first.

They were both smiling as they got dressed, Hunter wearing black combats and an olive t-shirt, looking like some smoking hot army soldier. Evie put on her borrowed black tank top and dark jeans and pulled her hair into a high ponytail.

"Last night and this morning…Hunter, we didn't use protection."

"It's ok, demons don't carry diseases, and I can't get you pregnant."

She stopped and sat down on the bed. "Because you're a demon? But what if I'm not a human?"

"It doesn't matter the species, demons can't impregnate females unless they are fully bonded. Incubus are a little different in that we can if a female is in heat, but we can sense it, and you're not, so don't worry." He leant in and kissed her cheek, reaching out for her hand.

She looked at it. Being reminded that he was a sex demon wasn't a great start to their relationship. Could she even put a relationship label on it? She had no clue, but with the imminent threat of death still hanging over her, coffee was definitely needed before she started working on any of the other crazy stuff this new path in her life had suddenly led her down.

So she took his hand.

They both walked downstairs to find Viden and Kali sitting at the kitchen counter in a heated discussion.

"You guys want coffee?" Kali sprang away from Viden and reached for the coffee pot as soon as she saw them.

"Yes please," Evie replied as Hunter nodded.

"Breakfast went cold," Viden said.

"I'll make us some scrambled eggs." Hunter let go of her hand and walked around the kitchen island.

"So what's the plan here, Hunt? We just wait until this all blows over? Somehow, I don't think that's going to happen."

"I can go somewhere else if me being here isn't ok," Evie said, looking between Viden and Hunter.

"You being here is fine. I'll work it out." Hunter said, putting a saucepan on the hob.

The day consisted of them all recouping from their previous day, talking, and listening to music. It was...nice, she should feel guilty, but this was the closest thing she'd had to normality and proper friends other than Jax in years, and threat aside, she felt content here with these people, ironic that they were all in fact demons.

Chapter 15

"So any ideas yet?" Viden asked Hunter as Evie went into the kitchen for another beer for them all the next evening.

"I'm going to go and speak to Bacchus." His 72 hours were well and truly up, not that his time limit had been honoured after every other demon assassin had been clued in on the hit.

His sim was out of his phone, and he was MIA. If Bacchus hadn't known that he had stolen Evie away, then he sure as shit knew it by now.

Whatever Viden was going to say next was cut off by Hunter's burner phone ringing from where it lay on the table.

They all looked at it like it was a bomb about to go off.

Kali reached over the counter to turn the music down as Hunter got up and walked over to the table.

As Evie padded over from the kitchen. Hunter looked at the phone. "It's Ade"

Evie perched on the sofa armrest opposite him as he hit answer, putting it on speakerphone.

"Hey Adriel"

"Hey Hunt, look, I'm at the den. Bacchus wants a word."

~~~~~~~~

Viden leaned forward and gave Hunter a look as a rustling noise came from the phone at the exchange before Bacchus' tinny voice came over the line. "I know you have her. I was debating which torture technique to use on you first- well, I still am, but things have changed. It seems that this is your lucky day." They all looked at each other. "The one that had booked the hit has changed his mind. It doesn't happen often, but well, we have made an exception for him."

Him, Evie thought, fucking Drew.

"So that's it? The hits suddenly off?" Hunter asked, the lack of trust evident in his voice.

"Oh no, it's not off, just changed. He wants her brought in alive now."

Hunter's eyes found Evie's.

"That's not happening."

"You *will* bring her to me."

182

"You expect me to believe that as soon as she's there, you won't put another bullet in her?" Hunter growled.

"Why are you questioning me? It's just a girl. You've never hesitated on a kill before."

Evie hadn't considered the implications of Hunter being an assassin before, but hearing the words said out loud made her hesitate. This Bacchus implied that he had killed women before, which sent a chill down her spine.

"The whys of it don't matter," Hunter replied, looking down.

"If you weren't one of my best assassins, you'd already be dead for pissing me off- that and the fact that you're all god damn Enforcers. That won't stop me, though. If you stand in my way over this, I will rip you apart piece by piece, starting with your brothers, then your club, and then everyone you know. You have half an hour. Bring her in, or I put the hit back out on you. Oh, and you can forget about the payment. You fuck with me, I'll fuck with you. You messaged for the damned job. I've got two minds to add two years to your time instead." Hunter could feel Viden's eyes burning into him. "I'll text you the address to bring her to. Be there or else."

The line went dead.

Hunter was furious. He stood up, clenching his fists, and launched the phone across the room, roaring.

Viden got right up in his face. "Two fucking years! Is that what this job was worth? And you fucking messaged in? What the actual fuck, Hunter! Why would you do that?"

"It doesn't matter, V! It could have been the whole amount, and it wouldn't have changed a thing," he shouted back.

"Then you're a stupid son of a bitch."

"What's two years?" Evie asked. When Hunter wouldn't answer her, she turned to Viden and asked, "What's two years?"

"We have five years of service left to the assassin den...Hunter's payment for your hit was worth two years off his time. That sums it up, right? Oh, and he didn't need to take a job, he messaged in for one." He looked at Hunter.

"And you don't like being assassins?" Evie asked.

The look Viden gave her was answer enough.

"I'll do it. I'll go to them and bargain for the two years for you."

Hunter let out a humourless laugh. "You can't trust him. Anyway, he won't go back on his decision now."

"But there is a chance, right? I don't think we should rule it out. I can find out what this is all about and who's behind it."

"Giving you over to a demon war lord and god knows who else is not an option. We will think of something else."

Viden turned to Hunter and said, "Evie, Kali, do you girls mind if me and Hunter have a little chat alone?"

The two looked at each other.

"It's ok," Hunter said, walking over and touching her cheek. She looked in his eyes and nodded, standing up.

"I need to finish cooking still, so I'll be close enough to act as referee if needed," Kali said, walking over to the kitchen again.

"Ok, I'm going to head back upstairs," Evie said.

"I'll come up when I'm done here," he said, giving her a small smile. "Try not to worry about things."

Nodding again, she walked over to the stairs to go back up to the room that she and Hunter were using when she noticed Hunter's phone lying on the floor right by her feet.

Looking around, Hunter and Viden were already in a heated conversation, and Kali had her head under the counter. Seeing an opportunity, she casually bent down and picked it up, tucking it inside her jeans quickly. Glancing back around, she was happy to see that no one had noticed as she quickly ran up the stairs.

She shouldn't have been listening in on their conversation, but when she'd heard their voices drifting up the stairs and into the room where she was waiting, she couldn't help herself. She crept over and sat on the top step, just out of view. They were all in danger because of her, and their conversation had an obvious content; Viden thought they should do the exchange, and Hunter didn't.

She hated to think it, but she was with Viden on this. Maybe her curiosity would get her killed, but she couldn't bring down however many people she barely knew with her. It was probably just Drew getting out of his league like usual. She'd go with him and then find a way to get away and disappear like she had the last time. She could easily disappear off her own back. There really wasn't any need for anyone else to be involved.

Hunter wouldn't ever let her go, that was apparent. However many times she said it to herself, the thought of doing this without him terrified her, but the thought of him getting hurt because of her was worse.

Decision made, she walked quietly back into the bedroom, putting the trainers she'd borrowed from Kali on and lacing them up. Taking a last quick look around, she spotted Hunter's bag over in the corner. Hopefully, he'd have some type of weapon in there that she could take with her. Rummaging inside, she didn't find anything useful and was about to close it up again when she noticed one of his black hoodies sticking out of the top. Picking it up she inhaled, his amazing masculine scent wafting from it. Slipping it over her head, it dwarfed her massively, but it would keep her warm and act as a reminder as to why she'd gone off on her own.

She took Hunter's phone out of her pocket and looked at the screen. It had a crack on it, but an address flashed up, which must have been the location of where Hunter was to take her. She walked over to the window and slid the panel up, holding her breath. Luckily, it didn't make a sound. Peering over the ledge, she was elated to find a flat roof underneath and close enough that she could jump down without breaking her leg.

She looked behind her at the door, where Hunter and Viden's voices still drifted through. He'd get over this. He would.

How they had gone from being on cloud nine to this, she had no clue.

Viden's words drifted back to her 'it would take a while, but he'll get over it.' Even so, her heart hurt for the man she was leaving behind.

She slid out of the window, jumping down as quietly as she could onto the roof below, and walked to the end, looking over the ledge. The ground wasn't that far beneath her, so she sat down and swung her legs over, sliding off and then dropping down onto the grass. The impact jolted her knees, but she quickly recovered, jumping up. She was instantly thankful for all those hours she'd put in at the gym.

Putting her back against the building, she typed the address into Hunter's phone sat nav, and looked at the directions. Shit, it was over an hour away on foot, over an hour for Hunter and Viden to catch up with her, and in a car that would take ten minutes.

Ok, new plan. She set off in the opposite direction towards the gas station on the map, ten minutes from Viden's bolt hole.

She'd been walking for about five minutes, keeping to the grass and off the road, sticking to the shadows to avoid unwanted attention, all the while listening out for any sounds of pursuit. It was mostly woodlands and fields that surrounded the quiet road, but all the talk of demons and assassins had her jumping at every sound she heard.

188

Pulling Hunter's phone from her pocket, she dialled the number that was listed in his phone as Bacchus.

"I hope you have come to your senses." The same tinny voice came over the line as before.

"I believe you're looking for me."

There was a beat of silence. "Ahh, hello, Miss Logan."

"I'm willing to meet with you, but first I want your word that Hunter and his brothers will have no repercussions from any of this."

A dark chuckle came over the line. "I don't usually take direction, but in your case, I will make an exception. You're quite the wanted lady. You have a very high price tag on you, and you seem to have managed to get one of my best assassins under your spell. To say that I am eager to meet you is an understatement." His tone made her cringe inside, making her doubt her decision to do this.

No, she couldn't back down now.

"I have one more non-negotiable before I meet with you."

"I'm listening"

"You're to give Hunter the two years that's owed to him for finding me."

"He was meant to kill you, not find you, and then hide you."

"Those are my terms, and I hope that you're enough of a man to keep to your word."

"You drive a hard bargain." He blew out a breath. "Fine. How can I find you?"

Closing her eyes she told him where she would be.

~~~~~~~~

"She's gone." Hunter ran into the living room, where Viden was sitting.

He jumped up immediately. "What do you mean she's gone?"

Kali looked up from where she was plaiting up pasta into bowls.

"As in, she's not here anymore. The windows open. I think she's run."

Viden's phone chimed with a text.

"It's Adriel. He said good choice on the hit, and to meet him at the Cellar," he flashed the phone screen at Hunter.

He thought of the implications. Evie had gone to Bacchus. Of course she had. Her self-preservation was obviously nonexistent compared to her feelings of guilt.

"Fuck!!" He went full on cave man, swiping his arm over the nearest surface and knocking everything from it.

His eyes flashed all black, his Demon surging forwards as he went to the nearest wall. Pulling his fist back, he punched a crater-sized hole in it.

~~~~~~~

"Where is she!" His voice came out warped as he whipped his head around.

Viden pulled Kali behind him as he faced off with Hunter's Demon. Eyes black as cole and face distorted in anger. It had been a long time since Viden had seen Hunter as his beast. His own stirred at the sight and memory of their good old days, causing death and destruction. His saving grace was that Kali was near, and if anything kept him in control, it was her.

"It's ok. We are going to get her back, but we need Hunter in order to do that."

The Demon growled in response, a bone-chilling sound that had Kali clutching at the back of Viden's wife beater.

Seconds ticked by before Hunter turned back to the wall and the hole he'd created there. Breathing hard, he stared at it for a long while before slowly leaning down and resting his forehead on the space beside it.

"It's ok." Hunter's voice came out normal seconds later.

He turned back to face them, his eyes returning to their normal grey colour again.

~~~~~~~

Viden and Kali both breathed out a sigh of relief.

"Fuck, I'm sorry," he said, rubbing his hand down his face.

"Don't sweat it, I know it's involuntary." Viden said, slapping him on the shoulder before pulling him into a hug. "Bonded Demons are a force to be reckoned with."

Kali looked at them both, confused. "Bonded?"

"It's nothing," Viden said, not taking his eyes from Hunter. He knew he'd made a balls up for mentioning it in front of her.

Hunter looked to the floor, searching for his phone, but it was gone from where it had landed. He'd bet that Evie had taken it.

"V phone the boys and tell them everything," he said, wiping his hand down his face.

"What are you thinking?" Viden stared at him with those soulless eyes.

"Just call them Viden. I won't do anything stupid."

192

He was so going to do something stupid.

"Kali, carry on dishing out the food. I'll be back in a second." She narrowed her eyes at him but nodded.

As Viden got on the phone and Kali returned to cooking, he jogged up the stairs and into the room where he and Evie had been. He looked around before making his way over to the open window. Climbing out, he hopped down onto the roof and then down to the floor below, and then he did what he was best at.

He hunted her.

Chapter 16

She'd been waiting in the shadows at the Star gas station for ten minutes when a blacked-out SUV pulled up. Two thick-set guys climbed out of either side of the back of the car, both wearing black button-down shirts and black trousers. One ruined the smart look with a bandana tied around his head. At least it was black, Evie thought to herself.

A text came through to Hunter's phone, telling her to get into the SUV. She waited a little while longer, deciding that this was quite possibly the worst idea that she had ever had. She should be curled up, warm, and safe in Hunter's arms right about now, not stood in a dark gas station debating whether to get into a demon warlord's car or not, when said demons had been trying to kill her not 24 hours earlier.

It was obvious to her now that this was a massive mistake. If she'd just disappeared, then Hunter would have probably just been let off the hook in the end anyway.

She'd half decided to make a run for it into the surrounding woodland when one of the guys-Bandana from the SUV spotted her.

"Luc, she's over there," he called to his buddy, thumbing in her direction.

Coming around the side of the car, they both approached her with their hands out as if they could read her mind and knew that she was a flight risk.

"Hey there, Missy," the guy, Luc said as they stopped in front of her. With his bald head and goatee, he looked like a total sleezeball. He was a similar height to her but bulky. She decided that if she was going to run, then she'd go through him, he was definitely the weaker link of the two.

The other one, Bandana, was taller and had more muscle than fat, which she noticed as he looked her up and down with a bit too much interest. His dark hair stuck out from under his bandana, and his dead eyes creepily took her in, like he didn't have a soul in there.

It suddenly dawned on her that they were both most likely demons. Strange to her that the knowledge of Hunter being a demon didn't bother her, while the idea of these men being demonic scared the living shit out of her.

"The boss didn't say you'd be this pretty, but don't worry, we're not allowed to touch our subjects." He licked his lips.

"So what are you anyway?" Luc asked her.

"Now that would be telling." She tried to bat her eyelashes. She was used to giving off 'don't approach me for sex' vibes in her job rather than come hither vibes, but they didn't seem like the brightest tools in the box, so maybe they would let slip what was going on so she could decide how serious she was about getting into the car with them. "So where is your boss then?"

"We'll take you to him now," Bandana said, grabbing hold of her arm.

Shit, shit, shit.

"So this other guy is there too?" She tried to walk slowly to the car, but his grip was like iron as he marched her along.

"Guessing so," they were suddenly at the car door.

At the sight of the open door, her flight instinct kicked in, and she turned to try and run, but Bandana's grip didn't loosen, and then Luc was grabbing hold of her other arm. There went that idea, she thought.

Just as they were manhandling her into the back, she heard yelling.

"Evie!" Hunter shouted from the direction she'd come from. "Don't you dare get into that car!" He was running towards them.

Too late, Bandana spotted Hunter and pushed her quickly into the back, where the other guy was waiting to restrain her. Putting his back to the open door, he blocked Evie's view and route of escape. Grabbing a gun from his holster, he shot off round after round at Hunter before cursing and ducking into the back of the car too.

"You're still a shit shot, Karl!" Hunter kept running and almost made it, but the car's tyres squealed away, gaining momentum before disappearing around a corner a few seconds later, leaving him behind.

~~~~~~~~

Hunter ran for a few feet more before he realised that they were gone. Putting his hands on his hips, he hung his head out of breath. He'd done everything he could think of to save her, and she'd still done the unimaginable. Looking around in despair, he noticed the shiny black phone lying on the grass where it had been dropped.

He picked it up and dialled Bacchus. "Where are you taking her?"

There was a growl over the line as Bacchus said, "She's not your concern anymore, Hunter. You need to leave things alone before I break my word and regret calling the hit off of you."

"Your word?"

"She made me swear that you and your brothers would walk away from this without consequences if she gave herself up."

Damn her for making a shitty decision, but for the right reason, his heart felt like it was breaking in his chest.

"Just tell me where she is."

"Goodbye Hunter. I'll have a new job lined up for you in a few days," and with that, he hung up.

~~~~~~~

They had been travelling for around an hour when the car came to a stop. She had no clue of their whereabouts. The back of the car was totally blacked out with a screen separating the front, so she didn't even know who was driving them. The two demons sitting in the back of the car with her hadn't even glanced in her direction since they'd driven away.

Oh my god, Hunter, he'd found her. Even though she'd run from him, he had come after her.

Evie's thoughts of him were cut short as she was shoved out of the car by Bandana's rough hands. They were in some kind of underground parking lot surrounded by expensive-looking cars, she noticed as she stood up and looked around.

Bandana- Karl, as she knew now- got out of the car behind her but kept his hand firmly on her arm, obviously still thinking she would run.

"Well then. You must be the famous Evie. Quite the run around you have led my boys on." A man dressed in an expensive-looking suit approached them from where he'd just gotten out of a silver Mercedes.

He stopped in front of her. He was taller than her, but not by much, and looked 100% like a demon warlord or mafia boss if you'd asked her before all of this. His dark, thinning hair was slicked over, and he looked at her with far too much interest, instantly making her feel uncomfortable.

"I'm guessing you're Bacchus?" She tried to look at him as unimpressed as she could.

"In the flesh, and let me tell you, not many are privileged enough to meet me. I'm something of a celebrity in the demon assassin world. I just had to find out what all the fuss was about concerning you though."

"Forgive me if I seem to not give a shit, but I don't."

Fury danced along his features, and she thought she saw his eyes momentarily turn red, but he fought to control himself. "Ah yes, I can see why

Hunter became enamoured with you so quickly."
He smiled at her flashing gold fangs. "Now you
must forgive me for my part in this, as I don't think
my client has the best intentions for you." He
looked her up and down. "I don't think he is going
to be disappointed, and you're going to get me one
hell of a pay check."

She didn't hide the look of disgust she gave him.
"So, where is he?"

Bacchus ran his hand through her hair before she
could flinch away. "So impatient. Well, although
fleeting, it was nice meeting you. Good luck Miss
Logan." He said this before walking back over and
getting into the car he'd appeared in before it
pulled away slowly.

That was odd. Surely if this was an exchange, the
two parties involved would be present for the
handover? Why didn't a demon warlord want to be
present at his own payout?

The thoughts disappeared as another car
approached where she was standing, pulling to a
stop in front of her. The back door nearest to her
opened then, drawing Evie's attention to it, and a
tall, medium-built man with long white hair got
out. He was also wearing an expensive-looking suit,
like this was some kind of business deal.

The door shut behind him.

Not Drew. Shit that wasn't Drew....

Bandana pushed her forwards towards him. The white-haired man's eyes went to where he was touching her and narrowed before going back to her face.

As they came to stand in front of him, Evie went on instant alert. Goosebumps rose on her arm. This man was dangerous. No wonder Bacchus hadn't stuck around.

She moved to run, but Bandana was there to restrain her, pulling her back to his side by her arm. The white-haired man looked at her with such disgust that just as she thought he was going to kill her there and then, he stepped aside, opening the car door again and beckoning for her to get inside.

Taking a deep breath, she looked around for any sign of help, and when it was obvious that she was well and truly on her own here, she walked over and slid into the car. Her heart pounded in her chest.

The white-haired man turned to Bandana, reaching into his jacket pocket, where he took out an envelope and handed it over. The demon's eyes went to her, and she thought she saw a flicker of empathy for her there. He looked at the envelope in his hands and nodded to the white-haired man before taking one last look at her before walking away, leaving the other man to get into the car beside her.

Evie didn't say a word, she dared not even breathe. A panic attack clawed at her, but she willed it away with everything she had. Whatever happens, happens, she thought. It was too late for regrets and doubts. She just hoped that before this all ended, she would at least get some answers.

Chapter 17

Kane walked into the room where Hunter was pacing at the Den.

"Where is she?" Hunter demanded, before a tall male followed Kane inside, making Hunter stop dead. His Demon went on instant alert, clawing his way to either attack the stranger or run from there.

He couldn't get a read on what type of demon he was as he looked him over, reigning in his beast as best he could. The man wasn't built like he and his brothers were, but he could feel the strength and danger radiating from of him. His long white blonde hair was pulled back from his face, and his eyes were so dark that they looked black, which matched the expensive suit he was wearing, giving him an appearance of authority over Hunter's Enforcer uniform. He wouldn't have questioned the guys station, as it was quite obvious by the way he carried himself and the sheer power coming from him that Hunter was in way over his head here.

Hunter's Demon bristled again.

"What is your interest in this girl, incubus? I'm sure there are plenty of females available to feed your...nature." The blonde asked him as Kane went and leant against the back wall of the room they were in, crossing his arms over his chest. He looked at him like he was imploring Hunter to rein in his anger.

"She hasn't done anything to anyone. Evie doesn't even know about demons." He shook his head. "Let me guess the guy behind the hits name is Drew."

"Evie?" He narrowed his eyes at Hunter.

"You know we don't give out hit purchaser's information," Kane called over from where he stood.

"We do not know a Drew." The blonde man replied.

Hunter's blood ran cold. "You know who put the hit out on her, though?"

The white-haired male looked at him with cold detachment. "You feel something for her, but this Evie, as you call her, is gone. Although my boss realised that killing her was extreme, he is now helping her. She will not be returning to Foston Hall...ever."

"I swear if you've hurt her..."

"You overstep your mark, *demon*."

A deep sense of foreboding overtook him. "You say that as if you're not a demon yourself. So if you're not, then what are you?"

The white-haired man looked him up and down, as if this wasn't worth his time, and sighed in boredom. "I am exactly what she is," he smirked before unfurling wings from his back.

Actual mother fucking wings.

Hunter's mouth dropped open.

"Shit," he scrubbed his hand down his face. "You're an angel- like a legitimate angel."

The knowledge of what Evie was suddenly hit him, and the news blindsided him.

Kane walked over then, putting his hand on Hunter's shoulder. "Give us a moment please." He steered him away from the angel standing in front of him. "Look, I could get in serious shit for letting you back here with him. This stays strictly between us," he said softly. "The hit was put out by an angel. It seems she needs to be marked for ascension or something. Now that they have her, they're not going to kill her, but this stuff is way, wayyy beyond our demon asses. You go digging around, and you'll end up more than just dust- you'll wind up on the end of a meat hook with no one knowing where you are. Don't fuck about with these guys. I mean it Hunter, you're in for a world of hurt if you carry on down this path." He looked him dead in the eye. "Leave angels to angel business."

Easier said than done. Hunter thought, feeling his Demon's fear at being apart from her. Even with the knowledge that he'd bonded to essentially the worst possible species he could have, he was still desperately frantic to get back to her.

"Fuck that shit. It's not happening. There is more to this than you're telling me, so tell me what you fucking know now," he growled, fisting the front of the guy's shirt.

Kane ducked a look at the angel, who seemed to be looking over at them with curiosity, but he could obviously not hear what they were talking about-either that or he just didn't care. Even so, Kane dropped his voice further when he said, "You obviously have a death wish over this and are not going to listen to logic here. This is all I know...she's promised to some high-flying archangel when she's fully fledged. He wasn't all for the idea at the beginning, hence the hit, but he's since had a change of heart."

The news was like a punch in the gut for Hunter. He literally lost his breath. Some arsehole didn't want to marry her, so he'd decided to kill her. His demon saw red.

Noticing his reaction, Kane continued, "Hunter, just leave this be. Like he said, she's gone, and it would be a suicide mission to try and find her. You need to get out of here before Bacchus gets back and catches you. He was lenient on you before, but don't test him. It's better for you not to be seen for a while until this all blows over."

He stood for a while just staring at Kane, willing his Demon back and the anger to leave him. He had so much to process; his mind was spinning, and his Demon's frantic behaviour was making his thoughts jumble in his mind.

Finally, when he felt more in control of himself, he nodded to Kane, walked back over to the angel, and stopped in front of him.

He looked at the guy, and just before the awkward silence went on a little too long, Hunter stuck his hand out between them. "Sorry, I didn't get your name."

The angel looked down at his hand and snorted.

"Look, I pretty much bought you your pay check, and you're the first angel I've ever met." He thought of Evie, "Well, that I knew about."

"Astaroth."

When it was clear that he wasn't going to shake his hand, Hunter dropped it to his side. "Well, if you ever need an assassin, you know where to find us."

Walking past them Hunter left the den behind, and his only link to Evie.

It was early morning when Hunter walked into the Cellar through the back door in a daze. Wandering through the still-busy club, he ignored anyone who tried to speak to him. He had one destination, the VIP lounge, and one objective- to get wasted.

He reached their table without any drama. Falling down onto the leather seat, he rested his head back, looking up at the ceiling.

A couple of seconds later, one of the bar girls brought him over a bottle of beer and a bottle of Jack. It was Ashley, Theo had obviously given her the bar job. She looked at him like she was about to say something, but at his scowl, she thought better of it. Putting the bottles down in front of him, she left.

Smart girl.

He was suddenly aware of the seats around him becoming occupied, glancing up, his brothers were all there, even Viden.

"Tell us what's happening, Hunter," Theo asked softly, resting his hand on his shoulder.

"Not here. Let's go to the flat," he said, picking up the beer and the Jack before getting to his feet.

They walked through to the staff area, where the door to Viden's flat above the club was. Going through and up the stairs, they opened up and all waited for Hunter to speak.

Scrubbing his hand down his face, he sat down on Viden's couch as they all gathered around him. Every second that passed was a second that made him feel more like he was falling apart. What were they doing to her? Where was she? Was she scared?

He looked at them each in turn and then explained it all, from the minute he texted the den to the minute he got to this damn sofa. They all sat in silence and listened to every word.

It was Theo who spoke up first. "Hunter, who is this girl to you?"

He looked around the room again and knew that he should just let her go and tell them she was a bit of skirt that got complicated. Only Viden knew the truth, and he'd cover for him, but who was he kidding? They knew him and could see this was killing him.

"Fuck...I've tried with everything I have to deny it, but I'll level with you all. My chest feels like it's been cracked wide open, and my heart has been ripped from it," he said, dropping his head into his hands.

He wasn't one to share his feelings and shit with his brothers, especially ones that put them all in danger, but the thought of not seeing her and the unknown of what was happening to her right now outweighed everything. He couldn't live knowing that he had failed her.

"It's killing me to think she's out there alone, and God knows who is doing what to her. I don't want to drag you boys into all of this. I gave a shit that the den threatened you- don't for a second think that I didn't, and I wouldn't have let anything happen to you guys, but I couldn't sit back and do nothing. My Demon has chosen her."

They all looked at him as if he'd grown two heads, well Theo and Adriel did.

"Chosen her...as in bonded?" Adriel breathed.

Viden smirked and picked up Hunter's beer tipping it back. "It's good that you have finally come to your senses and told them. Now we just need to work out how we are going to get her back."

Hunter could hardly breathe. "I can't ask any of you for help with this. I've already put you all at risk." He mumbled before looking at them again. "I was a selfish bastard, and I'm so sorry, but this is so much bigger than it first seemed. There isn't anything I wouldn't do to get her back, but this is on me. You guys aren't getting involved."

"To hell with you, Hunt, when are we not in danger? At least this girl, whoever she is, has given you something to fight for again and some light in your eyes. You messaged the den for a job, right?" As he looked down, ashamed, Theo continued, "The job led you to her. I see that as a good thing coming out of a bad situation. The fact that you've bonded with her is big news."

"Theo is right, and like Viden says, we are going to get her back, no matter what the costs. If she means something to you, then she means something to us." Adriel said.

"It's not that simple, its bad. Look, I know we have been together a long time now, and I see you as my family above all else. Your loyalty knows no bounds, but seriously, this is something I can't ask you to get involved with."

Theo sat down, leaning forwards, resting his elbows on his knees. "Come on, Hunter, the suspense is killing us."

He debated lying to save them all the mess of this, but as he looked at their expectant faces, he knew they'd never let it rest, and they would never let him face this on his own. At that moment, he felt the love that he had for them all. Through all the shit they had endured, he would give his life for any one of them, and he knew without a doubt that they would do the same for him.

"You remember I said that I couldn't work out what she was?" He blew out a long breath. "I found out."

"Well, what is she?" Viden asked first.

"...She's an unfledged angel."

Well, you could hear a pin drop after that revelation.

Chapter 18

After being in the car for a few hours, Evie tried not to think about the fact that she could see the way they were going and all of their faces. Surely they should have blindfolded her or something, seeing as how she had technically just been sold off in some kind of business deal. It didn't bode well for their intentions for her, she decided.

She looked across to the man that was sitting beside her. He was frowning while looking out of the window, his chin resting on his hand. She studied his profile while he was preoccupied with his thoughts. He had a long, straight nose and ice blue eyes, a similar colour to her own. He looked around the same age as her too and was handsome in his own way, but the coldness radiating from him and the fact that he had just exchanged money for her ruined the appeal.

She considered trying to speak to him, but as his gaze swung around to hers, she soon changed her mind at the look he gave her, so she went back to looking out of the window at the open land as they travelled further and further away from Foston Hall and Hunter.

She had done what she had set out to do, which was to get him and his brothers off the hook from all of this, but she was angry at the fact that these men and the ones back in that parking lot had all somehow benefited at her expense. Why that Bacchus bastard seemed to think that he had some kind of claim to money when all he had done was get her shot and then have her picked up and delivered to these people was beyond her. Still, if it meant that Hunter and the others were off the hook, then she didn't care, they could keep the damn money. All she had to do now was concentrate on how she was going to get away from these people, or Drew, if he was in fact behind all of this. If he was, then he was going to have hell to pay if he'd promised money to these people and he couldn't afford to pay them. The vibe she was getting from them was more along the lines of murderers than those that would let something like that slide.

It was daylight when they finally pulled up to an abandoned building in the middle of nowhere. She'd not seen any towns or more than a couple of cars the whole way, and nothing at all the last hour of the journey.

Two men stood waiting by the doors to the building for them, both looking similar to the one that was in the car with her. They all had long hair in different shades of blonde and silver, and all wore expensive-looking suits.

Stopping by the doors, one of them stepped forwards and opened the car door nearest her.

"Get out," the man said from behind her.

She did as she was told and stepped out of the car, the man getting out of the other side and walking around the back to join her before it pulled away, leaving the way it had come.

Her life on the run had her acting on instinct as she looked around the area while she walked towards the house for possible hiding places, weapons, or anything else that she could use to help her get away. There was nothing other than a few sparse trees and shrubs around.

Her heart fell, as all she could see was flat land to the horizon. She burrowed her face further into the neck of Hunter's hoodie as the chill air swept around them, finding comfort in his scent as she looked to the road they had turned off, which was visible from where they stood. One road in, one road out. Even if she did manage to get away, there would be no hiding anywhere. Whatever was waiting for her inside, she would have to face and on her own.

The two men stationed by the door stared at her as she walked towards them as if they had never seen a woman before. They both nervously glanced at each other as she neared before stepping out of their way to let them walk through the doorway, making a move to follow them inside.

The man walking beside her stopped and turned to face them. "Astaroth would like you both to remain here while she is presented to him."

It was the first time he had spoken other than telling her to get out of the car since the parking lot. She frowned at his choice of words, presented as if she was some sacrificial lamb.

They took another look at her and then each other before returning to their stations outside the door. It might have been her imagination, but she could swear that they looked nervous as their eyes swept over the area. What these men would be nervous about, she had no idea.

The man put his hand to her back and steered her into the house before she could think about it further. It was a cross between a warehouse and an old farmhouse of some type. It didn't look big from the outside and was cramped inside, but it had a lot of rooms coming off of the corridor, which she noticed as she followed him, all the while memorising the escape route.

The place was run down and dirty, half derelict. It didn't look like anyone had been there for a long, long time, and definitely didn't look like the kind of place these men in their expensive suits would typically hang out.

She was still hyper-aware of her surroundings as she followed the man into a small, recently painted white room. There was nothing inside other than a plastic white chair in the centre over a small metal drain grill on the floor.

"Do I finally get to find out what all of this is about now?" She asked the man she'd followed into this dank place as he turned around and looked at her. He didn't answer her, he just grabbed hold of her arm and shoved her into the chair before crossing his arms over his chest and moving to take station by the door. She glared at him, but with nothing else to do, she looked around the empty room and waited.

Her mind drifted to the last few days and how this had all begun. Meeting Hunter at Sin, him helping her, and him trying to protect her. She'd been so foolish. She should have known to stay with him, he was the only constant in this whole situation.

She was going to kill Drew if this was all down to him. She was going to kill him. He was psychotic, and she was never going to be able to live her life in peace while he was a constant shadow lurking over her shoulder.

This wasn't his usual style at all, but she wouldn't put it past him if he did have money to pay whatever it took to track her down. This was the longest he had ever not been able to find her, and it must be driving him mad. He was all about control. Knowing what she was doing, where she was, and who she was with- but not knowing anything- was his worst nightmare.

This had to be him.

A long while later, she heard footsteps approaching. She straightened where she sat after slouching down through boredom. The white-haired man by the door instantly tensed before stepping out of the doorway to let this other man pass through. It was not a good sign if this guy was scared of whoever this was.

It was another tall, white-haired male, stockier than the others she noticed as he walked towards her with arrogance, projecting total authority.

His eyes instantly went to hers and narrowed. "I don't appreciate the troubles you have caused my men in finding you." He said, stopping in front of her.

He was joking, right? She thought as she looked up at him. "I'm sorry, but I don't appreciate a bounty being put on my head or being shot. I don't even know what any of this is abo.." she didn't get a chance to finish her sentence, as he backhanded her so hard that she was knocked clean off the seat.

She hadn't been hit like that since Drew used to beat on her while she was growing up. If this man thought that he was going to be able to subdue her through physical violence he was in for something else, she'd long ago learned how to block out physical pain, but still she couldn't help the grunt that came out of her mouth as her side screamed when she landed on her gunshot wound that hadn't quite healed yet.

"You won't speak unless I ask you too, understand?"

Nodding rather than answering him, he seethed.

"Don't make me regret calling off the death hit on you, not that it was really my decision to do so, but someone found out who and what you are, so I had to call it off to save myself some unwanted...repercussions."

Evie moved herself around so she was looking at him from where she had landed on the floor, not hiding the confusion on her face quickly enough. "What I am?"

He let out an annoyed sigh.

"*You* put the hit out on me? This is all down to you, not Drew?"

He flew across the room, raising his hand again to strike her, but as she flinched away from him, he seemed to catch himself as his eyes flicked to the other man by the door. Instead, he clenched his fist as he turned away from her.

"Your lack of knowledge infuriates me." Pinching the bridge of his nose, he closed his eyes. "You have been missing for quite some time, hidden away by your birth mother from us, but now that we have found you, you have a lot to learn." He let go of his nose and stood up, looking over to the man still as a statue by the door again. "Take her to the other room and tell Alastair to start working on her right away. I want her prepped, compliant, and in order before anyone finds out that she is here and before her ascension."

"But sir, don't you think that we need to tread carefully here?" The man by the door said.

"Danios, you are one of my oldest friends, and I thank you for looking out for me, but do not question me on this. It is more important that we act quickly to reach our end goal in all of this before word gets out." He looked over to her and said, "Firmness is the only course of action that will get us what we want in the time frame that we need it. I'll be gone for a while, but you can reach me in the usual way if you need to."

He took one last disgusted look at her and strode out of the room.

She looked over to the other man, Danios. "Please, you have to tell me what this is all about. I don't even know why I'm here."

He walked over to her and leant down to her ear. "Best you don't ask questions. Do as Alastair asks, and things will go easier for you."

Taking hold of her arm again, he lifted her up and walked her from the room, down the hallway, and into another room at the back of the building.

2 days later

Time moved slowly.

The man she had been taken to, Alastair, as it turned out, was a complete psychopath. She hadn't been very scared of him when she'd first met him. He was the same height as her and was skinny-looking. With his short blonde, greasy hair that he kept perfectly combed over, he wasn't very intimidating to look at or be around compared to the other tall men that had bought her here. She soon learnt, though, that he was, in fact, the one that she should be most scared of.

It was their first meeting, when she had been led into another empty room, but this time with a wooden chair bolted to the middle of the floor, not a plastic one. Alastair had gotten up from a leather bag he was rummaging in over in the corner of the room and walked over to her with a cold smile on his face.

"So you are Evie?" She looked him up and down before nodded at him. "Take a seat then," he motioned to the chair in front of them.

He'd watched her every move, making her feel like she was a fly under a microscope.

That's when she began to feel scared.

She'd watched her fair share of murder dramas and documentaries to notice the mannerisms and characteristics of a natural killer, and this Alastair had them all.

Looking behind her at Danios, who was blocking the doorway, she had little choice but to walk into the room. As she sat down on the chair, he moved towards her, pulling up a leather cuff that was attached to the wooden arm and quickly fastened it. Panic clawed at her, but quick as a fly, he was on her other wrist, securing it also.

"What is this?" She pulled at the restrains, but there was no freeing her arms.

"I'll be fine from here," he said as he walked over to Danios, and before the other man could reply, he shut the door in his face.

Turning back towards her, he stalked back to the seat where she was restrained. "So are you going to answer my questions, Evie?"

"Are you going to answer mine?"

"First things first, I won't have a question answered with another question."

She narrowed her eyes at him.

"Do you know why you are here?"

"I wouldn't be in this position if I did, would I?"

His eye ticked as he looked at her. "Very well, we'll move directly on to phase two then. Astaroth wants quick results, you see, so we are on a bit of a time limit, I'm afraid." He rubbed his hands on his navy overalls as he got up and went over to the bag on the floor again, busying himself inside as he ignored her struggles.

Sweat started to bead on her brow as she searched for any way that she could possibly get out of this situation, but as she strained against the leather cuffs with all she had, she realised that there would be no getting out of them.

Standing up, he turned and began walking back towards her, a collar of some type in his hands. She looked at the thick brown leather that had flashes of metal all around the inside as he got nearer, and her heart started to beat frantically in her chest.

He leaned towards her and fastened it around her neck, humming to himself, and as she felt the cold metal on her skin, she started to panic as he pulled the buckle up tighter, giving her the feeling of being slowly strangled. Every time she swallowed, she felt her panic rise at the constriction that it caused, and she suddenly realised that there was a real chance that she was going to die in this place at this man's hands.

"Relax, it's just a shock collar. We have a lot of work to do and only a limited amount of time to do it, so we must work quickly and efficiently," he repeated, making him seem a little unhinged. She couldn't even tell whether he was speaking to himself or to her.

What the hell was this place? She thought to herself, willing the tears in her eyes away.

"If you do as I ask you, then you won't get shocked, but if you don't, then..." he suddenly produced a remote control from his pocket and pushed down on a button on it.

Evie felt the electric current course through her right down to her bones, every part of her tensed as her hands involuntary clung to the arms of the chair, pain racking through her.

As the surge of energy was suddenly cut off, she gasped, trying to catch her breath. The tears that had been in her eyes before ran down her face as she panted through the residue of the pain and the brutality of her situation. She tried frantically to reach up and tear the thing from her neck, but her shackled hands remained where they were.

Unaffected by her struggles, Alastair turned away and went back over to his bag again. If the last thing he had got from that bag was a shock collar, she dreaded to think what else he had in there that he could use on her.

A sudden feeling of resolve went through her. She didn't care what was in that bag. She hadn't gone through all the shit in her life- foster placements, Drew, being on the run for years- to sit back and take this now. She glared at his back, deciding in that moment that he could go and fuck himself, along with everyone else here. They could do what they wanted to her, but she wasn't going to play this game with them.

They obviously wanted something from her. To hell with them if they thought she would ever give anything up, that was of course, unless it was Drew's head on a stick.

Chapter 19

Trying to work out the passage of time while she was in that room was pointless; she was never allowed to leave, and there were no windows to give any indication of day or night, so she just continued on in relentless misery. There was a bucket for her to go to the toilet in the corner, and so dignity had abandoned her also, and what little scraps of food she was given were sporadic to disorientate her, she was sure.

Alastair always half-drugged her whenever he was going to take the straps off her wrists and locked the door at all times, so there had never been any chance for her to escape. The shock collar was his main method of torturing her, but as time moved along, he got more creative with other ways to cause her to suffer.

He'd obviously thought that he held a trump card to her terror when he dropped the fact that he was a real live demon, turning his eyes black in an over-the-top display to try and scare her, but when she didn't react in the way that he obviously thought she was going to at the revelation, he began to frantically mutter to himself that they were all being duped and that their downfall was imminent.

Evie loved it- that she had made him panic so wildly.

He walked to his bag and took out his phone, still muttering to himself as he put it to his ear. "Sir, I thought you said that she had no idea of demons, because she most certainly does know of our existence. Yes, uh huh, well, you can obviously see what a predicament this leaves us in. You are due to marry this girl, and she most definitely knows more than you think she does."

Evie's eyes travelled slowly over to where he was walking backwards and forwards in the room. Marry someone? She thought, what the actual fuck?

"Yes, I think that is wise, Sir. No, no, I'll continue on until then." He ended the call and put his phone back in his bag before standing up and rubbing at his chin. He was nervous. It was the first glimmer of emotion she'd seen from him other than impatience and anger.

"Who am I meant to be marrying?" She asked.

He looked over at her, obviously annoyed with her question, but he sighed in frustration rather than shock her. "Let's not pretend that you don't already know Armaitas."

She had no clue of what he'd just called her and didn't know what would be worse, playing along that she did know or telling the truth that she had no idea what he was talking about.

As she remained silent, contemplating her next move, he filled in the gaps with a huff. "You are promised to marry Lord Astaroth," her eyebrows raised at the title, "apparently you don't know any of this, and apparently, you were hidden on Earth by your parents," he mumbled, turning away from her.

Hidden on Earth, as if she didn't originate from there? And why the hell would her so-called parents hide her if they couldn't even be bothered to look after her or to check that she was alright after all these years?

"I think you've got the wrong person," she said.

"Ah, but you do know about demons." She couldn't deny it as he had seen her reaction for himself. "You are the right person. It has taken Astaroth many years to track you down, but now that he has you, he won't let you go again."

It was totally crazy. It was the 21st century, for Christ sake, she wasn't going to be sold off in some marriage deal. She had morals, and they screamed at her not to lie back and accept that this would be her fate.

"By the look on your face, I'm guessing that you are not keen on marrying him."

She let out a humourless laugh, which he shocked her for.

He had spent hours upon hours teaching her of her supposed blood line and Astaroth's after that, but more than anything, he worked to break her spirit and make her compliant and submissive. To be someone's wife.

"Tell me your immediate family." This was the hundredth time that he'd asked her this question. She knew the answer he wanted, but she had never repeated the names back to him.

Looking at him in the eye with a defiant expression, she said, "Anna and Drew were my adoptive parents. I don't know who my birth parents are," the same answer she always gave.

He smiled at her coldly, and his eye twitched as he punched down on the button to her shock collar, but she was getting used to the feeling of it. Sure, it hurt like a bitch still, but after the first however many times he'd used it on her, she had become used to the different aspects of it- the pain, the loss of control, and then the after effect.

Alastair seemed to have noticed this over the past few hours, and as he stood over her, she could see indecision warring on his face. Seeming to make up his mind about whatever it was, he reached for her neck and removed the shock collar. Her skin must have been a mess underneath. Her sweat mixed with a regular electrical charge meant that she had burns, and as the cool air hit them, she sucked in a breath at the pain.

He walked over to his bag, placing the collar inside before rummaging around in it again. Standing up, he turned and started to walk slowly back towards her with something in his hand. She struggled to see what it was before he stuck her in the neck with a needle, plunging some unknown liquid into her veins.

"Ow," she said deadpan as he removed it, her head starting to fuzz immediately. Panicking, she tried to cling to her consciousness, but there was no fighting it. As darkness over took her, she went to the one place in her mind that she always did- Hunter- as she blacked out.

As Evie came back to consciousness, she felt sluggish as she willed her eyes to travel around the room. She was where she'd been to begin with, but instead of being strapped to the chair, she was now tied down to a hospital-type bed, Hunter's jumper that she had been wearing was no longer on her, leaving her in Kali's black jeans and tank top that she'd left Viden's bolt hole in god knows how long ago.

The loss of the jumper had her eyes watering. It was the one thing that had tied her to him still, and now it was gone. She blinked quickly, willing the tears away before Alastair got any satisfaction from them. She looked down at her arm, where a canular stuck out, and followed the tube to a bag of fluids that hung on a pole next to the bed. Spiked metal cuffs now surrounded her wrists and ankles, making it impossible to move.

"Things will go differently from now on. You are very stubborn, which wasn't anticipated, but I have ways in which to treat that," Alastair said, smoothing his already perfectly smooth hair down and looking at her.

She wouldn't let on that she was scared, but she was, and inside she wondered what fresh torture awaited her now, but he simply got up, collected his bag, and left the room, shutting the door behind him. Her heart pounded and her stomach cramped through a lack of food as she lay still, trying to figure out what was coming next.

A whirring and a cranking sound suddenly started up from the ceiling and walls before a blast of cold air came in through the air ducts and all of the lights went out. It was pitch black, so dark that even when Evie's eyes adjusted to the lack of lighting, she still couldn't see a thing. She panted through the fear, her body starting to tremble from the cold and fear of not seeing what was happening around her. She had always been afraid of the dark growing up, for that very reason, her mind always playing tricks on her, thinking that things were there in the darkness when they weren't.

She couldn't tell how long she lay there freezing in the dark. It felt like months, but it could have been hours. Nothing else came for her, but the ice in her veins and darkness around her were torture enough. She forgot what warmth felt like, and even though she willed her body to stop trembling, it just wouldn't. She wondered how many teeth she would crack from the constant chattering and clenching of her jaw. One thing became her strength and anchor as she lay in pain alone in the dark: Hunter. Everything she had been through, he had been there with her, and this was no different as she replayed every moment they had spent together to keep herself strong and lucid. It warmed her heart, if nothing else.

She cried more often as no one was there to see her, dropping her stone facade and letting the tears fall freely before they froze on her face and in her hair. She was starving- like literally starving- her mind fuzzing in and out of reality and consciousness. She wished death would just come and claim her already.

She was done with living.

"Well, don't you look pitiful."

Blinking her eyes open, Evie realised the room was illuminated, and as her eyes adjusted to the light, she saw Alastair standing over her in the same navy overalls he always wore.

"You will be pleased to hear that we are going to a new facility today, but I think you need a little wash down before we leave."

She waited for the feeling of shame to come. It wasn't her fault she'd been tied to a table for god knows how long, but the shame never materialised, all she could think about was that they were moving her. It was the worst possible time, she was too weak and malnourished to try and escape, but still, the thought of any chance had her clinging to a new hope.

Alastair lifted the back of the bed up so that she was sitting rather than lying down. Her back and joints screamed at the sudden movement after being left in the same position for so long. Lifting a bottle of water to her lips, she didn't hold back as she drank it down greedily. Her stomach spasmed at the cold liquid that hit the empty space. She couldn't remember the last time she had eaten actual food.

She noticed that the canular was now gone, leaving a red welt on the inside of her pitifully thin arm, so she didn't have that to worry about if she got an opportunity to run.

God, how long had she been here already? She wondered if Hunter was out looking for her, or maybe Jax was. Wishful thinking, she would tell herself every time her mind wandered to being rescued.

Her empty stomach rejoiced at something other than air being in there, and she knew the pain it brought her was worth it if she was going to have any energy to try and make a run for it when the time came.

"Well, then let's get this done," he leaned over, producing another needle, like when he'd drugged her before.

"No, please don't..." But she was too late with the plea as he stuck the needle into her neck.

She came too just enough a while later that she could just about make out her surroundings as she was wheeled on the bed through the corridors of the house. It was dark outside as she was pushed out of the small building through the same doors that she had entered through all that time ago.

The fresh air and being outside was like Nirvana to her. Looking up at the stars, she struggled to keep it together as she tried to commit every little thing about the night sky to her memory. She wished it had been daytime so she could feel the sun on her cold skin, but she would take anything she could get at the moment, and just breathing in the cool night air was enough for her. She'd obviously been cleaned by someone while she was unconscious and put into a cream slip of a dress, but she didn't care about that. She was more distraught at the loss of the last things that linked her to her time with Hunter, but she didn't have the time to dwell on it, as Alastair was there pushing the bed out with her attached to it, and like always, she wouldn't give him the satisfaction of her tears or her distress, so she quickly blinked her sadness away.

All too quickly, the night sky disappeared as she was pushed on the bed straight into the back of a van. Alastair wiped his hands down his navy overalls before he climbed in behind her. She couldn't see anything about her surroundings when she was in the van, but they weren't travelling for long before it stopped and reversed back. When it stopped again, two knocks sounded on the back doors, which made Alastair get up and open them. Evie lifted her head as far as she could to try and gain anything she could from her new surroundings. She knew that she was losing her chance of escape, but she was still so sluggish with the drugs running through her veins, and the spiked cuffs at her wrists and ankles tore into her flesh every time she tried to move.

They were backed up to some type of garage. Other than the red tail lights of the van against the wall, the place was dark inside. Shelves and old paint tins, brushes, boxes, and the like littered them. With layers of dust everywhere, nothing looked newly used. Another abandoned property.

Alastair wheeled her out and through a door in the back of the garage. It opened up into a large open space. Again, everything was old and covered in cobwebs. She guessed from the layout that they were in some type of outbuilding. He continued to push her along and through another door at the back of the area. He stopped the bed in the centre of the new space and applied the brakes. Walking back over to where he'd pushed the bed through, he pulled the double doors shut, locking them in together.

Looking around, she noticed work benches with different implements along two of the walls and an old metal barred enclosure at the back that looked like something you'd keep a big dog in.

There had been no chance of getting free while she was moved, but it hadn't deterred her. She knew the doors to go through to escape, so she would continue to wait, and the first opportunity that came along, she would get out of there.

Chapter 20

The torture started up again pretty much straight away after the move, but along with keeping her in the dark and cold sporadically, he also added knives and chains to the mix now. Evie didn't care. She stuck to her guns, refusing to back down and give Alastair what he wanted. She was sure the majority of people would have just given in way before now, just rolled over and become some arseholes wife forever, or even lied to get out of it later, but she wasn't one of those girls. She guessed it came from the abuse she'd grown up with. She'd fought too hard and for too long to give up now.

Alastair seemed to get off on the extra steps he had to take in order to try and force her into submission, but Evie could tell that he'd started to become frantic at trying to reach his end goal. He'd been so careful not to give anything about himself away, but more than once she had seen his eyes flash to black with annoyance, reminding her of Hunter.

Occasionally, a long-haired man would come in whispering into Alastair's ear or bringing in food, which Alastair sometimes shared with her. Their eyes would always travel to her, but they never said anything or tried to help her, even if she implored them to with her eyes.

Time moved along even slower now, but her thoughts still often travelled to Hunter. She'd given up all hope of rescue as the more she thought about him, the more she realised that, in reality, they had only just met. Still, she wondered where he was and what he was doing right this second. She tried to picture him sitting at her bar at Sin and replayed their first meeting there so often that it was etched in her memory. Even Jax wasn't likely to be out looking for her. He probably just thought that she had just skipped town. Even if he did think that it was weird that she had vanished without a word, he wouldn't be out there looking for her.

Not for the first time, her determination and resolve started to slip.

Still without windows or any natural light, she couldn't tell one day from the next. Alastair started to drug her more often, moving her into the cage at the back of the room for hours on end while he was gone. They were the good days. She could stretch and move around more freely, making her realise just how weak she had become, but Alastair wasn't a fool, he kept her in the dark, her hands and ankles chained, and the door to the cell had no locks on the inside for her to try and pick. The metal was impenetrable. She had tried for hours on end to find any weakness, but there was none. He would always return, blinding her with the lights and then drugging her, and when she would wake, she would be back on the bed again, strapped down.

On occasion, she would wake up with another long-haired man in the room, but Alastair hated it. He'd scurry around, muttering that he had everything under control and that he was on the precipice.

They had given him one week more to break her. Only one more week to get through, she thought to herself.

The next day, in a desperate bid, Alastair shared everything with her. It was his last attempt to convince her to just get with the programme, submit to him, and accept this stranger as a husband.

The shocking revelation was that she was apparently some kind of royalty, as was Astaroth. They had been promised to each other before either of them had been born. Her birth parents seemingly did not know of the other family's brutal nature before the deal was struck. When the news hit them that their precious daughter would be subjected to a life of misery for their political gain, through her demise, they decided that when she was born, they would hide her in the world of men in order to save her from their mistake of promising her to such a cruel family. The lineage that Alastair had drummed into her came into her head: Lailah, her birth mother, was a queen, and Raziel, her father, a king.

What were they king and queen of?

Oh, just Elysium or...Heaven.

She supposed that at least they had tried to save her from all this. It was just a shame that it wasn't enough. She could laugh at the whole thing, hiding her on Earth, so she was protected. What a joke.

She actually laughed out loud when Alastair told her that she was the same as Astaroth and the other long-haired men keeping her captive- an angel.

What kind of a warped world was this- that angels were all dicks, and demons- she thought of Alastair; well, some of them were dicks, but some were also good.

When Hunter had revealed that demons existed in the world, she supposed she should have questioned the whole angel thing too, but it had never even crossed her mind. She was shocked now that she knew and found herself wishing that she didn't.

She dreamed of returning to her normal, very human life- Sin, her bills, her shitty apartment- but more than anything, she still dreamed of Hunter and what might have been between them.

She hated to admit it, but as time went on, her determination started to waver even more.

Alastair kept her chained up to the ceiling most of the time now, using the same manacles that he'd used on her on the metal bed that sported spikes protruding into her wrists.

Her body was getting more sluggish; the fatigue had set deep into her bones. She no longer dreamt of escape or Hunter anymore, or dreamt at all. She was going to die in this place.

It might come sooner than she thought. She realised this as she listened to a conversation Alastair was having with one of the long-haired men and found out that he only had two days remaining.

Her head lifted slowly as Alastair walked into the room, rubbing his hands together excitedly.

Oh god, this wasn't good.

"After learning more about you, Evie, I have decided that we've been going about this all the wrong way, but luckily for you, I have worked out the solution." He grinned at her like a maniac.

241

"Now this is your last chance. If we don't make headway, it's the end of the line for you, I'm afraid, as I have other places to be."

Having already decided days ago that death was the favoured option, she welcomed it and didn't take much notice to the new direction he'd decided on. Well, she'd told herself that, but that was before two tall men that she now knew were angels dragged in a half-dead-looking girl. Evie recognised her immediately. It was the red-haired stripper Scarlet from Sin. As malnourished and beaten as Evie was, she still fought against her bonds to try and get to the helpless girl before Alastair came at her with a needle.

"Hush now. We are just going to switch your places, and then we will begin."

Evie turned into a wild banshee, fighting with all the strength she didn't have against the chains that held her, the movement causing the spikes of the manacles to dig into her flesh anew, blood oozing down her wrists. Adrenaline suddenly boiled to the top and gave her the strength she didn't know she still possessed at the sight of the other girl, helpless and brought into this situation because of her.

Alastair quickly reached for the chains, pulling them up tighter and dragging her feet from the ground. Evie couldn't keep in the scream as her wrists were shredded. He stuck another needle into her neck, pushing down the plunger, and there was nothing she could do about it. Evie glared daggers at him, just as the fight left her.

"I will rip you apart," she slurred, sagging against the chains. She realised immediately that this wasn't the same drug that he had used on her before as a he was fully conscious but unable to move.

A new panic clawed at her, she was completely vulnerable, with no way to defend herself if she needed to. Her eyes watered and spilled down her face, and she could do nothing to stop it.

Oh god, they were going to hurt Scarlet. There wasn't anything more that he could do to her with his knives, chains, and shock collars anymore. That knowledge kept Evie from the pending terror that threatened to take her over, as the tall man-Danios that had brought Scarlet into the room turned to look at her.

He looked her up and down from where she hung on the chains, and then looked to Alastair.

"This is taking too long, and you are marking her too much. Does Astaroth even know what you have been doing to her?"

"He gave me free rein to get results quickly," he said, going over to his bag and busying himself inside.

"And how is that working out?" He knew that Alastair was failing. "You are on your last 24 hours, demon," he said, putting his hands back on his hips as his eyes slowly travelled back over to Evie again. He was obviously feeling some kind of way about the torture she had endured. She may have mistaken the look, but he seemed angry and a little sad.

Knowing he was an angel and portrayed to be a protector in every version of literature that she had ever come across didn't change the way she viewed him now. Angels were the reason that she was here, and he could help her, but he didn't.

"Switch their places and then leave me to my work, please."

Danios snorted a humourless laugh at him, shaking his head while walking over to Evie. "We are all going to Hell for this," he whispered, this time definitely showing his sadness as he unhooked the manacles around her wrists from the chains that she hung from, looking at the bloodied mess left behind. She watched helplessly as he picked her up and took her to the pen at the back of the room, placing her carefully inside.

Indecision warred on his face. She tried her hardest to reach out to him with her eyes, to show him just how much she was suffering, but in the end, he still turned away from her.

"I'll be sure to report your progress back to my lord," he said as he walked back over to drag Scarlet across the floor to where Evie had just been.

Alastair hurried forwards with a pair of manacles from his bag and quickly attached them to her wrists before Danios held her up and hooked them onto the ceiling chain, her head lolling on her shoulders.

As Danios turned back to him, Evie could see Alastair's turmoil as sweat begin to run down his forehead to his neck. Good, let the fucker sweat, she thought as she watched what was happening from where Danios had left her.

"Astaroth won't want to be bothered with it. I'll clean her up once we're done here. Don't worry."

"She's skin and bones, Alastair, and these marks will take weeks to heal. If you don't want me to report it to him, then you need to make contact with him yourself. The clock is ticking. Mark my words, as soon as your time is up, she'll be taken from you, and you will suffer the consequences."

"Yes, yes, ok, I'll speak with him before starting here."

Just as the two of them went to leave, Alastair called over his shoulder, "You can keep each other company until you're fully awake and willing to cooperate. I'll see you both shortly," he said, looking nervously at Evie, before walking from the room, leaving the two girls alone.

With the sedative running through her veins and her earlier adrenaline surge leaving her just as quickly as it had come, she lost all sense of consciousness and fell into an uneasy sleep.

"Are you awake yet?" Scarlet's voice jolted Evie into consciousness.

Groaning, she tested her range of motion, and although sluggish, she seemed back in control as she flexed her fingers and pulled herself up on shaking arms, dragging herself forwards until she sat in front of the cell door and a fully conscious Scarlet.

She looked at the red-haired woman, who was always so perfect at Sin. The black dress she wore was torn, and her long red hair was a matted mess. She used her arm to push her hair from her face, revealing an ugly mark as if she'd been struck there. She'd obviously been crying, her eyes puffy and red, but as she looked at Evie, it was clear that she had put on her usual cold facade that she always wore at Sin.

Evie was still wearing the slip of a dress that she'd been put in when she'd first arrived in this place. It was browned with dirt and dried blood and did nothing to hide the pitiful state that her body had become. She was suddenly self-conscious of the way she now looked in front of Scarlet and tried to hide as much of herself as possible, pulling her thin arms around herself.

Scarlet's cold stare broke as she watched her with pity in her eyes. "I knew this was a bad idea. Probably one of my worst, but seeing you now...I know I made the right decision."

A traitorous tear slipped down Evie's cheek. "How did you end up here, Scarlet?" She croaked, her voice raw from not being used in so long and the after effects of the paralysing drug Alastair had used on her.

She suddenly realised what awaited Scarlet here and looked at her with fear in her eyes. "You must escape here, Scarlet! Forget about me and get out. Any chance you get, run and don't look back. Please, Scarlet, you don't understand what will happen to you if you don't."

"Beth," Evie looked at her, confused. "Seeing as how I'm probably going to wind up dead here, you might as well know my real name. I don't think there is any escape from this place. Evie you've been gone for weeks, like eight weeks."

The knowledge that she had been in this hell hole for eight whole weeks had her losing what little hope she had left. Her head dropped, and her hands came out as she clung to the metal gate separating her from her freedom.

"I was helping Jax look for you. That's how I am here." Scarlet's voice had Evie's head lifting. "He and those four guys who own that club, the Cellar-Adriel, Theo, Viden, and Hunter..."

Evie couldn't breathe at the mention of his name. "They are out looking for me? All of them?"

"Evie, they haven't stopped looking for you," she looked at her, smiling sadly. "Hunter stormed into Sin the night you left, and all but threw Jax around, demanding if he knew where you were, where some man had taken you. I overheard them and wanted to help." She moved her head to face Evie more straight on. "Me and a couple of the girls from Sin went to their club on the other side of town and started working there a bit. We started asking questions, trying to find out what had happened to you."

"Why would you do that?" Evie whispered.

"I'm not actually a bitch. Look, we are all some kind of fucked up to end up at Sin, but that doesn't mean we don't look out for each other. Even though you don't work the main club and I've been hard on you, you're still one of us, and we don't take lightly to our girls disappearing. Luckily for you, I got some information on where we are and managed to tell Hunter before they grabbed me."

Evie gripped on to the bars of her cell, desperate for the knowledge Beth had on this. "I would have gone straight to Jax, but that guy Hunter- he's got it bad for you, he would have ripped me apart for going to Jax over him first. Shitty situation aside, I'm kind of jealous. No one would tear the world apart looking for me like that." She gave Evie a small smile.

Yeh, they were in the shittiest of situations, but Evie couldn't help but give her a small smile back, her heart warming at the thought of Hunter still out there searching for her.

"If anyone can find anyone, he's going to find you. We just have to hold on until they get here." Beth looked over to where Evie sat, running her eyes over her. "What's happening here? What have they done to you?" She asked quietly.

Evie's eyes watered. She could deal with this hell on her own, but Alastair was right that she wouldn't let anything happen to Beth on her behalf.

"It doesn't matter now."

"Who are these arseholes? What do they want with us?" There were many different ways Evie could answer her, many lies, but only one truth, and the fact that Beth was here because she was out helping to look for her owed her the right to the truth.

Just as she opened her mouth to speak, the door to the room swung open, and Alastair strode in, looking distraught.

"Slight change of plan, ladies. Looks like we are going to be moving you before we can have any fun together."

He turned, pulling chains that were attached to the ceiling next to where Scarlet was, free of the beams, and gathered them into his arms. As he hurried himself around the room, putting things into his bag, he moved towards the door, and the girl's eyes met across the room.

They had just lost their only hope of rescue.

Chapter 21

"They have Scarlet!" Jax threw open the door as he stormed into Viden's apartment above the club. Looking around, he saw Adriel, who sat up from where he lay on the sofa, but no one else there.

"You do know that you can't just come storming in here, right?" He breathed out a sigh. "What do you mean they have her?"

"She was with Tessa, leaving their apartment to come here. Tessa said Scarlet went back in to grab her purse, but when she didn't come back, she went in to look for her. She saw her being dragged into the back of a truck. She didn't get the plate, but she's got the trucks description."

"Maybe it's a coincidence? Why would they want to take her?"

"I don't know, but it doesn't change the fact that they have. It's not a coincidence. Look, she said they were tall and had long white hair, the same description as you told me."

"Ah shit, look, Hunters not here," Adriel said, scrubbing a hand down his face. They were all exhausted from searching endlessly for the past few weeks with nothing to show for it.

Walking over to Viden's door, Adriel banged his fist on it. Seconds later, a just-woken-up looking Viden emerged from inside.

"What's going on?" He asked, pulling a shirt on over his head.

"The angels have Scarlet," Adriel replied.

Jax's jaw dropped. "What the fuck? Has someone forgotten to clue me in....angels? When did they come into the mix?"

"Where's Hunter?" Viden walked over to the counter, grabbing a glass from the cupboard and pouring himself some water, ignoring Jax.

"I think he was doing the demon club rounds again, seeing if he could get any intel. He said he was starting at the Oracle."

"Er hello? Guys? Angels?" Jax threw his hands up, looking between them.

Adriel and Viden looked at each other.

It was Adriel who spoke first, as Viden glared at Jax, leaning up against the kitchen counter. "So, it turns out that Evie is an angel, and the people that have her are also angels."

"What happened to this guy Drew we're looking for? And you didn't think to tell me that these people are angels before now! I could have asked around, known what I was looking out for at least."

252

"Yeh, like you're so in tune with your demon side," Viden snorted. They had done a bit of digging into Jax's past through their Enforcer connections and were a little shocked to find out that he'd stayed off the demon radar as far as they could see.

"I might not be a demon Enforcer or running a demon club, but that doesn't mean that I'm dead weight in all of this. I've known Evie for a year and Scarlet for longer. I'm involved in this whether you guys want me to be or not, and I need to know all the facts."

There was a beat of silence as they all looked at each other until Adriel blew out a breath. "Four days ago, Scarlet gave Hunter a location she'd found out from a demon who came into the club who deals in angel feathers, and there was talk of a group of angels up to no good about two hours from here." Jax walked forwards and sat down on the sofa, facing Adriel. "The demon vanished before we could question him, and when we went to check out the address, the angels were long gone, but she'd been there, Jax." Adriel's memory of Hunter when he'd stormed into the empty location, only to find blood and the smell of death in the air, was seared into his memory. If he hadn't seen it with his own eyes, he wouldn't have thought Hunter capable of the devastation one girl could cause him, but he guessed that was bonded males for you.

"We'll phone Hunter, get him to meet us all at Scarlet and Tessa's apartment, and we'll hopefully get a lead."

~~~~~~~

Half an hour later, they were all standing outside a shitty complex of apartments. Tessa, one of the girls that had come over to the Cellar to work for them, was with them too. She was scared but was determined to help, even more so now they were picking off her friends.

"My car was right over here, and I was waiting for her next to it." She walked across the parking lot, which, unfortunately for Scarlet, was out of view of the front entrance. "I heard a bit of a commotion, but that's usual for round these parts," she said, looking down at her hands "I should have known something was wrong. I shouldn't have left her on her own. I walked around the corner, and that's when I saw the black truck and a long-haired guy manhandling Beth into the back of it. She looked unconscious. Oh god, I hope she was just unconscious and not dead. I froze, and then I hid. I should have tried to help her." Tears started to fall freely down her face.

Hunter leant down, looking her in the eye. He was exhausted, but this was the most hope he'd felt since they went to that address Scarlet had given them.

Evie couldn't be dead. He wouldn't believe it.

"If you had, then you would have been taken too, and we wouldn't be right on their tail."

Jax walked over, and Tessa leaned into him for a hug. It seemed the security guard was some kind of hero to the girls from that club.

Jax took her apartment keys from her and passed them over to Hunter. "I'll take Tessa to the Cellar. Let me know if you find anything." He grabbed Hunter's t-shirt before he could leave. "I mean it, don't leave me out of shit again."

Hunter looked down at Jax's hands and raised his eyebrows. "I didn't leave you out of anything, you just weren't there when we got the information."

"You know what I mean." His eyes flicked to the very human Tessa, who couldn't find out about any of the logistics surrounding the girls abductions.

"You're going to find them, aren't you? Scarlet and Evie?"

Hunter and Jax both turned to Tessa.

"I know we all work at a strip club, but that's not who we are. We are survivors, and we're strong. Each and every one of us has lived through something to end up there, but it's made us who we are. They won't give up, so you can't give up either."

Hunter would never give up. He didn't know how he could put that into words for Tessa with the same conviction he felt in his heart. "I give you my word that I will never stop looking for them both. Wherever they are and whoever has them, I *will* find them, I promise you."

Tess stared into Hunter's eyes before nodding.

Jax put his hand on her shoulder and turned her to him. "It doesn't matter where any of you came from or anything like that. If any of you go missing or need my help, you know you've got it."

"Same goes for me and the others. Anything you're worried about, come to the club and find one of us."

Jax looked at him and gave him a slight nod, as if he needed his approval.

"We just want them found and safe, but I'll pass the message on to the other girls."

"Come on." Jax led her over to his red mustang. "I'll catch up with you later, Hunter," he shouted back, emphasising the fact.

It was going to be another long night, Hunter thought.

2 days later

256

"We need to move right now!" Hunter said, pacing back and forth across Viden's living room above the club.

"It's not that easy, Hunter. We need to get everyone into place first. We won't lose her this time. Viden is trailing them, but you'll fuck this up if you go out there and tip them off that we know where they are. You know this," Adriel said from sitting on the arm of the couch. "As soon as we have a destination, we will mobilise, but until then, you need to sit down and conserve your energy. We are all going to need you on form, not just Evie."

He was right. Hunter knew it, and his lack of female contact along with his bonding link was taking its toll on his energy and stress levels. His demon was MIA, which was probably a blessing. The longer Evie had been gone, the more he had regressed back, almost like he just couldn't handle the fact that she wasn't there and that she had chosen to run from him.

This new location had come in the way of an anonymous tip-off left at the club only a few hours before. Hunter had scoured the CCTV and found the long-haired guy that had left the scrap of paper that Viden had found and his cars registration, but his brother had immediately left the club to check out the location, refusing to tell anyone what had been written on the paper, just that it was a lead and that he was going alone to check it out.

The second Hunter sat down on the chair in the kitchen, the front door slammed open, and Theo walked into the room. Hunter immediately stood up again.

Theo looked at him and grinned. "Let's go.

Hunter didn't need to be told twice. He armed up quickly. Blades crossed his back, in his boot, and on his legs. He was already wearing his Enforcer getup, which consisted of black combat trousers, a black wifebeater, and a chest holster, which he added two extra guns to. He grabbed a small gun and strapped it to his ankle for Evie for when he found her.

The thought had him smiling. They were going to find her tonight, he knew it.

Theo and Adriel were right there with him grabbing ammo, guns, knives, and throwing stars. They armed up quietly and efficiently. They each already wore a healthy supply of weapons, always carrying their favourites. The others were just insurance for if things happened- guns jammed, knives got lost.

The door to the room suddenly slammed open, and Jax strode inside. All guns were suddenly pointed in his direction.

"I thought you weren't going to keep anything else from me."

"Fuck," Adriel said, dropping his gun muzzle. Hunter and Theo following suit. "We nearly fucking shot you."

"We would have told you before we left." Theo spoke up, holstering his gun.

Jax took in his surroundings. "You've got an address?"

Hunter looked at him and nodded once.

"They are my girls so I'm coming too."

This earned him a growl from Hunter.

"We need all the help we can get," Adriel said to Hunter, putting his hand on his chest to stop him from moving towards Jax.

"Evie isn't your girl," Hunter sniped at him as he turned away, grabbing his coat from the back of the sofa.

"She's not your girl either. You need to remember that."

The look Hunter gave him would have made any fully grown demon shrivel where they stood, but Jax seemed to have bigger balls than most and simply cocked an eyebrow at him. "It's true. It's totally up to her to decide what happens when *we* rescue her. If she doesn't want you around, then you'll have to go through me to get near her."

As much as what Jax was saying to him pissed him off, he couldn't help but respect the guy for protecting her.

"If you ever feel like reconnecting with your demon side, I'm sure you'd fit right in as an Enforcer."

The worried look didn't go unnoticed by him. Interesting, he thought, but Jax quickly covered it. "Was that an actual compliment?"

"Come on already," he replied, rolling his eyes.

The four of them left Viden's apartment a few minutes later, once Jax had helped himself to their supply of weapons. They jogged down the stairs to the door that led back into the demon part of the club and strode across the bar area into the main belly of the Cellar, where music and people surrounded them.

Dressed as they were all in black- combats, wife beaters, black boots, and black trench coats hiding their weapons- they were a sight to behold. Bigger than most of the others in the club, everyone moved out of their way. The demons moved the quickest, hoping that they weren't the ones on the brother's radar as they all looked sheepishly in their direction, but as long as they kept to the rules topside and didn't go around pissing off the wrong people or giving demons a bad name, then they were welcome in the Cellar and wouldn't fall foul of their Enforcer or assassin jobs either.

Hunter's eyes went over to Kali, who was working her usual area in the main bar. As soon as she spotted them, she ran around and caught up with them.

"You're going after her, aren't you?" She grabbed onto Hunter's arm in an attempt to stop him. "Look, I know that I don't know Evie all that well, but I want to come with you."

They all turned to look at her like she was crazy, even Jax. "She's a girl, and sometimes you guys can be a bit...much. If she's been through something, she might need me more than she will need any of you."

Hunter had tried to keep all such thoughts from his mind, but he couldn't deny that Kali might be right and Evie may be hurting in a way in which he could do more harm than good being around her.

"Fuck"

"Viden's going to kill us good if we bring her," Adriel said what they were all thinking.

"She has got a point, though." Hunter scrubbed a hand down his face and looked at her. "You keep out of the way, and you stick to one of us like glue at all times. I mean it, Kali, no bright ideas. Go and grab your coat and meet us out the back. We are going in Ade's car."

She nodded and took off towards the bar again. It was getting late now, so the club was winding down. The others would manage without her, but that didn't stop Hunter from worrying about all the working girls at the club. Since Scarlet had been captured, they had increased the security around the place and had at least one of them on the premises at all times, but with them all gone, the threat that one of the other girls would suffer the same fate felt too greater risk. He burned to run to Evie's location, but he hesistated realising that he had to ensure the safety of all involved this end too.

He turned looking to the others. "I'll meet you out back in five."

They looked at him and nodded, not asking any questions as they carried on their path through the club. Hunter peeled off and beat feet back to a different part of the demon area of the club. It was hidden from the view of humans by the strong metal door that was camouflaged against the club's back wall. They obviously knew that it was there, but just thought it was another VIP area or private area for the brothers. Neither wrong, really.

He punched the code into the security lock and walked in. Looking around, he clocked the twenty odd demons in various stages of drinking, dancing, lurking, and generally doing demon stuff. A few faces swung in his direction as he shut the door behind him, but they only nodded to him and carried on their business.

He spotted who he was looking for immediately. The young legion demon was lusting over Pixie, one of the succubus girls working the bar in the corner. He whistled sharply, and Levi's eyes swung in his direction, his smile instantly vanishing as Hunter curled his finger to say that he wanted a word.

Nodding to one of the booths that was unoccupied, they both walked over to it and sat down opposite each other.

"What's going on, Hunter?"

Levi was shorter and slighter than Hunter, but he held himself well. His blonde hair and blue eyes made him a firm favourite with the girls at the Cellar, along with the fact that he'd earned himself a hoard of demon warriors after his father had died. Hunter and his brothers had helped him out a few times off the record, when some of those demons had fought to gain control of the hoard, thinking that they were more deserving than the inexperienced legion boy was.

"I don't have long, but I need your help. Can you spare some of your warriors? I can't tell you what, but something big is going down, and I find myself in the middle of it. I won't lie to you, there are probably going to be casualties."

Levi frowned "You've never asked me for help before, but you've always been there for me. I know if you're asking, then it's something serious, so they are yours. Use as many as you need."

Hunter reached over the table and squeezed his shoulder. "Have six stationed around the club, keeping an eye on the bar girls. Make sure they all get to their cars safely at the end of the night, then mobilise another thirty, I'll send you the address as soon as I have it...and Levi, make sure they are all packing some serious heat."

"You've got it," Levi said as he walked away from him, pulling his phone out from his pocket and putting it to his ear.

Hunter hoped that he hadn't just made a big mistake.

Chapter 22

They had been in the truck for about an hour when Adriel turned off the headlights and pulled off the road and onto a dirt track.

Leaving the car hidden, they went on foot as they neared the area where Viden had told them to go.

Following Viden's phones GPS signal, Adriel led the way through the thick undergrowth until they reached a clearing. Ducking down behind a fallen log, they peeked over the top, looking across to the outbuildings and barns that stood in the darkness, all looking abandoned, but Hunter knew better as he studied the landscape, noticing the telltale signs that there had been recent activity there. Broken tree branches, the smell of gas in the air, and hand and foot prints on some of the dusty surfaces showed that people or something had been there.

Trying to get a little closer, they worked their way through the thick undergrowth again. Progress was painstakingly slow but necessary if they wanted to remain undetected.

There was the slightest rustle of a bush next to them, and everyone froze, just as Viden appeared from where they had just come from, showing with his hands how many and whereabouts the angels were positioned. Two in one barn, three in another; he kept going until there was a total of around fifteen that they knew about.

Hell yes, they had found them.

Hunter wanted to shout in joy and rush through the buildings, but he knew he couldn't and that he had to wait. His Demon pushed him to move and to find her, but he managed to keep him at bay. The guy wasn't stupid, he knew the score.

The sound of rustling suddenly surrounded them, and they all stopped, going on instant alert, but the shadows that were appearing around them were all demons. Hunter thought at first it was Levi's hoard, but as he started to see some of their faces, he realised they were demons from the assassin den. It seemed that Bacchus had switched sides again. Most likely, word had gotten out that he was doing angel's dirty work and he was covering his arse.

Bacchus wouldn't be there, of course, he never did anything himself, but oh, how Hunter longed to see the backstabbing bastard to settle the score. Payback was a bitch, and he was counting down the minutes until he came face to face with the demon warlord again. His Demon growled in agreement.

The assassin demons all nodded to them as they spotted the brothers, waiting like they were for the right moment to mobilise.

"Viden, did you tell the den about this place?" Hunter quietly whispered.

"I may or may not have given them a little tip that would have a few of them showing up here," he smirked.

So they didn't know this was angel business...Chances were, they were going to find out very shortly as their eyes darted around the area.

Everyone was in place. It was then that Viden seemed to notice Kali, who was crouched down behind Theo. Fury changed his features as he looked at Hunter, pointing his finger right in his face. Barging past him, he pushed Theo out of the way and grabbed Kali by her upper arm before frog marching her in the opposite direction of the farm. She slapped at his chest and managed to spin out of his grip, glaring up at him. Viden looked up to the sky, obviously trying to get a grip on his rage, before he stared down at her. As he looked at her, the anger on his face slowly turned to worry before he took hold of her hand and tugged her into his side, glaring at the others as they walked back over to them.

A sharp whistle sounded from the trees before a small demon made a run for it across the clearing, which drew all of their attention. He ran seemingly undetected towards the building that Viden had indicated had the most angels inside and looked to place something on the window ledge before taking off back in the same direction again.

The brothers all looked at each other.

A couple of seconds later, there was an almighty boom as the whole front of the barn imploded. It was followed by a succession of booms as each building was hit with some kind of explosive. It looked like the assassin den did know what they were going up against tonight after all.

They all drew their weapons, nodding to each other as they broke cover and ran towards the carnage. Viden stopped Kali before she could follow, grabbing one of his guns and pressing it into her hand. "You don't leave my side. Point and squeeze. If you get separated from me, you find one of the others or you hide. Don't make me regret this," he said, looking at her intensely, like he wanted to say or do more, but instead took off in the direction of the chaos and all the others, with Kali by his side.

The angels appeared from the wrecked buildings and seemed to just keep coming. Viden's first count was way out, as more and more of them seemed to appear from nowhere. This was obviously a serious angel operation of some kind.

Situated off to the left, Hunter noticed a hidden, dark, small building that had been missed by the assassin's explosives, but angels were appearing from there in a steady flow, seemingly undetected by the others. He decided that was where he was headed as he peeled away from his brothers.

He shot off round after round as he moved, and even though they all hit their marks, the bullets didn't seem to do anything other than piss the angels off, as white blood oozed from the wounds where they had been hit. Hunter frowned at that new revelation.

Fights were erupting all around as he ran across the clearing. White robe wearing majestic creatures they were not. They were all tall, most had long white hair, some had dark hair, and they all wore fighting clothes in all black and red, similar to the demon's fighting apparel- layers of leather covering them as protection.

Taking cover, he watched as some of the den's demons tried to overpower one of the light-haired angels, who was now in the way of his end destination.

Hunter watched from behind the short wall he was crouched next to. The angel was fighting them with a short blade that had light emanating from it.

Whenever Hunter got the chance, he slugged the guy with another bullet, but like before, it didn't slow the guy down it just added more white blood. The angel didn't even notice him as he grabbed one of the other demons around the throat and easily broke his neck. Dropping the crumpled, unmoving form at his feet, he turned and grabbed another, slamming him against the floor. These guys were strong, and the demons were quickly becoming outnumbered.

Three of them suddenly jumped on the angel in an attempt to overpower him, causing his bright blade to fall to the floor. Finally, through sheer force of will, the angel fell to his knees. With the height advantage now on their side, one of the remaining den demons, Goose, grabbed up the fallen angel's blade and managed to get a clear shot at the angel's neck. Pulling the blade across his throat, white blood seeped out, followed quickly by dark red as the angel's eyes flew wide before he finally stopped moving. Goose wiped the sweat from his forehead with the back of his hand. Breathing hard, he turned and noticed Hunter.

"You've got a damned death wish over all of this, going against the den first and now you're here with angels?" He breathed heavily.

Hunter smirked at him. "You don't even know the half of it."

"And I don't want to. I'm only here because Bacchus told me I had to be. The first chance I get, I'm gone. All this shit with angels, not my scene, man." He backed away from him, but not before throwing the angel's blade to him.

Hunter caught it easily. It felt light in his hand, the weight all in its hilt. Being the same length as his forearm it felt like a natural extension of his arm.

"Angel blade, the only thing to kill them," Goose took off, running towards the other den demons who were fighting another not far from them.

Hunter looked around for his brothers and caught sight of Jax and Viden engaged in a fight with a dark-haired angel the same distance away as the building he was heading towards. Kali stood off to the side, squeezing off ammo every time she had a clear shot at him. Any other being wouldn't have stood a chance against them, but this one wasn't even slowing down. White blood covered him as his various wounds oozed.

Hunter looked towards the building that he had been heading to, and in a split second, he changed direction and ran for his friends instead. As he reached them, he went straight on the attack. Using Jax and Viden's distraction, he ran behind the angel and sliced the back of his legs with the angel blade. White and then red blood seeped out. The angel roared in pain as he went down onto his knees, but not before stabbing out with his own blade, catching Hunter in the shoulder as the tip pierced his skin. Burning hot fire spread in his veins, but he didn't waver as he grabbed the guy's long hair, pulling it back so it bared his neck, and in an ark-like motion, he stabbed him straight in the chest all the way to the hilt.

The angel looked at him in the eye with hatred and fury, his lip curling up as the light of life left his eyes. Hunter felt no remorse as he let go of his hair and pulled the blade free, leaving the body to drop to the floor.

He shrugged his coat off with one arm, leaving him in his muscle shirt, and reached up, his hand coming away from his shoulder, bloody.

Viden was there, pushing his hand away and checking out the wound. "What's with the shiny blade?" He nodded to the angel blade still in Hunter's grip.

"It's the only thing that will kill them. Bacchus' men have more, so grab what you can." He looked at his shoulder and said, "I'm not sure what they do to demons, though."

"It's not deep. You should be fine." Viden said, leaning down and swapping his blade for the one the angel had dropped.

The sound of vehicles brought all of their heads around just as five vans full of demons pulled up.

Viden looked at Hunter and raised his eyebrow in question. "Let me guess, you went to Levi? You know the payment he'll require for this Hunt."

"Yeh, well, I'll deal with that later if we get out of this. Let's get the boys. My bet is Evie and Scarlet are in that one." He nodded over to the building he had been heading to before.

They found Theo and Adriel, picking up angel blades as they went from dead and dying demons, obviously having worked out that they were the only way to kill them too. By the time they reached them, all six of them- Hunter, Viden, Theo, Adriel, Jax, and Kali- had angel blades in their hands.

Levi had delivered all right and sent not just thirty demons but more like fifty. They were holding their own against the angels, quickly working out their weapons were of little use and switching out to the brightly lit blades instead.

Hunter didn't feel bad about leaving them to hold the fort as he joined the others, running full speed towards the building in question. They came to it from the back, avoiding the front door where the angels had been appearing from before, and peered into the broken, dusty window.

Through the darkness, Hunter could see steps that led down into the floor with two angels standing guard at the top, just inside the doorway where the doors were now closed.

Hunter looked at his brothers and grinned.

They took their usual pairs. Hunter went with Viden and Theo with Adriel, Kali went where V went, and so Jax went with the others. Splitting up, Theo's group went around the front and walked through the front doors as if they owned the place.

"Hi gents, what have you got down there?" Adriel nodded towards the stairs.

The two white-haired angels sneered at him, "Cambion scum."

"Now that's no way to speak to my brother, is it?" Viden said, jumping through the window at the back, closely followed by Hunter and then Kali.

The two angels were surrounded, but they still looked at each other, smirking.

"Which one of you wants to die first?" Viden asked.

They both attacked at the same time.

Oh, they were strong all right, but no match for the brothers. The angels fought as trained warriors, disciplined with precise moves. The demons fought dirty, which is what gave them the advantage.

Sidestepping an attack, Adriel jumped up onto one of their backs, forcing his chest down and onto Viden's waiting blade. When he dropped down dead, the other seemed to realise that he may not survive this and attacked with renewed strength, sweeping his arm out, slamming Jax and Adriel against the wall as he grabbed Hunter by his shirt, throwing him exactly where he wanted to be- down the stairs.

The angel turned and stalked towards Kali, reaching for her, but Viden moved quickly and sliced straight through the angel's arm. As it dropped to the floor with a thud, he bellowed in pain, blood gushing from the wound, but he wasn't incapacitated for long as he snatched his other hand out and grabbed Viden by the throat, lifting him off the floor. Staring him in the eye, Viden was just about to lose consciousness when the angel jerked. His mouth opened, and his eyes went wide as a bright blade tip appeared, followed by a river of red blood gushing from his mouth.

The hand holding Viden up went slack, causing him to fall to the floor, coughing and gasping for breath.

The angel dropped face down next to him, revealing a bloody Jax standing over him, still holding the blade where it had penetrated the back of the angel's skull. He was breathing hard as he reached out his hand for Viden to take, helping him up.

"Thanks, man." Viden clapped him on the back as he stood.

"Guys, you might want to see this," Hunter called up from down the stairs.

They all jogged down the metal steps to where Hunter was standing. He was leaning on the railings on a platform, looking down. They all looked in the same direction.

The stairs carried on down another three flights, and at the bottom, there seemed to be row upon row of rooms or cells. A solid stone wall ran down the middle with a corridor either side of it, and then rusty metal edges created cage-like rooms one after the other, all ringed at the top with barbed wire.

It was an angel prison.

They were at an angle in which Hunter couldn't see into the cages from where they were standing, but there were so many.

They all looked to him.

"She's down there, I know it."

He went to go down the next flight of steps when Theo grabbed hold of his arm and said, "We don't know what else is down there. We keep alert and in pairs."

Hunter looked to Jax and asked, "Are you with me on this?"

"You bet." He held out his arm, which Hunter grasped onto with his, and they all took off down the steps together.

At the bottom, they branched off, one pair going up one corridor, another going down. This was a quick rescue mission, not an Enforcer job.

The rooms were dark, wet, and mostly bare. They all had stone floors with drains in the centre, no windows, no natural light, just the buzzing orange glow that came from the corridor strip lighting.

They looked in every cell, methodically working their way along. It wasn't until they came to the last cells in the rows that people started to appear inside them. They were dirty, some chained, all thin, and malnourished with various wounds.

Hunter swallowed audibly.

It was then that he started to shake. He'd never really experienced true fear until recently- well, until he'd met Evie. He felt it now. True fear. It ate at him as he looked at the faces of those locked away in this place. Not one of them raised their heads or even looked in their direction, it was like they were hollowed-out husks, forgotten about in this place. Sure, they could go along, letting everyone go, but who knows who or what they would be releasing.

Stick to the plan, he and Jax said intermittently when one of them stared for too long at one of the unfortunate people within.

Jax was searching the opposite cells when Hunter walked past the last cell on his line. He was just about to turn the corner when he moved back to it.

Peering into the darkness, he saw what his brain refused to see at first.

Shit, had he found her? The shock of the image made him think so, but his mind wouldn't process what he was seeing.

Hanging in the dark cell from manacles around her wrists in the corner of the stone jail was the unmoving, naked form of a girl.

His girl.

Oh god, she was dead. They were too late.

Jax was suddenly there next to him, staring at the same image, refusing to see what was right in front of them.

"Evie!" Jax bellowed next to him, grabbing onto the metal bars, causing a loud clang of metal that reverberated through the space. She jolted from the noise and began to tremble.

She was not dead. She was alive!

Hunter's eyes closed briefly with relief.

"Evie," He breathed.

Slowly, she lifted her head at the sound of his voice. As their eyes met through the bars, tears fell down her cheeks. She let her head drop back down on her shoulders and let out a sob. Hearing the noise, Hunter went full bonded male on the bars that separated her from him. With a roar, he launched himself at them, pulling with all his strength until he felt them begin to give way, and then all of his brothers were there helping him, all five of them pulling with everything they had.

The bars bent straight out of the wall, landing with a loud clang and they all sprang into action, but Hunter just stood there, rooted to the spot. He couldn't seem to get his feet to move, all of the thoughts of what they had been doing to her staring him straight in the face. He hadn't been there to protect her like he'd promised he would be.

The sound of Theo and Adriel yanking at the chains from where they were fixed into the wall holding Evie up had his feet finally moving towards them. As he reached her, he lifted his hands up to her face, wiping the tears from her cheeks with his thumbs.

"I found you."

Her head slowly lifted again, her eyes speaking of the horrors she'd endured. Bruises covered her jaw, and old blood had dried in her beautiful blonde hair. Shit. He looked down, finding her fragile body a network of old and new bruises, cuts, and blood. That along with the fact that she was naked, had him seeing red. He couldn't help the growl that left his lips.

As an assassin and when his Demon had been in control, he'd seen some pretty horrendous things in his time and done some too, but all of that paled in comparison for him. His heart was literally breaking right there as he took her in.

His Demon's rage threatened to break free over what had been done to her, but he had to rein it in. There would be a time and a place for that, and at the moment, Evie needed him.

Chapter 23

At first, she couldn't tell whether she was in fact being rescued or if it was some fantasy that she had conjured up in the dark recess of her brain, but as the brothers pulled at the chains, causing the spikes in the manacles to cut into her already bruised and infected wrists, she knew that she couldn't be imagining that kind of pain.

Seconds later, Theo broke through the chains that held her, causing another wave of agony from her arms and shoulders as they fell from where they had been holding her up. She suddenly dropped, but Hunter caught her as the pain blinded her. He carefully unhooked the chains from the manacles that surrounded her wrists and threw them across the floor, away from them.

She hadn't realised just how much she had needed him until she saw him there in front of her and felt his strong arms surrounding her. The horrendous torture and abuse that she'd endured while she had been taken barrelled into her, causing her breath to catch as she let out another sob. Her carefully structured wall of self-preservation from what had happened to her began to crumble. As she struggled to cling to the corners of it as it tumbled from her, she grabbed onto Hunter's shirt in a frantic effort to cling to normality.

He gathered her bloodied hands in his and kissed her forehead as she breathed through the impending panic attack. His scent was all around her, and she breathed him in, which grounded her to the here and now.

Kali was suddenly there with a big woollen blanket. As the two girls looked at each other, Hunter took the blanket from her hands. "Do you think you can stand?"

Her thin, bloodied hands came up to scrub the tears from her face as she replied with a small nod. She forcibly put her feet underneath her and tried to take her pitiful weight. As her shoulder joint's screamed in pain, her legs shook under the pressure, but Hunter was there, wrapping the blanket around her and holding her up.

"We need to get her out of here, now," he said to his brothers and Jax.

She reached her hand up to touch his cheek. "I shouldn't have left you..." her weak voice mumbled as she dropped her head again.

"This is not your fault, Evie," he crouched in front of her, tipping her chin up so he could look into her eyes. "It's not your fault, none of it. I'm going to find the people who did this to you, and then I'm going to rip them apart."

She looked at him, willing strength into her body, as her lip trembled at his words.

It had only taken a matter of minutes to transfer her from the cell and into the back of their truck. Hunter had pulled the blanket up and over her head, shielding her from whatever lay outside, as he carried her close to his chest and into the waiting van before it peeled away from the outbuildings and whatever else lay out there.

She had no clue as to how they had found her or how they had managed to bypass whoever had been stationed around the area. She supposed they were answers she would get later on.

Alastair's 24 hours had run out while he was moving her without the other angel's knowledge. He had drugged her and Beth and thrown them both into the back of a van, she didn't know how long ago. She had started to become conscious during the journey and had overheard him talking frantically on the phone about two girls who had been arrested and needed to be moved to a more secure location due to the nature of their crimes. He gave them false names and told whoever was on the other end of the line that they were both demons. At the time, she didn't know what he was talking about- that was, until she was taken into that angel prison by him and abandoned there.

None of them knew her real name. No one asked any questions. She was processed. Her clothes were taken from her, and she was hung in that cell and fed once a day, and that was it, almost like they were just waiting for her to die.

Hunter reached over and gathered her bloody wrists in his hands. Her heart dropped at his wince as he noticed the spikes that protruded from inside the cuffs. She looked out of the van window as Hunter worked on the first one, her eyes swimming with tears as she tried to hold it together. Just another hour or so, and she could let it all out—what had been done to her and the fact that Hunter and the others had come for her.

She was safe, but she was cold, not being able to call up any emotions after her elation at being rescued. "It's over. Don't think about it," she whispered, to herself or him, she couldn't tell.

He freed her first wrist, prising the manacle open and throwing it to the floor. He brought her ripped wrist up to his lips and kissed it lightly.

"The fuck, it's over," he growled.

He moved on to her next wrist as she stared straight ahead, not seeing or feeling anything.

They sat in silence for a long while before she asked, "Where is Beth?"

"Beth?"

"That's Scarlet's real name. Where is she?"

"She's with Jax and Adriel in the car behind us. She was in one of the other buildings, but we got her out. She's safe. We are going to the bolt hole, all of us." Theo said from the driver's seat.

They were quiet again for the rest of the journey, which Evie was thankful for. Hunter didn't crowd her, but he was there, seeming to know exactly what she needed. His strength and protection, and the knowledge that he was there, was enough. He wouldn't let anyone near her, she knew that with total conviction.

She was desperate to see Beth, the two of them forever linked by the unimaginable horrors that they had endured, but she spent her time now building up the walls again that contained her pain.

Closing her eyes, she leant against Hunter's shoulder and let the soft movements of the van lull her to sleep in his safe embrace.

Two hours later, she was sitting, arms around her knees, in the shower she'd been in weeks before at the bolt hole. The water was slowly getting colder as she sat, staring into space.

She'd sent up a private prayer of thanks for all the dark marble that had hidden the worse of the blood that ran down the plug hole, but now that it was all washed away, she didn't feel any cleaner.

The emotional breakdown that she had been holding out for never came, or maybe this was her new reality- the deathly quiet and the loss of feelings and emotion. Was she broken? Had they finally done what they had set out to do to her? She willed herself to feel something, but it just wouldn't come.

With a sigh, she stood up on shaky legs and turned off the water. Bruises and redness ran from her ruined wrists up her forearms, she noticed as she began to inspect her body of the abuse it had endured.

She had lost all faith in anyone finding her after they had been moved that third time by Alastair. She wasn't an idiot, he was hiding them so he would avoid any repercussions. She would direct all of the pain, the betrayal, and the suffering right back at him and at them.

The angels.

Hunter had said that he was going to rip them apart, but not if she got there first.

The glimmer of an emotion boiled in her subconscious, and she grasped onto it with both hands.

Feeling something finally, she grabbed the fluffy towel from the top of the toilet seat and wrapped it around herself, opening the door.

Hunter quickly stood up from where he was sitting on the end of the bed facing her. "How are you feeling?"

"Numb," she replied honestly.

Their eyes met in the tense reality of the situation; he'd been left, and she'd been tortured. Two beats of silence passed before they both walked into each other's arms, embracing, and in that moment, she broke apart, literally crumbled into a million pieces. It was like he was the missing link to her past self and all of her feelings and emotions, and in his embrace, it all came barrelling back to her.

Hunter held her as she cried, using his strength to help show her that she would survive this.

When the tears ran out and exhaustion kicked in, he pulled the duvet back for her to crawl into. Leaving the damp towel on, she felt his heavy weight dip the bed behind her as he wrapped his arms around her, caging her in.

He seemed to catch himself and drew back quickly, but she stopped him with a hand on his arm. "I need to know you're there. I can't feel alone right now."

He tightened his arms around her again.

"Just don't turn the light off, ok?" she whispered.

~~~~~~~~

Days passed.

Evie switched between sleeping, eating, and sitting in Hunter's arms, never leaving his room. Her physical wounds were healing, but he feared her mental ones were brewing beneath the surface.

Hunter didn't know how to deal with this kind of thing. His only experience was his own shitshow of a life early on, so he did what he had wanted and needed back then- he left her alone, but not on her own. He hoped that it was what she needed right now, but he had to find out why all of this had happened before the chance of retribution slipped away from them.

He stopped pacing the hallway and sat on the floor with his back against the wall opposite the door that she was behind, going through her own hell. He willed the image of her in that cell from his mind, but it was there every time his eyes closed. He was worried that it would be etched there for eternity.

Kali came up the stairs and stood in front of him. "I've just come from seeing Beth. Do you think that Evie is up for a visit?" She nodded to the door.

"I'm not sure what she needs right now, Kali, but you can ask her."

She nodded, popping her head into the door before disappearing into the room.

Hunter's head hung from his shoulders.

Fuck, this hurt.

"You couldn't have done anymore for her, brother." Viden said as he appeared at the top of the stairs, coming over to sit down on the floor beside him. "But I get why you're hurting. She won't open up to you. Don't take it personally. She'll get there."

They sat in silence together for a long while, it was late at night and Viden fell asleep quickly next to him.

Hunter was pulled from his thoughts as the door in front of them opened softly a while later. Viden didn't stir as Evie emerged. She paused at the sight of the two warriors sitting on the floor side by side before nodding down the hall for Hunter to follow her. It was the first time she had left the space, and he was eager to give her whatever she needed right now.

Getting up smoothly, he followed her into one of the other rooms and pulled the door shut behind them before he instantly worried that she might not want to be trapped inside. But as she turned and opened her arms up to him, he released a breath he didn't realise he was holding and had her in his arms a second later.

"Kali fell asleep after we spoke." She said into his chest.

"Did it help?" He asked.

"A little, yes."

"Will you tell me?"

"I don't even know where to begin, Hunter," she sniffed into his black muscle shirt, and his heart cracked more as he felt her tears wet it.

He walked over to the bed and sat on the edge as she climbed onto his lap and nestled into his chest. His strong arms came up around her shoulders, holding her close, even though his wounded shoulder from the angel blade screamed at him.

After a while, she started to speak.

"So the guy who put that demon hit out on me was actually an angel who I'm suppose to marry." She blew out a breath. "It seems that he didn't want a wife at first, but then changed his mind to wanting a compliant one. I'm some sort of hidden heir to something that everyone knew about but didn't know where I was, or something like that. Well, that was until he found out the adoptive name I had been given." She sniffled some more. "At first, they took me to some warehouse." Reaching up, she rubbed at her nose. "There was a demon there. He worked for them."

Angels working with demons. He didn't tell her that he'd found out as much at the den while he was looking for her, as this was her story to tell, and he was desperate for the information on what had happened to her after having searched so hard and for so long. "Do you know what this demon's name was?"

"It was Alastair. He hurt me, Hunter. He was their torturer."

He swallowed the growl that was trying to break free from his Demon and took a deep breath. "What did he do?" He didn't want to know- he needed to know to fuel his revenge.

Evie was quiet for a long while, reliving the past few days.

As she sat in silence, he asked the one question he dreaded above all else. "Did they touch you?"

He swallowed the bile rising in his throat at having to ask her. The thought of anyone hurting her like that was too much to bare.

As she started sobbing uncontrollably, he couldn't stop himself from launching up in anger, putting her down on the bed.

He was going to kill them. His Demon surged forward with the need to maim and kill them all.

"No! Hunter no. They didn't. Please..." she grabbed onto his arm to stop him from leaving.

~~~~~~~

His anger would get him killed.

This she could keep to herself. She needed to in order to survive it. The thought of that guard taking it upon himself to teach her a 'proper' lesson when she was moved that last time would be buried in her mind forever. A place she would never, ever revisit.

Hunter gathered her up again in his arms and sat back down. "The thought of them hurting you like that was tearing me apart." He shook his head, looking to clear his anger, and went for another angle. "Tell me more about this Alastair. What did he look like? Sound like? Smell like? Anything that could help me work out what type of demon he is. It will be the key to finding him." He wiped the tears from her face.

"He wasn't tall...not heavy-set. He was wirey, but he had strength." She remembered some of the beatings he had given her. "He had short blonde hair cropped close to his head that he wore slicked over, and he had a red tattoo on his neck," she pointed on her neck to the location of the tattoo.

Hunter watched her with interest.

"What was the tattoo of? You're sure it was a tattoo and not a brand?"

Evie considered this, "It could have been a brand, but it had defined edges. Maybe a brand and a tattoo on top? It was a circle but split into two halves, with three horizontal lines in the middle."

Hunter leaned over to the bedside table and pulled open the top draw. After rummaging inside, he pulled out a small pad of paper and a pen. Passing them to Evie, she took them and started drawing. Hunter watched her intently as she sketched. She turned the pad around, flashing the image at him. He knew demon brands and knew some demon tattoos, but this was a mixture of two.

"You mind if I keep hold of this?"

She shook her head. "Do you think it will help?"

"I think that this is the key to me finding this demon, Alastair." Hunter said, folding the paper up and placing it in his jeans pocket, wincing at the movement.

"You're hurt?" She asked, pushing his shirt to the side and looking at the red welt there.

"Angel blade, it's nothing, don't worry about it."

They were both quiet again for a while.

"You came for me..." she said in a quiet voice.

"Evie, I would have done anything to get you back. I *will* do anything. Don't ever think that I won't be coming for you. When you're away from me, wherever you might be, I will always be making my way back to you."

She looked up at him, tears falling freely down her face again.

He leaned forwards, hugging her into him. "These last weeks- without you- have made me realise that you mean something to me. Something more than I first thought."

"You know what I am now," she said, ashamed, as if not knowing what she was was his only reason for sticking around. He supposed that it was what he'd led her to believe in order to get closer to her.

"I do." He leaned back, looking into her eyes. "I'll let you into a secret. I've never really cared about what you are. From the moment I met you, you've been mine, and I've been yours." He took a deep breath. There wasn't ever a right time to admit to someone that you'd bonded with them, but he felt that she had a right to know the true depths of his attraction to her.

He reached up and rubbed the back of his neck.

"Uh oh," she smiled.

"What?"

"You're nervous about whatever you're about to say to me. Rubbing your neck, it's your tell."

He immediately stopped, dropping his arm back down to his side.

When he didn't say anything immediately, as he tried to figure out how to drop this bombshell, her smile dropped.

"Did something happen while I was gone?"

"What?" He caught on quickly to what she meant, "Oh no, no, nothing like that."

As her face relaxed, he decided just to go with it.

"So here's the thing...demons bond when they find the person they are meant to be with, whoever or whatever that may be and I think that's happened to me with you." He looked up into her eyes. "I *know* that's what's happened to me with you."

She sat quietly, a little crease appearing between her eyebrows. "So kind of like soul mates?"

"The demon equivalence to soul mates, yeh," he rubbed the back of his neck again.

"Ok," she said.

Shit, he'd put too much on her. She had only just been rescued and was healing and he dropped that on her.

"I shouldn't have told you that I'm sorry."

"I'm not a demon or a human apparently, and I have no idea if angels bond, but if we did, I think you'd be the equivalent to mine. You kept me sane in that place, Hunter, the thought of you got me through it."

His hands came up to her face, and their foreheads touched as they just sat together, feeling each other's warmth.

As they looked into each other's eyes, she reached up to touch his face, tracing under his dark eyes that had been starved of energy since the night she had been taken.

"Have you...have you been looking after yourself?"

He knew what she was asking but couldn't believe she was asking it. "No Evie, just the thought of it..." he shook his head. "No."

"I'm stronger now, and kissing me it helps?"

His eyes instantly dropped to her lips. "You have no idea."

"Tell me."

He hesitated, wondering whether he should divulge just how much she affected him that way.

"Kissing you...it affects me differently." At the worried look on her face, he quickly added, "in a good way."

"Because of this bond?"

"Maybe, but I'm not so sure. I've never heard of a demon bonding with anything other than another demon before."

"So that's why you stuck around," she smiled.

"You have no idea," he said again, smiling back at her.

She moved towards him first and kissed him. It was gentle from both ends, all the stresses and worries from the past weeks being erased as they were both lost in each other's embrace.

Hunter's whole body trembled as he recharged. He'd never get enough of this- of her. As they broke apart and Evie looked into his swirling silver eyes, he felt something within him shift.

"Evie Logan, I think I'm falling in love with you," he blurted out.

She looked at him, shocked.

Fuck. He'd just said exactly what had come into his head at that second, without taking into consideration the fact that she was still healing and had just found out a shit-tonne of information about herself. Talk about an overload.

All that had happened to her, and he drops the L-bomb right after he admits his Demon is almost fully bonded to her.

He was just about to apologise when she whispered, "I love you too, Hunter."

His heart soared.

He'd never felt like this about anyone before, and the fact that she was feeling the same for him was just too good to be true.

"I vow to you that these son of a bitches will pay for what they did."

Worry transformed her features.

"You're a demon, you can't get involved with angel business. I learned that while I was there, Alastair would mumble it continuously. Please, Hunter, I won't lose you over this."

This Alastair bastard was scared of demons finding out he'd worked for angels.

Perfect.

Hunter smiled at her. "I'm going to the Guild. You remember me telling you that I'm a demon cop? Well, angel's getting demons to do their dirty work, like Alastair was doing for them? He was right to be shitting himself over being found. Not to mention the fact that an angel put out a demon hit on you. They fucked up in the worst possible way. Demon law is as important as human and angel law, and they have been itching for an opportunity to take on Elysium. The Guild is going to be gunning for them big time, and I'm going to be the one leading the charge."

"Hunter…"

"I'm a bonded male, Evie, well, almost. For whatever reason, my Demon has picked you, and that comes with my unbridled protection. If that means I have to fight angels, then I will, but unlike them, I'll use the law to my advantage and get them on my side first."

She didn't look happy about it but nodded anyway.

He hugged her to him again and said quietly, "You know that Beth's been asking for you ever since you both got here…"

Chapter 24

As the sun set on the sixth day of Evie's freedom, she finally worked up the courage to go and see Beth. She felt awful that she hadn't been before, but she was terrified that the sight of her would send her back to that dark place that Hunter was helping her move on from.

Padding quietly down the long corridor, she made her way to the room he had told her that she was in and took a deep breath as she knocked quietly.

When no answer came, she held her breath and slipped inside. Every light was on in the room, momentarily blinding her as her hand came up to shield her eyes as she looked around the room, noticing all the blinds were down, the bed a mess, but everything else seemingly untouched.

"Beth?"

She waited for a reply and was about to leave when she heard a small voice from behind the bed.

"Evie?"

Walking around the foot of the bed, she saw Beth sitting in pyjamas on the floor, wrapped up in a blanket. She looked worse than the last time she'd seen her- bruises on her face and her red hair crudely cut short- but it was her eyes that haunted her. They looked at each other. The worries Evie had vanished at their reunion.

The tense silence stretched on until, in two quick strides, they were embracing and crying into each other's arms.

"Are you ok?" They both said at the same time. Laughing and crying, they stared at each other as the laughter died.

Silence surrounded them again.

"That was shit, wasn't it?" Beth whispered.

Evie gave her a small smile. "I'm not planning on doing it again anytime."

The last time they had seen one another was in the back of that van. Alastair had attacked Evie while Beth was still sluggish from the sedative and powerless to stop him. He'd beaten her until she had lost consciousness, and when she had woken up, she was being processed by the angels for their prison, with no sign of Alastair or Beth anywhere. Soon after that, she had been moved into the cell where Hunter and the others had found her.

"What happened to you?" Evie whispered, "I always thought you were somewhere near. I used to call out for you in the dark, but you never replied, and they weren't all that hot on noise where they kept me."

Beth sat down on the end of the bed and pulled Evie along with her. They both sat cross-legged, facing each other. She absentmindedly played with a loose strand on the comforter as she recalled what had happened to her.

"That was the last time I saw you when he went crazy at you in the back of that van. He beat you so badly. I screamed at him to stop when I came to- so loud that, in the end, some of those long-haired men came out to see what the noise was and ended up dragging him off of you. They took you away then, and Alastair pushed me out the back of the van and drove off, leaving me there."

"He just left you there?"

"He was panicking, and that made me happy," she smiled. "Before they brought me into that room with you and Alastair at the start, they kept me for a day or two at some other place where two of those long-haired men stayed, I think. I heard some really really weird stuff down there...stuff about you Evie."

"Let me guess, angels, demons, murder plots, birthrights...have I left anything out?"

"Yeh, that about sums it up. At first, I thought maybe I was dead or that I was hallucinating. That was until angels and demons were all I heard about. They kept me next to one of their rooms that they all met up in, so I heard a lot. They went from saying that they should never have trusted a demon to saying that they should never have been involved with any of it. I listened to everything they said in the hopes that if I got away somehow, then I would be able to find my way to you." Evie reached over and took her hand. "I don't think we would have ever gotten out of that place. They were frantically looking for where Alastair was holed up for fear of being found out. I didn't even know whether you were still alive until they started discussing what to do with you, as he was failing with the mission. They were worried about your ascension and that they were all going to be found out and killed. They were still talking about what to do with you when they got a call from some guy they called Astaroth. The most I could work out from that conversation was that some people had worked out you were alive. They all panicked and left straight away, and they never came back again. That's when I was moved into that room with you."

Beth was gripping her hands as if she were likely to be torn away at any moment.

She tried to think of what this new information meant to her- the possibility that other angels knew that she existed. That probably wasn't a good thing. "Have you told the others about this?"

"No, I wanted to speak to you first. I appreciate them rescuing us from that place, but it was me and you living it, and it's your information, not theirs."

"Thank you. I need to work all this out somehow. They have done so much already. I haven't told Hunter about the royal stuff, and I don't think I should until I find out all the facts."

They spoke for a long time after about nothing much at all- idol chat with the occasional question about demons and angels thrown in by Beth.

Adriel had brought up a coffee for the two of them. His awkwardness around Beth didn't go unnoticed by Evie. She smiled at her, raising her eyebrows as he left.

"He's been checking up on me, that's all," she blushed.

"Oh sure, don't worry, I doubt humans having relationships with demons is as bad as angels having relationships with them."

"You mean he...he's a demon?"

Evie laughed, and it felt good. She would survive this, she thought.

~~~~~~~

Hunter stopped just outside Beth's room. The sound of Evie's laughter had him closing his eyes as relief flooded through him. Hearing them talk about relationships between angels and demons

304

though was just something he didn't want to think about right now. They could deal with that later.

He scratched the back of his neck before remembering what Evie had said about his tell and dropped his hand back down again.

Walking over, he knocked on the door frame before leaning in. Both girls looked exhausted, but they were strong.

Evie's eyes lit up as she noticed it was him. He'd never get tired of seeing that.

"Can I get either of you something to eat?"

Hunter brought them food regularly, but it mostly went untouched, neither of them regaining their appetites even though they were both so painfully thin.

"I might come downstairs, actually." Evie replied, looking at Beth, "Will you come with me?"

Hunter looked at her. Neither of them had ventured downstairs since they had arrived days ago. Evie was a warrior, and even after all the hell she'd been through, she was still trying to help Beth. She was still wearing the t-shirt he'd put on her the night before of his. It hung like a dress off her, hitting just above her knees. His eyes travelled down to her bare legs, which still sported the bruises and marks of her time in that hell hole. Hunter's Demon rejoiced at having her close again, content to share her with him at the moment, but the sight of the marks on her was still a bitter pill to swallow.

"Are the others down there?" Beth pulled his attention away, asking him.

"Theo is downstairs."

She wasn't quick enough to hide her disappointment. It was no secret that she and Adriel had grown closer since they had come here, apparently him being the one to storm into the cell where she was being held and acting all knight in shining armour to rescue her.

Evie had listened to him tell her Adriel's account of it. She didn't really remember much of that night herself, which was definitely a blessing.

~~~~~~~

"If it makes you feel any better, Ade is on his way back with takeout."

Evie narrowed her eyes at him. "What kind of takeout?"

"Chinese...we pretty much ordered everything from the menu, so there will be plenty."

Not likely Evie thought, knowing how much food Hunter put away, but still her stomach rumbled at the thought of Chinese food.

She looked at Beth, giving her a hopeful look that she would say yes to coming downstairs with them.

Evie wanted to go back to Hunter's room. She could think of nothing she would like better then to curl up with him in bed and hibernate for as long as possible, but she knew that it wasn't healthy and that Beth was probably in the same boat, but on her own.

"Who can say no to Chinese?" Beth gave a small smile.

They walked back to Hunter's room so she could pull some trousers on before they all wandered slowly down the stairs together.

"Hey, there they are," Theo called over, sitting up from where he was slouching on the sofa.

Evie looked around the open room, the space looking more lived-in since she had been there last- before she had handed herself over to Bacchus.

As she looked around, her eyes stopped on one new addition.

Sitting on a stand in the corner of the room was her goldfish from her apartment. She walked over to him and crouched down, pressing her finger against the glass as his little chubby body swam over, his mouth forming a quick succession of O's as if he had missed her as much as she had missed him. Her eyes watered at the normalcy, at her life before all of this staring her in the face.

"You bought him here?" She turned around to look at Hunter and Theo.

Hunter shrugged. "It wasn't like I could leave him at your place all alone."

She walked over to him, and he pulled her in close, kissing the side of her head.

"Thank you," she said, smiling up at him.

"No thanks needed. I like the little guy," he winked before setting her down on the sofa arm before moving over to the kitchen.

He was busy getting cutlery and plates out when Adriel came in carrying a good six bags of food with two bags of prawn crackers dangling down from his mouth. As soon as he spotted Beth downstairs, he smiled widely, causing him to have to grab onto the bags to stop them from falling from his mouth. She smiled shyly back at him.

They all ate together around the dinner table. Hunter kept the conversation light with stories from the Cellar and how he lived to wind up Jax. Evie couldn't be sure, but she was pretty certain they both liked each other. She missed Jax, but Hunter had told her that he'd been called back to Sin soon after they had arrived here, promising that he would return soon.

She looked around at them. It was nice. She supposed it was like how a family would act together, and she dared just for a second to imagine what it would be like in a future filled with the same.

~~~~~~~

Hunter was putting it off, calling in the Guild. At first, he thought having their help in finding Alastair would be invaluable, but the more he thought about it, the more he realised that he may actually be putting Evie and himself at greater risk by getting them involved.

The Guild's aim was to find demons who broke the rules. Yes, Alastair had broken the rules, but so had he.

Every day he was with Evie, he was breaking the demon and the angel's most sacred law- that neither would have relations with one another. He was dicing with death being with her, he knew that, and so did his brothers, but none of them dared question him about it.

Alastair was still out there. They had used all of their resources to find him, but they came up blank every time.

His Demon writhed beneath the surface, impatient to exact revenge on those that took her from him.

Soon, he thought.

It was time he called in the big guns to help.

He set up an official meeting for him and his brothers for the next day with some Guild superiors. Evie was safe with Jax, Kali, and Beth at the bolt hole. Hunter had just gotten off the phone to her.

He was so proud of her. She was with him every step of the way after that first venture downstairs, now sketching layouts and maps and giving descriptions of anyone she'd seen or heard during her time as their prisoner, and she'd given Beth the strength to do the same. Roles reversed he didn't know if he would have come back from something like that so quickly, but she was his warrior, refusing to back down or wallow in what had happened to her.

The meeting he'd set up was away from the Cellar. He didn't want them anywhere near Evie until he knew of their intentions when it came to the angel business, and even though she hadn't been to their club, the workers all knew her now, even just by her name and a picture they all had when they had been looking out for her, so any wrong answer would blow Hunter's cover story.

Viden, Adriel, and Theo were all with him at the bar that was a few blocks over from their club. They were all sitting around a small table with drinks in front of them, a tense silence settling over them as soon as they had entered.

"I know I keep saying it, but I appreciate you all being here for this." Hunter finally broke the silence.

"We wouldn't be anywhere else," Theo replied just as two Justice demons approached their table.

They were huge, minotaur-looking creatures to the brothers, who could see through their glamour, but to any humans looking their way, they were just a couple more beefy guys joining their table.

"Strange place to meet incubus. What happened to your club?" One asked in a deep, gruff voice as he sat down opposite Hunter.

"Too many ears there," he replied.

They all sat in tense silence.

"You wanted a meeting, and now we are here. What is this about, Enforcers?" The same one spoke, the other just standing there staring at them, his giant arms crossed over his chest like this meeting wasn't worth their time.

Hunter looked to his brothers for reassurance, and at their nod, he leaned forward, steepling his fingers.

"Ok, but hear me out first before you say anything."

They both grunted their disapproval at his order, but they let him continue.

Hunter launched into the story from the moment he'd met Evie. He missed out bits and gave vague truths here and there and he left out the fact that they had become intimate totally. He wouldn't give them any reason to dig into that one. His excuse for following her was none other than his incubus side being able to tell that there was something off about her and him wanting to bang her.

The Guild demons sat and listened to him, not giving away anything as they took in all the information given. The Guild already knew about them working for the den. Hell, they were the reason for it, all those years ago, when Viden had lost control, that had been the Guild's form of punishment, not for just him to owe the den but for his brothers too, which they knew hurt him the most. The Guild took care of business on the topside, and the den took care of business in the underbelly, staying on track, but there was often a hazy line between the two.

"Angels using demons?"

"I told you that it would be of interest to the Guild." Hunter replied.

"We need to talk to the boss about this, obviously." The chatty one said as he stood up.

The silent one reached into his pocket and pulled out a phone, passing it to his partner. They both walked away a little distance but turned, keeping their eyes on the table still. No blood rituals or sacrifices were needed here for contacting Hell. The underworld was a mere phone call away.

About twenty minutes later, they returned to the table.

"The boss wants to meet this angel girl, Evie. He's never seen or heard of a female of the species on Earth before...apparently they are quite rare." The chatty Justice said.

Hunter growled.

"You should learn to keep your hormones in check, incubus. This girl is the one consistent in your story, is she not? He wants to find out what all the fuss is about. You *will* bring her by order of the Guild to the location we give you at the time allocated, or we will take her from you. Do not forget relationships between demons and angels are strictly forbidden. The only reason we are not dragging you down to hell to stand trial over it is because you didn't know she was an angel before. If we get even the slightest hint that this girl means something more to you, then you will be stripped of your Enforcer title and banished back to the pit to stand before the Judge."

His heart hammered behind his chest, but he feigned disinterest. "Tell me where and when, and I'll bring her myself."

They both nodded in unison. "We'll be in contact."

It wasn't until they had left the pub that Theo leant across the table, taking a long drink of his beer. "He won't do anything to hurt her, Hunt. He's the chief of the goddamn Guild, he won't risk pissing off any angels." He said.

"Evie's an angel, and she's going to be pissed off." Viden said, as Theo glared daggers at him.

Chapter 25

"Tell me again," Hunter asked, reaching over to hold her hand as he drove them to the location the Guild had given him two nights ago.

It was a small bar just outside of town, where she was to go in alone. It was early evening and still almost light outside, the nights were so much warmer now that spring was officially here.

Evie sighed "You tried to sleep with me. I said no, and then you were following me, acting all creepy. To be fair, not much of this is a lie," she smirked at him.

"Har har"

"Then I tell him about the angels, concentrating on the fact that Alastair," she swallowed audibly at his name, "was working for them...doing their work."

"That's my girl," he squeezed her hand. "I can't come in or stay near or he will know I'm hanging around, and we need him to think you're nothing to me, so I'm going to go and wait at the Cellar with the others."

Evie tamped down her panic at the thought of Hunter leaving her there. She needed to keep it together for this, knowing his hands were as tied as hers were. This was the first real time she had left Viden's bolt hole, and fear gripped her every second she was out in the real world. She was thankful to the brothers for allowing Jax free rein to come and go as he pleased from their secret location. Having him near was a huge comfort to both her and Beth, which they both desperately needed.

They were quiet for the rest of the journey, both lost in their own heads about what had passed and what was yet to come. She absentmindedly picked at the dressings that surrounded her wrists. She was still healing, but it was a slow process.

All too soon, they pulled up opposite the bar 'Joes' where the meeting was to take place. It looked more up-market than she was used to, and she was glad that Hunter had persuaded her to change out of her jeans to wear a long, plain black dress with long arms- to cover her bruises and heels instead.

He reached up and rubbed the back of his neck, looking over at her.

She had to pull it together, if not just for her, then for him too. She willed her hands to stop with the consistent picking at the dressings, but Hunter had noticed and seemed to see how she was so tightly strung that there was a real possibility of her snapping at any second.

He slammed the car into drive and sped away from the bar, pulling down the next road, which turned out to be a dead end. He stopped, killing the lights and looked around.

Turning in his seat, he pulled her across the centre console and into his arms. "Don't trust anything he says, nothing, you hear me? He is a master manipulator and a prince of Hell. We just need the Guild on our side to bring this Alastair bastard in, nothing else." He pulled back and palmed her cheek. "As soon as you're done, call me, and I'll come here and pick you up. You'll be ok, Evie."

He looked like he wanted to say more but instead kissed her as if he were searing the memory of her into his soul. Resting their foreheads together, they both sat for a few seconds more before she pulled away and grabbed her bag, getting out of the car. She turned to see him watching her walk away.

Punching the steering wheel, he spun the hilux around, driving back out onto the main Street. He drove past her slow enough that she would reach the bar before she went out of view, but not slow enough to draw attention to himself.

Her eyes flicked in the car's direction one last time as the red tail lights carried on down the street as she placed a hand on the bar's door, pushing inside.

Inside the bar was dark, the walls were a deep red with mahogany wood furnishings, and the lighting was mainly candlelight. She looked around, noting that there was no one else in the room beside her. The only noise was the cracking of wood piled high on an open fire place to the left.

Small circular tables were set out for dinner service with silver plates and cutlery, and in the middle of the room was a wraparound bar with drinks lining the back wall.

It was really nice inside, the colour combinations reminding her of what she could remember of her visit to Hunter's club, the Cellar. Maybe this was another demon hangout, she thought. It would make sense for the meeting if it were, given the fact that there were no other patrons inside.

She was about to choose which table and seat to take- being nearest to the front door, she thought, when a tall, stout fellow appeared from behind the bar area, polishing a glass.

"Sorry, private function tonight, Mam." He looked her up and down and said, "Oh wait, are you here to see the Boss?"

"Um, y-yes," she stuttered and chastised herself. She wanted to appear strong, not weak. Clearing her throat, she tried again. "Will you announce to him that I have arrived."

"So you are this famous Evie Logan?" A voice rumbled from right behind her. It was like nothing she had ever heard before. Every hair on her body stood on end, and a new rush of fear swept over her. She couldn't describe it, but she felt that whoever and whatever this being was, he was her polar opposite and didn't belong here.

Her eyes travelled over to the man that was standing behind the bar, and she could see him visibly tense. He placed the glass he was polishing down and walked around the countertop, but not close enough to interrupt.

Evie swallowed and slowly turned around to face the tall man before her. He was dressed in a black suit, which, paired with his dark eyes, dark hair, and chiselled jaw, made her think at first that he was handsome, but as she looked more closely at him, his image wavered for a split second to reveal a dark swirling form with blood-red eyes behind the mirage.

Her heart hammered behind her chest. She was ok. She was going to be ok, this was just a business meeting between two people. She was safe, and she would never be taken anywhere against her will ever again.

"I am Evie Logan," she said, sticking out her hand in a bold move and praying that it didn't tremble.

The man looked down at her hand and then slowly back to her face again. "Forgive me for not shaking your hand, it's just that our two kinds don't particularly mesh well when in contact." He looked her up and down again and said, "such a shame."

She quickly dropped her hand and followed his direction on where to sit- at the very back of the bar in the darkest corner.

"Welcome to my establishment once again, my Lord. As always, it's a pleasure to host yourself and your guest."

"Yes, Joe, bring my usual and then step outside, please," he replied, never taking his eyes from her.

Joe bowed low and scurried away.

"You drink wine, yes?" He asked her.

"Yes, thank you."

They sat in silence for a few moments before Joe returned, carrying a black wine bottle, pouring out two glasses of it, and then placing it on the table. He bowed again and then left the room.

"My Enforcers inform me that you are in fact an angel."

She nodded.

"But you are unfledged?"

She nodded again.

"How is it that you found yourself tangled up in demon business, then, Evie?" He gestured that she drink some of the wine, which she did. The flavour was the most divine thing she'd ever tasted before. It was dark and velvety and warmed her mouth and tongue as she swallowed.

She bit back the moan before it made its way out of her mouth, but he seemed to notice and smirked at her.

"There became something of a bidding war when the angels found me." She replied.

"You were hiding? What were you hiding from?" He leant forward and drank some of his wine, black smoke appearing from his mouth as he drank the liquid down.

Oh god, she hoped that she hadn't just poison herself with demon wine.

She looked down at the glass in her hand.

"Don't worry, it's quite safe." He smiled at her and motioned for her to continue.

"I wasn't hiding from the angels as such, it was more a human situation gone awry."

"Why concern yourself over a human?" He asked, looking perplexed.

"I was a young girl out in the human world alone," she caught herself before she said more than she and Hunter had planned.

He steepled his hands in front of him, noticing her pause no doubt. "Tell me what you know about angels, Evie. Your ascension is near?"

"I don't know what to tell you, Sir. I thought we were here to discuss a demon?"

He ignored her question. "I heard that some of your fellow angels have acted unfavourably towards you. Do you have any idea of the reasoning behind this?"

"They were fighting over who should claim me as their own," she said, referring to what Hunter had told her to say.

"You are quite the wanted celestial then?" He scratched at his chin, reaching across to take another sip of his wine.

A chill swept through Evie. Nothing scared her like the angel Astaroth did, but this Prince of Hell was certainly up there on the scare scale.

"Will you find the demon who the angel's paid to torture me?" She was keen to wrap up this conversation and get away from him as quickly as possible.

He took another drink of his wine, motioning for her to do the same as his eyes travelled to where her bandaged wrists were just visible under her dress arms.

"Ah, yes, Hunter showed me his demon brand…I will have him dealt with accordingly."

She was instantly relieved.

Hunter had told her the Enforcer's punishments mostly revolved around banishing baddies down to Hell- no better place for that piece of shit.

"You were not brought up with the knowledge that you are an angel?"

"An unfavourable marriage promise had my birth mother hide me rather than face retribution from her husband," she said, taking another sip of the wine. "I've only met a handful of angels, and those I have met I do not care for. In my eyes, I am human and always will be." She replied.

"Ah, but you are not, human that is," his eyes glowed red slightly before dimming again. "My Enforcer demon Hunter, do you have some attachment to him?"

"He saved me, and I am grateful. Nothing more," she said, keeping to the script.

Narrowing his eyes at her, he leant back in his chair. "Tell me, Miss Logan, do you know of our laws when it comes to angels and demons?"

She looked him in the eye and shook her head.

"Allow me to enlighten you then. To have relations between a demon and an angel is strictly forbidden."

She tried to hide her reaction but wasn't quick enough.

"It is one of the oldest laws in existence, and your Hunter runs the risk of being stripped of his clearance topside, meaning he would have to return to Hell indefinitely for being close to you. Do not think me a fool. I know what is between the two of you." She swallowed down the panic that was crawling up her throat. "What I am proposing is a trade."

She eyed him warily, Hunter had warned her not to trust him. Even still, the news floored her, and she would do anything to avoid Hunter being punished like that because of her.

"What trade?" She replied quietly.

"You say that you do not see yourself as an angel and you are in love with a demon. The way I see it is that you have two options. One is to stay as you are but never see the incubus demon again..."

"And my second option?" She asked.

"You become a demon yourself." He shrugged nonchalantly.

Evie stared at him blankly. "How is that even possible?" She breathed.

He leaned forwards, steepling his hands on the table again. "You have heard of the term fallen angel?" She nodded. "You give me your wings, take a quick trip into Hell and back, and then you're free to stay with Hunter however you wish."

Now this sounded way too easy. Hunter would flip his lid at her even considering the possibility, but what was her other option- to lose him forever? Condemn him to a life in Hell?

He should have told her. He should have come clean about this before they had become so close.

She did have another choice, though, as she remembered back to when she had decided to disappear in order to protect him. Was this any different? She could still do it. It would break her heart and change her forever, losing him, but she could, and she would do it to save him, but was her angel status really worth losing him over? Giving up her wings would be a surefire way of sticking her fingers up at them, for all the pain they had caused her, but turning into a demon herself?

"I'm feeling generous," his voice pulled her from her musings. "Your ascension must be soon. I'm going to give you a couple of weeks to decide," she blew out a sigh of relief. "There is one stipulation. You must not speak to Hunter or any other Enforcers about this deal. If you breath a word of the offer I've given you, then the deal is off and Hunter will be dragged down to Hell. I have eyes and ears everywhere, Evie, remember that. One of my Justice demons will come to you when your decision is required. Take care, Evie, and make the right decision."

He gave her one last wavering look before his corporeal form fuzzed out, becoming smoke and black mist. The Prince of Hell's red eyes remained focused on her for a few seconds more, watching her reaction to his new form before it imploded in on itself, disappearing before her eyes.

She looked around, and the owner of the bar, Joe, appeared seconds later from wherever it was that he had gone. He looked over at her suspiciously before taking out a cloth and going back to cleaning the glasses while keeping his eyes on her.

Her hands were still shaking as she pulled her phone from her pocket.

Three missed calls and a text message all from her man.

Call me as soon as you're out of there. I need to know that you're okay.

She looked over to the man behind the bar and turned her back to him, hitting redial on Hunter's number. He picked up on the second ring, asking, "Are you ok?"

She closed her eyes, savouring the sound of his deep voice.

"I'm alright. Your boss is super terrifying, though. He said they were going to call in Alastair," she said quietly, even though the barman, Joe, was far enough away that he wouldn't be able to hear her.

There was a rustling sound through the phone, as if he were getting up and pulling on a coat. "I'm coming to get you."

She closed her eyes.

"It's not safe," she said, willing her voice to stay calm so as not to give her away. "I mean, anyone could be watching us. I'm going to get Jax to come and pick me up, and before you argue, I need to talk to him. I have to sort out business at Sin, I've got all my human stuff I need him to help me with, and I need to check in with Beth."

She had moved into Jax's place, and he wouldn't tell any of the others where that was, saying it was none of their damned business. She had a feeling he was hiding from someone too, much like her and some of the other girls who worked at Sin. He and the brothers had become close after her rescue, but this was a non-negotiable for him and they hadn't pushed the matter.

Evie could feel Hunter's indecision warring with him through the phone. She imagined him running his hands through his hair, trying to get a hold of himself.

After a while, his voice came through the line.

"He'll pick you up from there?"

"I won't move until I see him, I promise, and I'll get him to drop me at the Cellar when we're done." Tears pricked her eyes, and she had to swallow them down.

He grumbled "I don't like it." He was quiet for a second. "Keep your phone with you. Any sign of trouble, call me, and I'll be there." She smiled at his possessiveness. "I mean it, Eves, the angels are still out there. I'm not taking any chances with you. I only just got you back."

"I'll be careful, I promise, I'll let you know as soon as I'm with Jax and when we are on our way to you."

"Make sure you do," he growled.

How could she say all she wanted to him without giving away the fact that she most probably wasn't going to see him ever again.

"Hunter…"

"Yeah?"

"….it's nothing…I'll see you later. I love you."

"I love you too," he said, ending the call.

How would she give him up, she thought, as she pulled up Jax's number.

Five minutes later, Jax's impressive frame was striding through the bar towards her. She put her empty wine glass down from where she was sitting studying it, and stood up.

Joe looked him up and down from behind the bar suspiciously.

Spotting Evie, his face softened as she walked to meet him halfway, embracing him in a hug.

"Hey, baby girl, I'm glad you've finally decided to stop hiding from me," he said, squeezing her.

"I wasn't hiding. Hunter has just become a little more protective after the whole angel torture situation."

"But not tonight, apparently?" He raised his eyebrows at her, looking around.

"No. Tonight, I need you, but not here. Can we go to your place?"

He rubbed the back of his neck, reminding her of Hunter. "He's ok with this?"

"He knows you're picking me up. Jax, he's on a strict need-to-know basis. Promise me that you won't speak a word of any of this to anyone." The look in her eyes was so intense that Jax nodded his head.

"My cars round the back, lets go," he grabbed her hand and pulled her out the rear entrance of the bar, half dragging her over to his sleek red mustang. She didn't question the fact that he had known where the back entrance of the bar was, he'd obviously been there before.

As soon as Jax peeled the car away from the curb and hit the highway, Evie fired a text to Hunter, telling him that she was with Jax and not to worry.

His reply came back almost instantly.

Be careful.

Jax's phone went off with a message. Pulling it out, he read it and chuckled, flashing the screen at her.

I'll feed your inside bits to Viden if anything happens to her.

330

"This is obviously not something he's done, then."

"No, nothing he's done."

"I'm going to regret saying this, but…he's a good guy. You could do a lot worse."

"Like you?" She raised her eyebrow and gave a sad smile.

"Hey, I'll have you know I'm a catch!"

"Total panty melter."

"Just a shame not your panties, hey?" he smirked at her.

Her face lit up with a smile as she rested her head back on the seat. Jax was always so easy to be around. He would help her, she knew he would.

"I told you that you're more like a brother to me."

"Ouch," he said, placing his hand over his heart as her smile widened.

"Its good to see you smiling again," he said, looking at her, his face sobering. "When I found out that you'd been taken, it ate me up inside. I always knew that you were special. I just didn't realise how special."

They were both quiet for a while then, until he spoke again. "Don't let the fact that it was angels that hurt you put a dampener on the fact that you yourself are one. It's truly amazing, and you're part of a dying breed."

"That's just it, Jax. Other than my experience with them, I know nothing of angels. Do you know anything about them?"

If giving it all up was one of her options, then she needed all the facts, even if it would make her decision harder.

"I don't know much, but I'll tell you what I do know and what I've learnt along the way. My mum told me that angels were to be feared but also respected in all ways, that they are elite warriors- watchmen stationed throughout the continents. Their wrath is most commonly known to humans as karma. You do something wrong, and karma will punish you in mysterious ways- that's angels at work. Later on in life, while I was going through a wild streak, I met one and got talking to him. He taught me that there is a strict hierarchy between them- the royals are at the top, descendant from the original Archangels, next are Archangels, then watchers, and lower angels. The lowest are the nephilim- they are angel blood mixed with humans, and at the bottom of the pile are the fallen." Evie looked down at her clasped hands in her lap. "I'm guessing, with all the interest in you, that you're right up there at the top somewhere. Hunter suspects it too, no doubt."

He went quiet, obviously debating whether to drop the no angels and demons together bomb.

She saved him the turmoil. "What are fallen angels?"

"They are disgraced angels, Evie. A demon fucks up and they get sent back to Hell, but an angel fucks up- like seriously fucks up- then their status, job, birthright, along with their wings, are ripped from them, and they are tossed down into the pit- Hell Evie. Most don't survive very long, as demons don't much like the beings that punish their natural behaviours, and in Hell, the rules that protect angels topside don't count anymore. If they do survive then they are reborn as demons themselves. I don't know much about it other than they lose all knowledge of their lives before falling."

Evie swallowed the lump in her throat. Well the Prince of Hell had failed to tell her that little nugget of information.

Chapter 26

"So what happens to the fallen angels after?" Evie asked.

"What do you mean?" Jax looked across at her, the glow of the car's interior lighting his face.

"After they fall? What happens to them?"

He shrugged his shoulders. "They just find their place in the human world. Angels won't have them, and demons won't either."

"And they never remember?"

That earned her a frown. "It's part of their punishment, Evie. They return to how they were before they ascended." He sighed. "There is a story of two angels, Arlain and Seph. There aren't many female angels around, and so most have more than one suitor at a time."

She already knew this from Hunter.

"They were both watcher angels, and they were very much in love, but Arlain was very beautiful and the object of many other angel's desires, mainly an Archangel named Rayel. He knew of their feelings for one another, but he announced that he would be taking her for himself and that she had to forsake Seph. When Rayel arrived to claim her, she wasn't there. Seph killed Rayel to protect her from him, and he was cast out, stripped of his wings, and sent down to Hell as punishment for his crime against the Archangel. Arlain found this out and ripped her own wings off, following after him down to the pit. She was sure that if they stayed together, their love for each other wouldn't be lost, but the higher powers were furious at Arlain's lack of care for her angel status and did the only thing they could to keep them apart. They received the most extreme punishment. Arlain was banished to Hell, and Seph was banished to the ground floor...Earth."

Evie felt tears spear her eyes at the unfairness of their punishments. Just for being in love, they were punished.

"To further their suffering, they made them keep their memories of each other. If there is one thing I can teach you about angels- about what you are, Evie- it's to play by the rules." He looked at her sideways, "which brings me onto another subject- you and Hunter."

"I know what you're going to say, Jax. I know angels can't love demons."

He looked shocked. "Did Hunter tell you?"

"He doesn't know that I know." She looked over at him. "I need to keep it that way."

He eyed her suspiciously. "What are you thinking?"

She debated whether to tell him. He was going to give her shit over it, but she needed another perspective.

She took a deep breath before she spoke. "There is only one way that we can be together. I just need you to remind me of who I am at the end of it."

He sat trying to figure out what she meant when it dawned on him.

He pulled the car over, slamming on the breaks.

"Hell no! Have you not been listening to anything I've been saying? You and Hunter will be the next story kids get told of how you were both punished for eternity over this. After everything you have been through, you will lose him anyway, Evie, and you will both suffer the worst fates because of it."

"What other options do I have? Tell me, please! I can't lose him, I love him," she cried.

His face immediately softened, and he reached over, pulling her into his arms.

"There must be a way," she whimpered into his chest.

"You're still technically human until you ascend. If you're still off the radar of all of the angels that matter, then they can't do anything to you for being together the time you have."

"Jax..." Terror filled her eyes, "Beth overheard the angels that took us. They already know about me, and I'm marked to ascend. How do I stop it?"

"Ah fuck...I don't know enough about this, Evie. It's sketchy details at best for demons. I've only ever met the one angel before all of this. We must have a bit of time. I'll figure it out." He tried to smile at her reassuringly, but Evie could tell it was forced. "Who told you of the angels and demons thing if it wasn't Hunter?"

She pulled back from him, wiping the tears from her face. "I met with the Guild boss tonight."

Jax's jaw hit the floor. "You, you met the G-guild boss? As in a Prince of Hell? Like just now? Ok, next time, Evie, lead with that. So he told you that you and Hunter can't be together."

"In a way," she said, looking down at her hands again.

"The suspense is killing me here. What did he say?"

"This stays between me and you, Jax. No one else promise me."

"I promise."

This was why she had called him- he was always there for her, no questions asked, always totally dependable. Even with the knowledge that she was an angel, he hadn't changed towards her, and she loved him all the more for it.

"He offered me a deal."

Jax's eyebrows shot up.

"He told me the same as you did, that Hunter and I would be separated because of the damn law, but that there was a way around it."

"By falling..." Jax finished.

She nodded slowly.

"I'm guessing Hunter and the others don't know that you're marked for ascension, just you and Beth?"

She nodded again.

"This is serious stuff. We shouldn't even be talking about it. I can tell you what Hunter would say, but you already know, and it's the same as what I'll tell you." He took her hands in his and levelled his eyes with hers. "You need to close the damn book on all of this, Evie. Turn the page and then close it, never to re-open, at least until we work out all this ascension stuff."

She thought of all the things crammed in her never-to-re-visit box, and a fresh wave of tears started back up.

"Hunter would never want you to do this, I promise you. Every time, he will pick you over himself. Don't do this to him or to you. Take this car, Evie, and go somewhere far away from here. There's ten thousand dollars in the boot, take it and hole up somewhere. There is a burner phone in the glove box. I'll find out about this angel business, and I'll call you."

Her breath hitched. Could she really do this right now? Walk away from Hunter, possibly never to see him again.

Jax's eyes softened at her look of despair. "I'll explain it to him. I'll miss out the details, but he'll know the whys of it." He smiled sadly at her. "I love you, Evie. Not in the way he does, but I'll always be here for you, that will never change."

He leaned over and kissed her cheek before opening the door and moving to get out of the car. She scrambled to grab a hold of him to stop him from leaving her.

"Jax no, I need time to think about this. It's too much." She grabbed hold of his t-shirt, making him fall back into his seat.

He turned and looked her dead in the eye. "You know that if you go back to him now, then you will never leave. It needs to be now, Evie. Go, live. I'll work out the other stuff, and we will deal with it whatever it is, but you need to cut Hunter out for his own good."

Damn him for being right. She thought as fresh tears ran down her face, "Jax, I only just got him back."

He palmed her cheek, wiping the tears away, only for them to be replaced by new ones. "You are a warrior. How long have you been running for Evie?"

"You know about all of that?"

"I take my security job very seriously, and that includes looking after all the girls at Sin. I do background checks on everyone just so I know what to look out for. I know about Drew...I am in awe of you, Evie, at your strength to survive."

"Hunter has a lot to do with that, you know."

"I know, but you were also a survivor long before you knew him, remember that."

"Jax...his demon has bonded to me."

He scrubbed a hand down his face. "I guessed as much. Has he completed the bonding?"

"How does that happen?"

"You would know if it had. I've no idea what would happen if a demon fully bonded with an angel, though. Let's not find out, hey?"

She took a deep breath and cut the waterworks, managing a small smile. She found that place within herself that she supposed was the survivor in her "You're right."

"I'm always right," he winked at her, "about time you realised it."

Rolling her eyes, she took his hand in hers.

"Good luck, Jax."

"Why do I need luck?"

"You have to go and tell Hunter..." His smile disappeared. "I'd rather be in my situation than in yours."

"Fuck," it dawned on him what he had to do now. "I suppose I can't put it off forever. Travel North Evie...less angels."

He squeezed her shoulder, giving her a last smile before getting out of the car.

She leaned across the seat. "Wait, how will you get back?"

But he was already gone, as if he'd never been there.

~~~~~~~

Jax sifted to the darkened alleyway behind the Cellar. He hated it- not only did it hurt like a bitch, but it was also a beacon to all kinds of nasty, mainly his family, whom he had no interest in seeing after all these years. He kept his sifter and legion heritage hidden for good reason.

He thought of Evie and knew that she was strong enough to do the right thing. He just had to do his part now to ensure that she didn't hurt anymore than was necessary. That girl had been through so much, the fading bruises and healing cuts that still marked her skin were a reminder of the torture that she had survived.

Letting out a long breath, he walked around to the front of the club, ignoring the line of barely dressed humans waiting outside.

This was going to be a total shitshow, he thought.

He walked straight past the two demon doormen, nodding to them as he went. They had gotten used to him coming and going while Evie was missing.

Taking the stairs up two at a time, he made his way to the VIP section on the top floor. Hunter was there with his brothers at their normal table. They were all in deep discussion about something when Hunter's eyes came up and met with his. Whatever he was saying died on his lips as he surged up and came across the room at him.

"Where the fuck is she? You were supposed to be taking care of her!" They were practically nose to nose. His eye's flashing to all black.

"We need to talk," his eyes flicked to the others, "alone."

Jax's sombre tone had Hunter taking a step back and scrutinising his face before nodding over his shoulder, leading Jax through the door at the back and up into Viden's flat.

~~~~~~~

Jax went and stood in the kitchen, his hands resting on the worktop and his head hanging low.

"She's gone, hasn't she?" Hunter leaned back against the wall, resting his head back and looking to the ceiling. His eye's turning from black to grey.

"She found out about the angels and demons law—and no, before you say it, not from me. Hunter, she knew the consequences of loving you, and she chose your safety over her happiness."

Hunter started pacing then, scrubbing his hands through his hair. The implications of what Jax had said sinking in. He had just found her, and now she was out there on her own again because of some stupid law they had no power over.

He was furious.

"Fuck what I am, fuck what she is, fuck all of this! This is bull shit!"

BOOM! He looked up, finding that he'd just punched a fist-sized hole through the wall.

"You know that this is the only option," Jax said sadly.

Hunter's head dropped on his shoulders as he leaned his forearms against the wall. He closed his eyes, fighting to get control of his Demon before he ripped Jax's head off.

He stood there for a long while, just concentrating on breathing in and out and calming down. He could feel her moving further away from him. Could he do this? Live knowing that she was out there and all alone. Shit the angels, they were still after her. He could still hunt them if they were hunting her, though, right? That wasn't breaking any rules. Fucking rules- who even thought up the damn law that was now ruining their lives?

The thought suddenly came to him.

His eyes shot wide as he spun around to face Jax. "Evie's a royal," he breathed.

"I figured as much," Jax said, scratching at his stubble.

"What if she's *the* royal?" At Jax's confused look, he continued, "When we were searching for her, I heard some things about some angel legend. A royal that disappeared...I didn't think much of it, as it was so vague and from so many years ago. But what if..."

"No way. Even if she was Hunter, which is highly doubtful, it doesn't change anything."

"It would change everything...she could change everything."

Jax went over and perched on the sofa arm, confident now that Hunter was past the attacking him mode.

"I'm not following."

"Who wrote the damn laws?" Hunter walked over, standing in front of him.

Jax looked up and shook his head. "If, and that's a huge if, Evie is this long-lost legendary royal...you're talking about one of the most ancient of their laws, you'd need a damn good reason to go meddling in royal angel business and not just your dick."

"You said it- they are ancient, they need updating to more modern ways."

"And you really think that they are going to let Evie, a not even fully fledged angel who's lived her whole life as a human, walk in and demand they change laws that she doesn't even know or understand?" Jax gave him a come-on look.

"If she is the one they have been looking for, then I don't think they will have any choice other than to do as she says. This isn't just about me and her Jax...they are still out there looking for her. There isn't any reason for it unless she is important." He dropped his voice. "Jax, she'll spend her life running. She'll never be free of them, and in the end, they will kill her, or worse."

"Unless she falls," Jax said quietly.

Hunter frowned. "Where did that come from? No. That's not an option. No way. It's never going to happen. I won't allow it."

"But it is another option, and like you said, there's not much you can do about it if she chooses that path."

"You told her about becoming a fallen angel? What the fuck, Jax? I thought you gave a shit about her." He pointed his finger right in his face, snarling.

"Of course I didn't, you stupid sod! Your Guild boss gave her the idea. I'm guessing he made it sound a lot more appealing than the reality of it, though. He got in her head, and she asked me about it, but I managed to persuade her to go off the radar instead. She's always been on the run, Hunter. It's nothing new for her, and at least she will have a life to live."

346

Hunter's heart was breaking, but he knew without a doubt that this was their only and best option.

His Demon prowled just below the surface, wanting to take Jax out for taking Evie away from him.

It looked like he was going to be getting really friendly with a bottle, or five, of vodka real soon.

Chapter 27

Evie was back living her old life of being in a solitary loop of existing and not drawing attention to herself in a hidden location. Luckily, it was something that she was good at, but this time being on her own, now that she knew what was waiting for her a few hours drive away, it was a different experience.

It had been two weeks. She had found a shitty little house to rent with only one neighbour far enough away that the little old lady kept to her own business and didn't pry. It was quiet here- a small town of eight hundred, mostly farmers and old folk- from what she'd seen.

She'd lasted all of one night before she'd begged Jax to give her Beth and Kali's numbers in return for her sending his beloved mustang back to him. They had both been to visit twice now, and it had helped to restore her sanity.

She had pumped them both for information about Hunter.

"He's still searching for who hurt you." Kali had told her, with a sad smile on her face.

"But he's ok?"

The girls both stole a glance at each other.

"He's ok, Evie," Beth replied. "When you left, he struggled with it, especially after all that's happened, but he's got good people helping him through it."

"Do you think you'll ever come back?" Kali asked.

"God, I hope so. I can't live like this forever, knowing he's out there and I'm here, both of us being miserable."

They both never liked leaving her, especially Beth, but they always promised to come back and always set the date before they left so she had something to look forward to.

Evie was so proud of Beth and her ability to bounce back from their traumas. Other than sitting around spending Jax's money, Evie had only managed to wallow in her own self-pity.

She had a shower, washed her hair, and wandered into the kitchen. Hopping up onto the worktop, she eyed her phone.

Reaching across, she pulled it towards her. After picking it up and putting it down a few times, she found Hunter's phone number. This number she'd gotten from Beth. Not even Jax knew she had it.

Pressing call, she put the phone up to her ear and closed her eyes, willing her heart to slow down.

It rang four times before Hunter's deep voice came over the connection. "Hello?"

As she sat in silence, she dared not even breathe.

"If you're some prank caller, I will find you and beat the shit out of you, but if you're not, and it's you..." He breathed out heavily. "Shit, I miss you so damn much."

A tear slid out of the corner of her eye.

"Stay safe, I mean it. I'm not going through all of this for nothing..."

She hung up on him. She couldn't bare to hear anymore in case she thought to hell with the whole thing, and ran back to him. It was a thought that went through her head a lot recently, but she had to stay strong.

Wiping the tears from her face, she jumped down from the counter and went in search of ice cream to cheer herself up.

~~~~~~~

"I know you speak to her, Kali. How is she?"

"Don't torment yourself, Hunter," she said, putting another vodka bottle down in front of him as he sat on the bar stool in front of her.

Both their eyes travelled over to Jax as he strode across the club's dance floor, making his way towards them.

It was 3 a.m, and the last of the Cellar's patrons had just filtered out of the doors and into the waiting taxis, leaving just the workers remaining.

Hunter turned back to Kali. "I can't tell if I want to kill him for spending time with her or I want to thank him for keeping her safe."

Kali smiled at him sadly as she continued to wipe down the second-floor bar and tidy things up for lockdown.

"Anything new?" Jax said as he reached them, resting his arms on the bar top.

Hunter looked at him sideways as he tipped his vodka bottle up. Jax looked worried, as always, that today was the day that he was finally going to get a beating for giving Evie the means to run away.

"You want a beer, Jax?"

"Sure, thanks, Kali."

She popped the top and placed it down in front of him as he took the bar stool next to Hunter.

"Are you two going to play nice, or do I need to stay?" At the sound of their grunts, she shook her head. "I'm going to go finish off upstairs then."

Good luck with that, Hunter thought. Viden was up there 'relaxing' after working an Enforcer job. Hopefully he'd patched himself up enough that she didn't need to play nurse for him. Oh god, it looked like he was going to have to go back to his apartment tonight.

Jax swung around to face him. Ugh, this dude was still here.

"I told you if I found out anything, I'd let you know," Hunter grumbled.

"Uh huh, forgive me if I don't believe you when you say that. She asks me about you, you know."

That had Hunter freezing with his bottle half-way to his lips.

"I can't keep fobbing her off all the time. If I tell her you're breathing, I do in fact have to make sure that you are breathing."

"As long as that's all you're telling her," he said, thinking about his recent alcoholic tendencies and pushing the vodka bottle away.

"I don't want to make this harder on her than it already is, and me telling her of your recent path of self-destruction wouldn't do either of you any good."

Hunter grunted at him. "I have it under control. If you'd just give me her number, then I could talk to her. Surely that's not against the rules."

"You know it is." At his glare, Jax continued, "I'm not the rule-maker here. I'm just helping her to protect you. I'm doing this for her benefit, not yours."

"And here's me thinking that we had all bonded over killing angels."

Jax laughed. "I don't hate you anymore. I think that's progress."

"I still hate you, so maybe not," Hunter smirked.

Jax's phone started to ring.

Quickly hopping up from the bar stool, he fished it out from his back pocket. As Jax looked at the screen and then at him, Hunter thought that it must be Evie calling.

He considered grabbing the phone from him just to hear her voice, but before he could make a move, Jax was off, calling over his shoulder, "I'll...see you later."

He beat feet away from the bar as if his house were on fire.

That was weird Hunter thought.

~~~~~~~

The next day, Evie went through the same motions as always, spending most of the day looking out of different windows, paranoid that the angels would find her. They made her arsehole of a foster dad Drew look like a kindergarten teacher, but that didn't mean that she didn't keep an eye out for him too. She guessed that that would be an unbreakable habit of hers forever.

A shrill noise went off from next to her, where her phone lay on the table. Evie checked the time. For the two weeks that she'd been gone, Jax always called her in the morning at 9 a.m. and then again in the evening at 7 p.m. on the dot. It was 3:39. p.m.

She scrambled to pick it up before it stopped ringing.

"Any news?" She asked.

"Not good news, Evie, I'm on my way to you. This needs discussing face-to-face."

"Oh, come on Jax, don't leave me hanging like this."

"Honestly, Evie, I'll be at yours in an hour."

With that, he hung up, and she went about pacing the house she now resided in for an hour. She was waiting for him at her side door when he pulled up in his mustang.

The look on Jax's face had her ushering him inside quickly and then shutting the door behind them.

"It looks like I'll have to sit down for this," she said, pulling out two wooden chairs and sitting down on one.

Jax went and stood behind the other, leaning on the back of it.

He scrubbed a hand over his dark hair. "Hunters screwing. He knew I was coming to you and wanted to come too. Viden and Theo locked him in the flat at the Cellar."

Evie's eyes went wide at that mental image.

"That's not why I'm here, though. I managed to speak to that guy, the one Beth found out your kidnap location from, the one that deals in angel feathers."

She fell back into her seat.

"It's shit. I warn you."

"Jax, what hasn't been shit recently? I'm a big girl. Spit it out."

When he didn't say anything immediately, she narrowed her eyes at him.

"Jax, come on. Tell me."

"The angels who took you into their jail would have sent your blood up to the top floor to activate your angel gene for ascension. They would then have received a date for when that would happen. They obviously didn't tell you this date?"

She shook her head. "What happens on this date? I float up to heaven?"

He looked up at her through his dark hair and said, "No, you drop dead."

Well, shit.

"Your human side has to die in order for your angel side to be fully fledged. That's the way it works."

"Let me guess there isn't any way of stopping it?"

He shook his head slowly.

"Is there any way to find out the date?"

He shook his head again.

"So I'm just going to drop dead at some unknown time and then be this fledged angel? What does that even mean?"

Jax moved to her, pulling her chair around to face him. He kneeled in front of her. "If there was anyway around it, I would have found out. He was positive there was no way out once activated and even the Guild's little deal with you, you'd have to ascend before you fell, so it's all just part of the motions. They would have known you had to die in order to keep their deal."

"How long do you think I have? And how long am I likely to be gone? I will come straight back, right?"

"He said it could happen in days to a month or two, depending on how much business they have up there. As for how long you'll be gone and what happens, I have no idea. I'm sorry, Evie."

It seemed like such an un-angelic thing to do, harvesting souls, but then there wasn't anything angelic about any of the angels she had come into contact with yet, so why change now?

"Jax, it's been weeks since I got to that prison." She searched his face frantically. The look he gave her scared her more than anything else.

"Beth's going to come and move in with you, so you're not alone."

So I don't die alone, she thought. "I can't do that to her. She's been through enough already."

He scrubbed his hand down his face. "I'll move in then. You're not going to be on your own in this."

"Let's hope it happens sooner rather than later then." Her attempt at humour fell on deaf ears.

"Give me a few hours to pack some stuff, and I'll be back."

"Does Hunter know?"

He stopped in his tracks.

"No, and I think it might be better to keep it that way."

She nodded numbly, and as soon as she could, she ushered him out of the door so he could go home and pack.

She walked around the apartment with a strange detachment, stacking the books that she had managed to buy neatly and throwing what little washing she had into the machine. She wondered about her apartment back in Foston hall and what would happen to it and all her belongings once she died. At least her bills would disappear- one bit of good news in this shitshow.

Beth had told her that Hunter had been to stay there a few times so it didn't get broken into, and he was still looking after her fish at the bolt hole. The thought had her smiling.

She walked into the bedroom, pulling on her favourite baggy jumper that she'd managed to get Beth to bring and her bed shorts. It was getting close to 10 p.m. now, and she was emotionally exhausted. She didn't know how much more bad news one person could take.

There was a soft knock at her front door, and Evie went on instant alert. Jax had a key, and Beth and Kali wouldn't come without texting or calling first. This was someone else.

She flattened herself against the peeling wallpaper and crept over to the window that gave a good vantage point of the front door, one of the reasons she had picked this house over the others.

She held her breath as she peered through the thin curtains. Seeing who was waiting on the other side, she ran to the door and pulled it open, and for five long seconds, they just stared at each other.

"Evie..." Hunter was there right in front of her.

He walked through the door, backing her up and pushing it shut behind him.

She looked at every part of him, her eyes starved for the sight. "Oh god, I've missed you," she breathed.

He reached for her. "I..."

"I don't want to talk. I just want you."

He didn't need telling twice. He had her backed up against the wall quicker than she could blink and was kissing her like a starved man. His hands roamed everywhere before he reached around to grip her hips. She was with him on that, wrapping her legs around his waist and grinding into his obvious need for her.

He trembled as he recharged from their kiss.

Eyes swirling molten silver, he carried her over to the kitchen counter, propping her up. She kept her legs well and truly wrapped around him, needing him close to her. He paused then, pushing her long hair back from her face, his eyes travelling over her as if she'd disappear at any second. Oh god, she hoped Jax had kept to his promise and not told him.

"I need you," she breathed.

Hunter was so on board with that as he flicked open his jeans with his free hand, pushing them down to release himself. He was so hard he hurt as he pulled her shorts out of the way and pushed against her. This was something he didn't rush, he was big compared to her, and after the ordeal she'd been through with the angels, he obviously didn't want to hurt her. He pushed in inch by inch. She helped him by spreading her legs wider to accommodate his size.

It was hard for Evie not to regress back to that night in the prison where she'd been attacked, but this was Hunter. She breathed him in, keeping her eyes fixed on his face as she locked the box to that memory, her mind wholly focused on him and what he was making her feel.

"Fuuuck" he groaned when he was fully inside, her moan sounding through the room.

She reached up, gripping onto his hair, as he reached under her legs to grip onto her arse as he thrust into her.

She pulled his shirt off over his head before doing the same to her own, kissing his shoulders and neck as he strained. Leaning back on the worktop, she gave him better access to the rest of her body. His silver eyes roamed over her before he dipped his head to her breast, biting the tip before sucking it into his mouth while palming the other one.

As she started to slip on the counter, he couldn't get a purchase on his thrusting motion, so he withdrew from her, pulling her off of the kitchen side, spinning her around, and bending her over it instead. Grabbing onto the side of the sink, she gasped as he filled her again. Holding her by her hips, he set a bruising pace.

Leaning down over her, he bit her on the shoulder, making her come hard as he spilled himself inside her.

They were both panting as they came down from their high. He'd made her forget, just for a little while, but she was so thankful for it.

Withdrawing from her heat, he tucked himself back into his jeans before leaning down and passing her the top she'd thrown off as she turned around, leaning on the counter. He looked uncertain, like he'd done something wrong, his eyes travelling to her neck and where he had bitten her.

She reached up and rubbed at the sore spot. "It's ok, Hunter. I liked it." She felt herself blush.

He moved his hand and rubbed at the back of his neck, still looking uneasy.

"I'm sorry I left," she whispered as she pulled her top on over her head.

His eyes travelled from her neck to her face, and he blew out a breath. Reaching out, he hugged her to him, putting his arm around her shoulders. "I know why you did it. What I don't know is why Jax suddenly told me to come to you after all this time. Why now?"

She closed her eyes, dropping her head onto his shoulder. She knew why. He'd sent Hunter in his place to be with her so she could say goodbye to him properly.

Her phone pinged from across the counter, pulling it over as she looked at the screen.

It was a message from Jax.

It's up to you whether you tell him or not, but I changed my mind...I think that you should.

I hope I don't live to regret this.

Jax

She closed her eyes again, bringing the phone up to her forehead.

Turning to Hunter, who was watching her intently, she said, "I might be able to shed some light on that."

God, she hoped she had the strength for this conversation and that she was doing the right thing by telling him.

"Let's move over to the sofa."

As they went over and sat down, Evie turned, so she was facing him. "I love you."

He smiled at her. "I love you too, so much."

She returned his smile, but hers was a sad one, and she couldn't help the tears that sprang into her eyes.

His smile faltered as he looked at her. "Hey, what's going on? I know we're on the Guild's radar but we are safe here. We've got time to work something out."

She took a deep breath. "Jax spoke to the angel feather dealer."

Hunter's eyebrows shot up.

"There isn't any easy way of saying this, but we've run out of time. He found out that I have to ascend to become a fully-fledged angel. Bad news is that I've been marked for ascension, worse news is that in order to ascend, my human body has to...die."

363

He frowned at her. "And he tells me I keep him out of shit...I'll go and speak to this guy and find out a way to stop it." He got up, heading towards the door.

She turned towards him and said, "By the time you get back, I'll probably already be dead."

He stopped with his hand on the door handle.

"There isn't any way of stopping it. Jax has already looked. I'm on an unknown timeline here, but its borrowed time at best."

"So what...we're just supposed to sit here and wait for you to die? I'm not going to do that, Evie. What happens after? You come straight back here? You stay up there forever? You're asking a lot of me." Hunter scrubbed at his hair.

"I'm not asking anything of you. I'm telling you, it will happen, Hunter. Everyone dies."

"Give me something to fight Evie- something to punch, stab, shoot..." he said as he walked back to the sofa, gathering her up in his arms. "I can't just sit here and wait for you to die,"

They sat in each other's embrace. If only this could be their life, just sitting and enjoying each other without some imminent threat on the horizon.

Hunter moved back, holding her at arm's length. "Shit, I hate to have to talk about this now, but if it is the case of any minute, then I need to talk to you about something too."

She nodded to him.

"Ok, so while I've been digging into the angel's business, I found out some stuff...I think that you're part of some royal angel bloodline. There is a rumor that there is a lost member of the Arcana family that was hidden in the human world as a child. I can't prove that it's you, but there are too many coincidences, and it would make sense that you were promised to some other angel arsehole before you were born. If that doesn't scream royal, then I don't know what does."

She knew that he was right from what Alastair had shared with her.

"If you are Evie, then you may have the ability to change their laws, even make new ones." He took her hands in his "You could change the law that is stopping us from being together."

Chapter 28

Evie stood in the kitchen after changing into bed trousers and a tank top, contemplating the possibility that she was in fact this long-lost royal angel that may have the ability to change angel and demon laws, while Hunter was in the shower.

So much was spinning through her head, but mostly she was worried that Hunter was there with her.

Being apart from him had made her feelings that much more stronger, but his Guild boss's threat of sending him back to Hell indefinitely scared her more than anything. He'd said that he would know if they were together.

She knew that out of all of her shitty options, becoming a fallen angel was probably the worst one, especially coming from that arsehole who hadn't divulged all the facts to her. Instant red flag as to why he is so keen for her wings and for her to fall...

Suddenly, warm, damp arms reached around her, pulling her from her thoughts as they wound around her middle from behind.

She turned to face her demon.

His black hair seemed even darker wet, the stubble that had grown in giving him a roguish look. His strong, tattooed shoulders and chest tapered down to the towel he had wrapped low around his waist. He was so handsome, and he loved her. She couldn't quite believe it.

He reached up and ran his large finger between her eyebrows on her frown line. "Other than the obvious, what's wrong?" His voice rumbled.

Oh, let me list them, she thought- impending death, possible royal angel, angels trying to kill me, Prince of Hell blackmailing me- she looked into his beautiful eyes.

"You shouldn't be here," she replied.

At his frown, she continued, "Hunter, you're risking everything by just being here with me."

"I don't care. I want to be selfish for a little while and have this with you. How can you still not know that none of it means anything to me. Evie, even if we only had tonight, I'd still risk it all anyway. If what Jax found out is going to happen, then I'm going to be with you through it, no question. We have dealt with so much shit that something good is due to come our way."

"Maybe us finding each other was the good thing? Whatever happens to me now, I'm not sorry because it brought you to me."

As they looked at each other, his eyes suddenly turned black. She sucked in a breath. "Hunter your eyes..."

"Not Hunter," his voice rumbled, warped, and low.

Evie had rarely seen Hunter's Demon, and when she did, he'd freak out that he'd lost control around her, but here he was staring at her through his eyes.

She'd had demon sides explained more to her by Kali, Viden, and Hunter while they had been in the bolt hole together. The female demons very rarely heard a peep from their other side, where as the males always walked hand in hand with theirs. Their testosterone activating their demon side, hence why they tended to come out more at times of heightened aggression and arousal. Kali had told her that a demon was always present in males, but they were never fully in control. At the same time, Hunter had told her that wasn't always the case for him and that it was one of the reasons he had chased her in the beginning, because his Demon had wanted her and had bonded with her.

Maybe this was the chance she could find out why.

"Um...hi," she said shyly.

"Hi," he smirked. "It's nice to be able to finally talk. My other side is a little protective of you."

This was still Hunter, she reminded herself, just a different version of him.

She was surprised that she wasn't scared.

"I've seen you a few times."

"Not enough before he suppresses me. All this extra energy you have been feeding me, though, well, I've been storing it up so I could at least have one conversation with you before being pushed back behind the wall again."

"A conversation? I thought demons were all about the murder and mayhem."

"Not when it comes to you..." he reached for her, gently pushing her hair back from her face.

"So you don't fight him for control so you can hurt me?"

"I'd never hurt you," he frowned, looking at her seriously, his black eyes like orbs of obsidian, as he took in her every feature as if he was starved of the sight of her.

She could see why people would run in terror from them, but she was drawn in. Looking deeply, she saw Hunter and the Demon and knew that they were one and the same.

She loved them both.

His nostrils flared, seeming to sense her revelation, and then he leaned forward and kissed her long and deep.

After a second of hesitation, she kissed him back. It was like kissing Hunter, but at the same time, not. He was more raw. She felt his passion and pent-up frustration right down to her bones as he owned her completely.

He pulled back, looking at her with total male satisfaction as she clung to his bare shoulders. "Bond with me, Evie."

"I don't even know what that means."

He growled, "He won't tell you because he doesn't want to push you. I want you, over all others, I'd choose you alone to become my mate."

"But I'm an angel- not only that, I'm forbidden to be with you."

"I don't care."

She looked into those black eyes as he stared at her so intensely. "Can Hunter hear this conversation?"

He shook his head slowly.

"W-what if I fall? Become a fallen angel, I mean. I wouldn't remember who I am, but we could be together."

He smirked at the idea. "I wouldn't let you forget who you were."

"Give me time then. Let me work through all of this, and then I'll come back to you both."

"You'd better," his voice rumbled as he kissed her again- the kind of kiss that would forever be seared into her memory.

"Tell Hunter to stop holding back on me," he said, taking one last lingering look at her as a shudder went through him.

Leaning down, he rested his forehead against hers, closing his eyes. Panting hard, he opened them.

Grey eyes stared down at her.

"Fuck," he breathed. "Are you ok?" He looked down at her, searching for any sign that she was in distress. "I couldn't get control of him."

She reached up, cupping his face in her hands. "I'm more than ok. He's been storing up energy so he could overpower you...Hunter, he only fights you so that he can be seen by me. I think he likes me," she said, giving him a shy smile.

"Oh, he likes you alright, but I'm not sharing," he chuckled.

She laughed out loud. "I don't think we have a choice."

His eyes flashed black again briefly, and the Demon's grin came out. Hunter growled, pushing him back, a second later grinning himself. "Well, at least now we know he won't force you into consumating the bond."

"He wouldn't be forcing me. I want to."

Hunter scratched the back of his neck.

"Uh, do you now."

"Yes, but I want to know everything there is to know about it first, the good, the bad, and the ugly."

"We can do that."

"I don't care how long we have left of this chapter. I'm not going to stop doing the things I want to do just because there is some impending doom hanging over me."

He reached up and brushed the hair back from her face. Evie smiled up at him, using his distraction to her advantage as she reached down for the corner of the towel on his hips. With a quick tug, she pulled it from him before taking off like a chased rabbit.

"Oh, you're asking for it now," he took off after her, butt naked.

She let out a squeal of delight as he chased her around the small house.

All too soon he caught her around the waist, pushing her face first into the wall between the living room and bedroom, pinning her small frame with his larger one.

"Now now, there are consequences for getting a sex demon naked and then running from him."

He reached down in front of her into her pyjama bottoms and was elated to find her still wearing no underwear.

His need for her pushed against the top of her bottom. With no barrier, she felt every inch of him like a hot brand, seeking what only she could give him. Her head tipped back onto is pec, and she let out a moan.

"I want to be gentle, Evie. I do, but I can't. I'm sorry, I can't," he said, pushing a thick digit into her, causing her head to fall forward, her forehead resting on the cool wall in front of her.

He kissed the junction between her neck and shoulder as he added another finger, stoking her fire.

She was panting hard, just holding on to reality. As she was about to peak, he removed his fingers, pulling her trousers down and pushing himself against her. She arched against the wall and him, pushing back, just as he thrust forward, giving her every inch of himself. She cried out in pleasure and pain, the best combination, as he thrust into her.

Reaching up, he ripped the tank top she was wearing in half, throwing it to the floor behind them. The missing fabric was quickly replaced by his large hands, which came up to grip her breasts, squeezing them.

He couldn't balance how he was positioned for long, his strong hand slapping out onto the wall by her head. Pulling her leg up so he could push even deeper into her, she couldn't stop the orgasm that barrelled through her.

Looking over her shoulder, she saw Hunter's eyes were black. Holy shit, his Demon was fucking her. The thought had her orgasming all over again.

His pace turned frantic before he slowed and then went rock solid, all of his muscles going rigid as he groaned, his body straining as he started to breathe heavily.

Putting her leg back down, he pushed against the wall, allowing her to do the same.

He slowly withdrew and turned her around to face him. "That was..."

"Yeh, it was," she smiled as they clung to each other.

"So I guess I don't have to work so hard at keeping control now?" He chuckled.

She smiled up at him. "No, but you're going to have to buy me some more clothes." She bent to pick up her shredded top, hanging it from her finger.

"That I can do," he said with a boyish grin.

Walking into the bathroom, he came back out a second later with his black t-shirt in his hand.

"Arms up," he said. As she complied, he put it on over her head. "So what have we got to eat?"

"I wasn't expecting you, so I've not got much," she said, walking over to the kitchen

"Are you saying I eat a lot?" He raised his eyebrow at her.

"Yes!" She laughed.

Hunter ate three and a half pizzas *and* garlic bread in the time it took Evie to eat half of his fourth one.

Being together like this, being a normal couple, she could get used to. It gave her hope that no matter what happened next, they had gotten this far together, and his strength and her determination were a force to be reckoned with.

Whatever the future would hold for them, she was happy in this moment.

He was snoring softly on her bed facing her, his expression that of total relaxation, a few hours later.

Watching him for a few seconds more, she got up, being careful not to disturb him as she crept out of the room silently. It was still dark outside, but she didn't want to sleep any longer.

Walking quietly into the kitchen, she reached into the cupboard, taking out a cup and placing it on the work surface before opening up another cupboard and taking out a tub of hot chocolate.

Smiling to herself at the memory of how the day had gone with Hunter and the ache between her legs, she vowed that she would continue on with optimism for however long they had left here together. He was right- they were due some good news in all the recent bad.

Jax had done the right thing by sending him here. Hunter made her feel alive and like there was something out there worth fighting for, and she needed that right now. When she'd been with the angels, the thought of him had saved her. She would never have held on for so long if she didn't know that he was out there living.

Realising that he was her strength, she knew now that if she did fall after ascending, the thought of him would bring her back. Always.

She was just turning to get the milk when a rough, calloused hand came up and covered her mouth.

Her eyes went wide in shock as an arm wrapped around her waist, holding her flush against the cold, unfamiliar body.

"Hello, Evie," a voice she would recognise anywhere whispered into her ear.

Drew.

Shit. Looking all around her frantically, she saw where he had entered the house. Broken glass littered the floor by the open back door that she had failed to see before. He obviously meant to leave in the same way as he dragged her along towards it. She tried to shout out to Hunter, but only a muffled noise came out around his hand as he clamped it down even tighter, cutting off her air supply.

Tears streamed down her face as she reached out blindly, trying to get a hold of anything. As he pulled her along past the counter, she flayed her hand out and managed to grab hold of a kitchen knife, and without hesitating, she stabbed down, hitting him in the thigh.

As he grunted and stumbled, she knew she'd got him good, but it didn't stop him from grabbing the knife from her as he carried on dragging her outside and to his waiting truck.

She fought with all she had, grappling with him, shoving and kicking anything she could to gain the upper hand, but he held her with an iron grip that she just couldn't break free from as he pulled her over the grass. She dug her heels into the mud, determined that if she was going to get taken, she would give Hunter every clue she possibly could as to where he'd taken her.

"You're going to regret that, you little bitch," he spat at her.

She kicked out her foot and managed to kick over a metal bin in the yard. As the loud clang vibrated through the garden, she used his surprise at the sudden noise to knee him in the groin and run for the house.

"HUNTER!" She cried, tears blurring her vision as she ran back through the door, just as he stumbled sleepily from the bedroom, shirtless and rubbing at his eyes.

~~~~~~~

It was like watching a horror movie in slow motion, Hunter thought. One minute Evie was running towards him, and the next there was some bastard plunging a knife down into her back. He couldn't get to her fast enough. He reached for her, but she was just too far away from him.

As her momentum faltered, her mouth dropped open at the shock and the sudden loss of mobility as she fell down to her knees, barely breaking her fall with her arms as she fell to the ground face first.

Hunter didn't even think- he just acted as he launched himself at the man. One of his hands grabbed onto his head, the other his shoulder, as he wrenched his head one way and his body the other, breaking his neck with a loud crack.

Dropping the dead weight, he raced back to where Evie had slumped down onto the floor.

Shit, shit, shit, the knife was a big one, and he'd stabbed her right between her neck and collar bone. He went to grab it to pull it free, but stopped just before he touched it. He knew that removing the blade could do worse than leaving it be, but he was panicking.

There was so much blood.

Rolling her over carefully, her eyes rolled in her head before she blinked them frantically, shaking her head from the fog that clouded it.

"Dre...Drew," she coughed out, spraying blood everywhere.

"Shh, it's alright, he's dead. He won't hurt you again." He gathered her up into his arms, cradling her to him. "Shh," he rocked her as she cried, blood beginning to seep into his trousers, where he kneeled next to her.

"I'll get help," he said, going to get up, but her hand reached up to grip his arm, stopping him from moving.

"It's too....late..." She panted, "...love you..."

As her breath hitched a couple of times and she jolted and then went lax, he squeezed his eyes shut.

He didn't want to look, but he had to. Leaning back and looking down at her, seeing her blank expression, his world fell apart. A noise he'd never heard before rose up and out of him before he could stop it. The sound was filled with all of his pain, anguish, and heartache. It was filled with all that they had endured and all they had been through, only for her to be taken away in the cruelest of ways. How could she be there in his arms one minute and then gone the next?

"Evie," he whispered through the tears streaming down his face. "Evie, you'd better goddamn come back to me. This isn't the end. This can't be the end."

He didn't know how long he sat clutching her in his arms, it was long after she had turned cold, but he couldn't bring himself to let her go.

He looked up, seeing the bastard who'd killed her lying in a puddle of her blood. His sightless eyes were staring straight ahead. He wanted to rip every part of him to pieces for taking her from him.

He reached across and felt his pockets, pulling out a silver mobile from one and numbly dialled one of the only numbers he knew by heart. It rang twice before Viden's voice came over the line.

"Yeh?"

"...V"

"Hunter? Is that you?"

"I need you, brother."

"Where are you?" The sound of Hunter's voice made Viden sound frantic.

He ended the connection, dropping the phone onto the floor as he hugged Evie's lifeless body back to his chest again.

As darkness was replaced with sunlight, he heard footsteps approaching. His Demon growled in warning.

"Hunter?" It was Viden.

Looking up, he saw that they were all there. Theo, Ade, Jax, Kali and Beth.

He was more than numb.

Taking in the scene, Viden kneeled down beside him and said, "Brother, you need to let her go."

"I don't think I can," he croaked.

He couldn't bare to look at her face again. He couldn't see her lifeless eyes staring back at him, no longer seeing him.

Theo kneeled in front of him and said, "Pass her to me, brother." He held his arms out.

As panic threatened to override him at the possibility that this would be the last time she would ever be in his arms, he forced himself to pull it together as he passed her over.

As Theo took her, Viden was there, embracing him as he dragged him away from where he'd been sitting all night. His joints and muscles screamed from the movement, but he welcomed the pain.

His jeans were soaked in blood, the red covering his hands and lap. He stared at it, feeling a weird attachment to the liquid that was once keeping her alive.

After a little while, Viden asked, "Who was he, Hunter?"

"Drew...he was her foster father. I think he was trying to take her, but she got away from him."

"There is a truck out the front, so that would make sense."

"I wish I could kill him again. He didn't suffer enough...I should have avenged her. He should have suffered."

"You did avenge her. He's gone."

Hunter's eyes tracked to where Theo had taken her. They were over by the front door, wrapping her in a white blanket.

"We need to leave here," Viden said.

"Wait, I need to know..." he said, looking over to Jax. "Will she...can she still come back from this?"

Jax looked at him, wiping tears from his eyes.

"I wish I could tell you, but I just don't know. In theory, her human body has died, so she should ascend..." He coughed to clear his voice. "But it's not how it's meant to go down. I don't want to think it anymore than you do, but she may just be...gone."

No, that just wasn't a possibility, she would never leave him like that. This couldn't be the end of their story.

She'd survived angels and demons, only to be taken by a human with his own sick agenda. She hadn't deserved any of it. Just because she had been born into the wrong family, she had never stood a chance.

Now he had to pin all his hopes that the very bloodline that ruined her life would be the one to save it also.

He had to believe.

Believe in her.

Believe in them.

...and believe above all else that she would come back to him.

Hunter

EVIE

Book 2 of The
Enforcers available
now

ACKNOWLEDGMENTS

Thank you!

To my readers, thank you so much for taking the time to read my first novel! Hunter has been a true labour of love for me, and I'm so excited to bring the brother's world to life in the next few books.

Hunter began as a series in which every brother would have their own book, but he and Evie had other plans for the direction in which they travelled.

Au contraire, that doesn't mean that Viden, Theo, Ade and yes, even Jax are going to get their own stories told.

Each and every chapter I write, I learn and grow along with my characters' feelings for each other, and I can't wait to share their journeys through my books with you all!

The biggest of thank you goes to my wonderful soulmate and husband. You came along and showed me what true love was when I'd given up hope. I love you always.

As always, I thank each and every one of you for the support I receive. I've got no education in writing, and I self-edit and publish, so there are going to be mistakes. Thanks for sticking in there!

Please leave a review of the good, the bad, and the ugly, as I rely on feedback to help my writing grow.

Many of these lines were written during my down times while working in the prison service. The true heroes of this world are working to keep the streets safe as a forgotten service, much as Hunter strived to do in my books.

You all truly do not get the appreciation you deserve, so here is my acknowledgment to you all.

My brothers, you never walk alone.

In a time when the world was torn apart, Hunter and Evie came together.

ABOUT THE AUTHOR

Alice is an English writer who enjoys life in the Buckinghamshire countryside, surrounded by her menagerie of animals. Having spent most of her working life on farms, she can be found either with her horses, reading books, or writing them.

Growing up with great friends around her, she found her passion for writing stories when she would indulge her guilty pleasure in the world of LOTR fan fiction.

Thankfully a lot has changed since then!

Made in the USA
Columbia, SC
07 February 2024

d9962ec7-821c-479f-aa46-f681b6713873R01